Praise for *LIVE* in Person

"Fitzgerald is such a master at building believable characters that it makes you wish you could sit down and have a beer with them... suspense, romance, family tension, friendship and even an adorable little puppy! A must read if you enjoy diving into and losing yourself in a good book."
—Cindy Mommer, Editor

"Fitzgerald's *LIVE* series is so engaging and intriguing that she can't possibly publish the next novel fast enough. I'm hooked. Give me more now."
—Kerry Alan Denney, author of *SOULSNATCHER*

"As with the two earlier books in this series, I couldn't put this one down! Suspenseful, funny and a love story, all wrapped in one!"
—Chris Hebert

Praise for the *LIVE* Series

LIVE Ammo "Talented Lynda Fitzgerald provides an exciting journalistic investigative mystery that has an Ann Rule true crime feel... *LIVE Ammo* is an exciting thriller that deserves to be on the bestsellers lists."
—Harriett Klausner, *Mid-West Book Review*

"A fascinating read. I could not put this one down."
—Terry South, *Quality Book Reviews*

"An altogether great read. A delightful mix of romance, thriller and mystery will keep most readers riveted for hours."
—Olivera Baumgartner-Jackson, *Reader Views*

"Lynda Fitzgerald has written another page-turning, intriguing mystery. *LIVE Ringer* is the kind of thriller that makes your palms sweat, your mouth dry, and makes you just a little bit afraid to read it when you're home alone. *LIVE Ringer* is the best and most intriguing thriller I've read in a long time. I hated to put it down."
—Vicky DeCoster, *Author of Husbands, Hot Flashes, and All That Hullabaloo!* and *The Wacky World of Womanhood*

"*LIVE Ringer* is a fascinating, nail-biting read. Allie is a wonderful character—and so is her dead aunt. Lynda Fitzgerald has told a spell-binding story, complete with good people with dark secrets, with compassion and great skill."
—Alice Duncan, Author of Hungry Spirits

"Fast-paced and eerie, *LIVE Ringer* kept me guessing. Fitzgerald tells a fine yarn, indeed, and peoples her story with characters who are both endearing and exasperating – rather like life itself."
–Fran Stewart, author of the *Biscuit McKee mysteries* and *A Slaying Song Tonight*

Allie Grainger from Lynda Fitzgerald's *LIVE* series is a character I'd like to get to know in real life. She's warm, funny, and spirited. Lynda Fitzgerald's skill at storytelling will pull you into Allie's world and you'll be hooked.
—Brittiany Koren, Editor at *Written Dreams*

ALSO BY LYNDA FITZGERALD

LIVE Ringer

LIVE Ammo

If Truth Be Told

Of Words & Music

An Irreconcilable Difference

For Fran —

LIVE in **Person**

My favorite author —

A NOVEL

Hugs!
Lynda Fitzgerald

Lynda Fitzgerald

Crystal Dreams
press

LIVE in Person
by Lynda Fitzgerald

Published by Crystal Dreams Press
6 Old Colony Dr.,Whitby, ON. Canada

http://www.crystaldreamspress.com/

This is a work of fiction. Any reference to living people or
organizations is purely coincidental.

Book Design: Carolyn Prior
Cover Design: Nicolle Brown Designs

Paperback   ISBN-13: 9780971565821
ebook   ISBN-13: 9781591462941

Published in Canada. Printed simultaneously in the United
States of America, the United Kingdom, and Australia.

CIP data available from the publisher.

Acknowledgments

A special thanks to my daughter, Nikki—you
make me proud.
And to my critique group. You keep me humble.
And finally to Cindy Mommer for faith,
friendship, and all your stellar editing work.
I'm grateful to you all.

The Promise

*H*e knew how to terrorize; it was what he did best. Some people were born to heal, some to lead. He was born to strike fear in those who crossed him. He'd studied the art in childhood and perfected it during his years as a cop. Now, he was a cop in jail, but not for long.

Allie Grainger. The name tasted sour on his tongue, but his thoughts of revenge rendered it almost sweet. Because of her, he'd lost everything. Now, Allie Grainger would lose—everything.

■ ■ ■

One

ALLIE FELT LIKE A SCHOOLGIRL going to her first dance—except she was thirty years old, divorced, and she did not intend to dance with this man, at least not vertically. Her cheeks burned at the thought, but not from embarrassment. Rand Arbutten was hot.

For months, they'd tried to get together. From that first kiss in her kitchen last August, they knew they'd end up in bed. Even Rand's seventy-year-old grandmother Frenchie knew they'd end up in bed, but so far, it was no-go. Something or someone—his schedule, her schedule, her friends, his family—always intervened. Then, his law firm sent him to New York for eight weeks, something about multiple depositions and interviews in some big case he was working on. They'd had a number of steamy conversations during his absence, but that's as far as it had gone.

Rand lived and worked fifty miles west in Orlando, which didn't make it any easier, but as he said, "What's fifty miles of good road?" He spent two days a month as a figurehead at the newspaper where Allie worked, but that only complicated things. Everyone at the paper seemed to know what they had in mind and, intentionally or unintentionally, managed to thwart them. Even Myrna, her friend and acting editor, wasn't cooperating this time.

Allie had spent the past Christmas with Rand, his father Cord Arbutten, and Grandmother Frenchie, but that was in a family setting not conducive to grabbing him by the hand and dragging him to bed, tempted though she was. Although Frenchie would have applauded them. Cord, too, probably.

She stepped out of the shower and wrapped herself in a bath sheet. Nothing would ruin today. Rand was in town for twenty-four hours, and she planned to spend twenty-three of them with him in bed. That would give them an hour to eat so they could keep up their strength.

Silky pink undies, a semitransparent pink peasant blouse. Deep burgundy Capris and matching toenails. No shoes. She didn't plan to be on her feet for long. She laughed aloud. Could it really be happening? Could today be the day?

She had it all orchestrated: a slow walk on the beach, a bottle of Chablis on ice for when they returned. Music—something sexy with plenty of saxophone. Maybe a little Sade. Fresh, scented sheets on the bed. She'd even fed and walked Spook hours early so he wouldn't be needy once Rand arrived. Her cowardly Lhasa Apso would probably disappear to his favorite hiding spot behind the living room sofa when Rand got there and not emerge until after he left, but it didn't pay to leave these things to chance.

A spritz of Jo Malone 154, a splurge on her last

visit home to Atlanta where her mother dragged her to Nordstrom's. Allie had paled when she learned the price, but her mother told her it was time to ratchet up her self-esteem, and for once, Allie agreed. Besides, with all the money her aunt had left her, she could afford it.

Rand told her the scent made his knees weak. She smiled. All the better.

Her best friend Sheryl probably wouldn't barge in. Her hours were erratic as a sheriff's deputy, and Allie hadn't seen her in more than a week. No, today and tonight belonged to Rand and her.

As she walked into the living room, she heard tires crunch to a stop in her oyster-shell driveway, and the breath whooshed out of her lungs. What was wrong with her? It wasn't as if she were a sixteen-year-old virgin, although at the moment, that's exactly how she felt.

She restrained herself from racing to the door and flinging it wide, but it was a near thing. When she saw Rand's outline through the frosted jalousies, her heart hiccupped. Even though it was January, sweat broke out on various parts of her body. God, she was a mess! Frenchie was right. It was high time they got this over with so they could begin to behave like normal human beings again.

She counted five after he knocked before opening the door. They stood, regarding each other, Rand big, dark, and tall on her puny front stoop, Allie drinking in everything about him, from his tight jeans to his narrow waist and broad chest to the stunned look on his face.

"*Jesus*," he whispered. "You look sexy as hell."

"So do you," Allie managed before he stepped

through the door and closed it with his foot. She heard the deadbolt click as he reached for her with the other arm. Then, it was a tangle of clothed limbs, murmured words, and pure sensation. She heard "God, I've wanted to..." and "waited so long..." and half-heard many other phrases, but she didn't care what he said at the moment. It was all about the doing.

His lips came down on hers. His hand slipped under the back of her loose blouse—the primary reason she'd worn it—and caressed her skin. She ran her hands over his face, his neck, and pulled him closer.

After what seemed seconds or hours, he said, "*Whoa.* Wait." His breathing was ragged. "Give me a minute here."

Allie didn't even have enough breath to gasp. She stared up at him. He ran his hands up and down her arms and gulped in several breaths. "Not yet. Not this way."

Allie looked up at him in confusion. When she could form words, she said, "Then when? And how?"

That brought a strained laugh from him. "Soon. Today, I mean, but this isn't how I want our first time to be. Flying clothes and groping hands. I want it to be—*Oh, hell,* forget it." He crushed her against him again, and his lips came down on hers.

This time, Allie pulled back. "Wait." She put her hands against his chest. "Wait," she gasped. "You're right. It should be memorable."

He pulled her to him again, his embrace looser. "It'll be memorable. I can promise you that."

Allie felt her blood pressure soar into the stratosphere. She managed to bite back the "*No, now,*" that sprang to her lips, but he was right. She, too, wanted this to be the ultimate romantic experience.

Allie averted her eyes. She didn't know what to say, what to do. At least Spook would be a topic of conversation, but as usual, he was nowhere in sight. "Where is he?"

"Who?" Rand seemed almost back in control.

Allie envied him. "Spook. My dog."

"I saw him run behind the couch when I came in. Not much of a watchdog, is he?"

Allie stiffened. "He was abused. He can't help it."

Rand grinned. "I wasn't criticizing your pup, Allie. Not all dogs are watchdogs. It doesn't make them any less lovable."

"Do you like dogs?" It stunned her that she was ready to jump in bed with the man, but didn't know the answer to this question. Suddenly, it was important to her that he did.

He shrugged. "I never had one when I was growing up, of course. No pets allowed at a military academy."

Allie winced. Rand's father, Sheriff Cord Arbutten, had put Rand in a military school when he was twelve and threatening to turn into a juvenile delinquent. It had almost destroyed their relationship permanently, but it turned Rand around. Witness an honest attorney. What could be more rare?

"But we always had a few strays around campus," he said. "We fed them and played with them. So, yeah, I like dogs—a lot."

Allie felt a smile split her face. "Good." She wasn't raised around animals, either. Her mother maintained they were filthy beasts with fleas and who knew what else crawling all over them. Allie knew that Spook was clean, and she'd never seen so much as a black speck on him. "Me too. Now."

After that, she couldn't think of a thing to say. Rand stood there staring at her. She began to regret that she'd worn the nearly transparent blouse.

Finally, he spoke. "Would you like to go for a walk on the beach?"

She couldn't believe it. That was supposed to be her line.

■ ■ ■

RAND HELD HER HAND as they descended the wooden steps to the beach. Her backyard—the Atlantic Ocean in all its glory. He kicked off his shoes at the bottom of the stairs and draped an arm loosely across her shoulders. She put her arm around his waist as if they'd been doing this for years. The beach was almost deserted, compliments of winter and the early hour. The sun worshipers were still donning their bikinis, and the snowbirds usually slept late.

Winter or not, the sand felt sun-hot under their bare feet, the water warmer than the air. They said little. The moment was too pure to sully it with words. The slap and hiss of the waves set their leisurely pace, and Allie knew she'd never been happier.

When they reached the Cape Canaveral jetty, they turned and retraced their path, footprint into sandy footprint. Theirs were the only tracks, but that would change soon. The condos springing up on either side of her tiny house would soon be completed. Then, an extra few hundred or so people would share her little stretch of paradise. She didn't know how she would bear to sell her aunt's house, but…

"I've told you before, Allie. Sell the thing."

Her Aunt Lou had been dead for almost a year, but they had these conversations in Allie's head. They began when she returned to Cape Canaveral, and at first, Allie believed it was her imagination, a product of desperately wanting a little more time with Lou. But enough things had happened that she was now convinced they communicated. Their talks were infrequent and brief, but they gave Allie a measure of comfort.

"Honey, it's only a house."

"It's not only a house; it's your house. It's all I have left."

"That's not true. You have our memories, a life-time of memories. I left them in trust for you. Those are what count, Allie. Not things."

"God, I miss you."

"Who?"

Allie blinked. Had she spoken aloud? She almost didn't answer. Rand once thought her aunt had caused the breakup of his parents. He knew better now, but was he ready to hear about Allie's ghost? She'd mentioned these talks with her aunt once to Marc Frederick, her former boyfriend who lived in Miami. Marc had humored her and dismissed what she said. Allie never mentioned it to him or anyone else again.

"My aunt," she offered. Let him ask if he wanted to know more.

He did. "Tell me about her. I know you worshipped her."

Allie leaned her head against his shoulder. "You're right. I did."

He took her hand, and she squeezed his fingers.

"She was so inherently kind and wise. With a family like mine, that meant a lot to me. She was honest almost to a fault. She lived her life her way and didn't care what others thought." Allie shook her head. "That's not true. She did care, but she didn't let it make her crazy."

He stopped. "Like you do?"

She lifted her chin. Then, she chanced a peek at him and saw his lips twitch. She smiled.

They continued to walk. "I talk to her sometimes." She waited for his derision.

"You mean have actual conversations?"

"Yes."

"What do you talk about?"

Allie looked up to see if he was humoring her, but all she saw was curiosity and decided to take a chance. "It's never the same thing twice. Just now, we were talking about my selling the house."

Rand stopped in his tracks. "You mean right now? Just a second ago while we were talking?"

Allie laughed. "Not *while* we were talking. While we were walking and not talking. She thinks I should sell the house."

"You mean the house you're living in now?"

Allie nodded.

"Why?"

"Because of all the condos springing up on the beach. It's not going to be the same."

He walked along for a moment in silence. "She's right, you know."

"I know she's right, but it's hard. It's something of hers. I don't have much left."

Rand pulled her close and tightened his grip. "Of course, you do. You have the memories of all the years you spent with her. Those are what count."

Allie smiled. Great minds.

Rand leaned down and brushed his lips across hers. "You're wonderful, you know?"

Allie put her arms around his waist. "Why do you say that?"

"A million different reasons. You're beautiful."

"You think so?"

He pulled her closer. "Stop fishing. You know damn well I think so." He stroked her back. "You're determined. I love that. And..." His lips came down on hers hard. Allie went lightheaded. She clutched him tightly to stay on her feet.

Wolf whistles from above caused them to jump apart. Allie squinted up into the sun and saw workers hanging off a half-completed building. Some waved their hands or caps. Others seemed to be making gestures of some kind. Her face burned.

Paradise, indeed. "Let's go," she said, taking Rand's hand.

Back at the house, they brushed the sand off their feet as best they could and let themselves in the back door. Allie started toward the kitchen and the wine, but Rand took her shoulder and turned her around.

Allie caught her breath at the intensity in his eyes. He rested his hands gently on her shoulders. "I don't quite know how to say this, but…" He stared at some spot over her head, and then looked back at her. "Allie, I've never known a woman who appealed to me the way you do. It's not just your physical beauty. I mean, hell, there's plenty of that, but you're so much more. I don't know how to say it."

Allie smiled up at him. "You're doing fine."

His face remained serious. "You're so much of what you describe about your aunt. You're inherently kind. I watched you back when you were trying to prove my father didn't commit murder. You're fair and honest, even when it's hard. You work to protect others, even if it means putting yourself at risk."

He was talking about the last summer when Rand's mother had committed suicide. Rand had been convinced his father killed her, and Allie had almost lost her life trying to prove differently.

"I know you were married before, and you want to take this slow and easy, but—oh, hell." He ran a hand through his hair.

"Just say it." The words came out breathless.

"I—I think I'm in love with you. I know it's too soon. I don't mean to pressure you—"

Allie beamed up at him through moist eyes. "I can take the pressure. Oh, Rand…" was all she managed before his lips came down on hers.

Allie fell against him. When the kiss finally ended, she said, "You really know how to sweep a girl—"

They both froze at a knock on the door. Rand looked at her with raised eyebrows, and she shook her head. She wasn't expecting anyone, and that was an understatement. She considered ignoring it, but whoever had decided to invade her privacy wasn't going away. Another knock—harder this time.

Pulling away from Rand, Allie yanked open the door—and gasped.

Two

THIRTY MINUTES INTO THE TRIP. Approximately, because he wasn't allowed to wear a watch. Sidney had counted in his head the seconds since they'd left the Seminole County Jail complex. Shit, it was only because the deputies transporting him were his buddies that he wasn't in full restraint. The wrist restraints were bad enough. Most of the transports wore leg shackles, too, but everyone knew Sidney was a pitiful cripple. God knew he'd played it up enough over the months. One look at his mangled ankle, and they'd tossed the leg shackles aside. Sidney had spent months convincing them that he was just a harmless broken deputy who got busted for trying to protect his boss.

Busted in more ways than one. His body was so twisted and wrecked from being rammed with Levine's cruiser that it was agony to roll out of bed every morning. It wouldn't be so bad if he was a good boy and took his pain meds like the bitch nurse in the psych unit told him, but he consistently cheeked them, knowing he'd have a better use for them in the future.

This wasn't his first transport to a hearing. Hell, the prisoner transport van felt like a second home.

He'd had a half-dozen hearings while the county tried to decide what the fuck to do with him. They were pushing for two counts of attempted murder and a score of lesser offenses, but his lawyer pushed back just as hard to get him off on diminished mental capacity.

Sidney chuckled. Sure. Diminished mental capacity. So, if he was nuts, how had he fooled the shrink assigned to him? Not only that, but he'd convinced the guards that he was not only lame, but also their friend. He'd played up the injuries, moaning when he put his weight on his right foot, wincing when he stood. It wasn't all an act. It hurt like hell, but he could take pain. What he couldn't take was humiliation brought on him by Allie Grainger.

Two thousand. About thirty minutes into the trip. He couldn't leave it too late. He had a lot to do once he got on home territory. The first thing was clothes. He'd requested that he be allowed to wear civilian clothes to the hearing, but that was denied, just as he'd figured it would be. Only prisoners going to trial got to wear civvies so they wouldn't look like guilty scum when they came before the judge, and they had to change into those at the courthouse. But, hell, was worth a try.

At least, he wore the navy jumper. General population. Not high-risk red or, God forbid, work-gang orange. A dark jacket to conceal the lettering on back, a patch here, and a clipboard there, and he'd look just like any other anonymous drone going about his job. Then, a vehicle. Nothing fancy. It wouldn't do to stand out. He grinned. Wheels wouldn't be a problem. He could hot-wire anything with wheels in no time flat—another of the many talents he'd perfected over the years. Shit, when he was a kid, he used to hot-wire his mom's car three times a week. No one caught him then, and no one would now.

"You OK back there?" came Raymond's voice over the speaker.

"Breakfast is playing hell with my guts, but other than that, I'm just ducky."

He heard Raymond chuckle. Raymond wasn't a bad guy. Young and inexperienced. Sidney hated what he had to do to him, but hell, that was the breaks. You did what you had to do. Besides, after his escape, Raymond would no longer be his bud. Neither would any guy he'd worked with. He was finished in Brevard County.

Six months ago, he'd tried to protect the sheriff from a reporter's prying eyes. How the hell was he supposed to know the sheriff didn't kill his wife? Everything pointed to it, and he'd been so *sure*. Hell, the sheriff's own kid was sure. Sidney had shadowed the bitch as she and the little bastard went around collecting evidence—to hang the sheriff, he'd thought. When he finally closed in on them, Levine followed and rammed him with a goddamn police cruiser. She was a dead woman walking, too, but not his first priority.

Twenty-two thousand, twenty. The trip took a little more than an hour. He planned to make his move about forty-five minutes in. That should put them close to I-95 and the rest stop he'd talked the guys into letting him use before. It was generally deserted, and his plan hinged on that. If not, he'd wing it.

The guys knew he was always having stomach issues, some real, some not. Another thing he'd built up, planning, always planning for this day. He knew they weren't going into the john with him to wipe his ass. They weren't that kind of buds. He smiled. Thank God, Seminole County kept him in isolation for his protection. They did that with cops. Otherwise, he might have a few of those kinds of buds too. He was good in hand-to-hand, but his injuries had weakened him, and a lot of those guys were brutes. He knew because he'd locked up their kind for years.

He felt bitterness sour in the back of his throat. That bitch. She'd taken it all away from him, the sheriff's respect—hell, his friendship. Sidney knew Cord Arbutten had looked on him as a son, easy to do since the sheriff's own son was a nasty little prick who never gave his dad the time of day. He thought of his own father, glued to his recliner with no interest in Sidney once he realized Sidney didn't want to be a firefighter like him. No, Cord was his dad. Had been his dad. Shit.

Almost time. Once he was free, he'd head back to Brevard County. He knew they wouldn't catch him. He was too good. He'd almost never been caught as a kid. He remembered when he used to hang with the Cape Canaveral bunch. He was always doing something to them—gum in their hair, snakes in their shoes—and the only one who ever caught on to him was that bull dyke-bitch Levine.

The seconds ticked in his head. When the time was right, he bent over at the waist, clutching his belly, and screamed.

Three

"LEN?" ALLIE FINALLY SQUEAKED OUT. "What are you doing here?"

Len brushed past her into the house. "Aren't you glad to see me?"

Rand looked from Allie's face, which must have expressed her shock, to Len's smug one. He stepped forward and held out his hand. "Rand Arbutten."

"Rand, this is Len. My—"

"Good to meet you, Rand." Len shook his hand, barreling over her words, as usual. "I haven't heard Allie mention you, but I'm sure that's just an oversight." He looked around before putting his suitcase on a chair.

Rand looked from Allie to Len to the suitcase and seemed to size up the situation. He took a step back, his face a blank mask. "Allie, it was good to see you. Why don't you give me a call when you're free?" Then, he was out the door.

For a moment, Allie couldn't move. Then, she started after him. "Rand, wait..." But he was already in his car. Seconds later, he drove away without a backward glance.

"Well, well," Len said, chuckling. "Did I interrupt something?"

Allie spun on her brother. "What the hell do you

mean showing up here unannounced?"

Len frowned. "Mother said you'd become a garbage mouth. Too much time around that cop girlfriend, she said."

Allie was so furious that all that came out of her mouth were incoherent sputters. Len could reduce her to a stammering fool. He always had. At one time, Allie believed it was Len's superior intellect. Now, she knew he was just a blowhard steamroller who delighted in besting everyone. Another lawyer, but a far cry from Randall Arbutten.

"I asked what you're doing here," she finally managed.

Len, impeccable in a lightweight suit perfect for the Florida winter, leaned against the doorjamb. Allie knew he was posturing, but that didn't make it any easier to bear. "I have business in town and decided to pay a visit to my sister. There's nothing strange about that."

Allie was still too much in shock to pretend to be anything else. "Nothing *strange?*" Her fists clenched at her sides. "Len, I haven't seen you since I moved down here a year ago. You didn't even make an effort to come by when I was in Atlanta over New Year's. Nothing *strange?*"

Len brushed his coat sleeve. "I was busy over New Year's. Some of us have social lives," he added, his tone dismissive. "Nothing's changed much, has it? You'd think with all your money, you'd at least buy some new furniture."

Allie gritted her teeth. "I like this furniture, and how the hell would you remember what was here? The last time you were here was when you were thirteen, and that was for two whole days before you went whining to Mother and Dad about 'the awful sand and sun and nasty bugs.'"

"Actually, it was sleeping on the couch so my precious sister could have a private bedroom that put me off. Lou always favored you."

He sounded so much like a petulant five-year-old that it took Allie a moment to get back on track. "I asked you why you're here."

"I intend to stay here with—"

"*No.*"

Len had been studying the room, taking everything in, assessing its value, and no doubt finding it wanting. Now, his gaze snapped back to Allie. "What do you mean *no?*"

A flash of power. Allie had the upper hand with her elder brother, a rare and exhilarating experience. She crossed her arms. "No means no. You are not going to waltz into my house and—"

"A house that should be half mine by right."

"Bullshit."

"Garbage mouth. You know, overuse of profanity is an indication—"

"...of a limited vocabulary," she finished. "I know, Len. We have the same father."

"Hard to believe. You act just like Lou."

Allie smiled without warmth. "It's Aunt Lou to you, and if that was supposed to be an insult, you failed miserably. I'm proud to be like her."

"The woman was a mere step above trailer trash."

Allie felt her face burn, and it took all her control not to slap him. She took a deep breath, then another before she walked to the front door and flung it open. "Get out."

"You don't mean—"

"I said out. Get out of *my* house. For that matter, get out of my life. You've never been a brother to me. It's a little late to start pretending."

Len stepped back and cocked his head. "Is our little Allie growing a spine?"

Her cheeks burned hotter. "I have a perfectly good spine. I also have a legal right to this house."

"And all that money."

"And all that money," she echoed. "You spent your entire life ridiculing Aunt Lou. Why did you expect her to leave anything to you?"

"I'm as much her family as you are."

"You were as much a nephew to her as a brother to me. You criticized everything she did or said. You, our mother, and, yes, even Dad sometimes. Her own brother. It made me sick. You all hated her because she thumbed her nose at you and went her own way."

"We didn't hate her," Len said, standing straighter. "We didn't care enough to hate her. We scorned her."

Allie trembled with fury. Tears hovered near the surface, but she'd be damned if she'd break in front of Len. She struggled to calm down, but her voice still shook when she spoke. "OK, Len. You scorned her, and she left her house and money to me. That's the way it is. That's the way it's going to stay. Now, I want you to leave *my* house."

"Or what?"

Of all the insufferable, pigheaded *jackasses*. "Or I'll call the police."

"On me?" He scowled. "For what? I'm your brother, for God's sake, your own flesh and blood."

"Being my brother gives you no rights. You're

an uninvited person who barged into my home
and won't leave when I ask you to. Whatever
our biological relationship, that's breaking the
law." Allie wasn't sure it was breaking the law
in the strictest sense, but Len did divorces, and
law school was a long way away. Maybe he didn't
know, either.

He hesitated long enough that Allie feared he
would call her bluff, but in the end, he sighed
and picked up his suitcase. "Exactly where am
I supposed to go? I have no reservations. I expected
to be welcome in my sister's home."

"You were wrong. I don't know. Go to a hotel. Go
to the Hilton in Cocoa Beach. There aren't any big
conventions in town. They should have a room."

Len chewed his lip. "Mother won't be happy
when she hears about this."

"I couldn't care less."

He started out but stopped on the threshold.
For just a second, Allie saw something in his eyes.
Anger? Panic?

"You haven't heard the end of this, Allie. That
money is half mine by rights. I could make a pretty
good case in court."

Allie took a step back. "Are you threatening me?"

Len smiled without humor. "I don't threaten,
baby sister; I take action." With that, he was gone.

Allie slammed the door behind him and stood
staring at it. Was the man insane? What did he
mean bullying his way in here and demanding
half her inheritance? Did he really think she'd fork
over a million dollars and half the proceeds for the
sale of the house? Because that's what he wanted.
He had no interest in the house per se, any more

than he wanted a long-overdue relationship with his only sibling. Money. That's what Len was after. But why? Didn't he have plenty? His law practice with her mother was successful beyond measure. He and Ella Faye didn't have kids. Why would he need more money?

After a moment, she saw Spook out of the corner of her eye, huddled beside the sofa. She scooped him up and held him close. "You poor little guy. I'm sorry that big, bad man scared you. You could bite him, you know. You have my permission."

Spook trembled in her arms. Or maybe she was trembling. She couldn't tell.

With only a quick peek out the front window to make sure Len was really gone, Allie slipped out the front door and headed to Sheryl Levine's house, across the street and a few doors down.

■ ■ ■

ALLIE AND SHERYL were friends during all the summers Allie spent in Cape Canaveral with her aunt. Both Sheryl and Joe Odum lived in the neighborhood then, and the three kids were inseparable. The fourth member of their group was Sidney Finch, a sneaky little worm they included in their games only because he made an even fourth. Sidney's idea of fun was leaving smelly fish in their shoes and dropping spiders down their shirts.

Joe, Sheryl, and Sidney had all gone to work for the Sheriff's office when they grew up, although Allie would have bet money Sidney would find himself on the other side of the bars. After the rampage last summer when he tried to kill her and several others, that's where he ended up, or at least, he was safely tucked in a prison medical facility awaiting trial, which allowed Allie to sleep nights. Joe had died a year ago at thirty, which had the opposite effect.

So, it was only Allie and Sheryl now, and Sheryl had been an absentee friend lately. Probably something to do with work, information Allie wasn't privy to. Sheryl's car wasn't in the drive, but maybe Libby knew where she was.

Allie knocked on the front door, then turned the knob and stuck in her head. "Libby? Anyone home?" Her eyes widened as Libby made her slow way into the living room, leaning heavily on a walker.

"Allie, dear," Libby called. "Come on in."

Allie grinned and gestured at the walker. "What's this? Where's your wheelchair?"

Libby giggled like a teenager. "Isn't it exciting? I made Sheryl promise not to tell you. I wanted it to be a surprise. I've been going to physical therapy. The boys take turns driving me back and forth. Some kind of new deceased officer fund is paying for it all. The doctors say there's no reason why I can't regain most of my mobility if I'm willing to work hard."

Libby Odum was Joe's mother who'd come to live with Sheryl after Joe and his father died within two weeks of each other. Not surprisingly, Libby looked a wan seventy, although she barely capped sixty. Her frame was petite and thin to the point of emaciation. A stroke had kept her in a wheelchair for years because she had no money to pay for physical therapy, and she was too proud to accept charity.

Allie was the anonymous donor of the new fund. She'd been half-afraid Libby would refuse the help, but it looked as if she was wrong. The "boys" Libby spoke of were sheriff's deputies—Joe's friends—who came by from time to time to check on his mom.

Allie's smile widened. "That's wonderful, Libby. What does Sheryl say?"

A shadow crossed Libby's face, or maybe being upright after so long was painful.

"I know she's pleased," she said, moving across the room. She reached for the chair arm and lowered herself to a sitting position.

Allie fought the urge to help her. She knew Libby needed to do this herself.

"Although I have to admit, I haven't seen much of her lately," Libby added. "She's been awfully busy. I don't want to mother her to death, but I do worry about her."

Libby hadn't seen Sheryl, either. That didn't sound good. Allie didn't want to put Libby on the spot, but she had to ask. "Any idea what she's working on? It's not like her to be so out of touch."

"I sure don't." She bit her lip, not meeting Allie's eyes.

Allie wasn't sure she believed her, but she wasn't going to press it. She only hoped Libby and Sheryl weren't having problems. Initially, when Libby came to live with Sheryl, Allie had feared her friend might have taken on more than she could handle. Libby was strictly wheelchair bound then, but until Libby moved in, Sheryl had spent half her time driving to Cocoa and back to check on her. Sheryl felt someone had to take care of the woman, and there was no one left, except her.

Something was wrong. Allie could feel it. But if Sheryl wasn't telling Allie or Libby was what was going on, whom would she tell?

Four

SIDNEY FELL TO THE FLOOR as he heard the door swing open.

"Jesus, man!" Raymond hung back for just a moment before jumping in the van and kneeling by Sidney. "What's the matter?"

Sidney rolled on the floor in a fetal position, groaning. "It's my gut. Christ, it feels like it's on fire." He clutched his belly, swallowing hard. "Man, I think I'm going to be sick."

"You wanna get out?" Raymond asked.

Sidney knew Raymond didn't want to clean the van after Sidney tossed his cookies, something Sidney did a few times before to prepare for this moment. In fact, he'd counted on it. By his calculations, they were no more than a few miles from the rest stop. "No, man, I don't think I can stand up right now. I need a bathroom. *Hurry.*"

He swallowed hard again, feeling real sweat drip down his forehead. When he threw himself off the seat, he twisted his crushed foot under him and almost blacked out. That wouldn't serve his purpose, but the sweat seemed to convince Raymond.

Raymond looked at Jake standing by the open door. "Get us to that rest stop ahead. I'll stay back here with him and let you know if we need an EMT."

All against regulations, Sidney thought, squeezing his eyes tight as if in pain. These boys were going to be in a heap of trouble after this was all over.

He waited until Jake started the engine and the vehicle was racing at full speed. Then he made a choking sound and rolled away from Raymond. As Sidney knew he would, Raymond leaned toward him to see if he was all right. At that instant, Sidney swung both arms with all his might. They connected with the side of Raymond's head, and he went down hard, cracking the back of his head against the steel bench opposite.

The dude was out. Strong pulse, though, and no blood. Good. Sidney didn't want to kill him. He hadn't done anything yet that would get him executed, and he damn sure wouldn't do it to a fellow officer. He'd reserve that for Allie Grainger, but not until he'd had some fun with her.

He only had a couple of minutes. No time to get Raymond stripped. He yanked and pulled until he got him out of his jacket, which was really all he needed.

He found the keys to his wrist restraints. Hands fumbling in his haste, Sidney unlocked the cuffs and snapped one on Raymond's wrist and the other to the bench frame, staying out of reach of Raymond's feet in case he woke up. Socks served as an effective gag. By then, Raymond was regaining consciousness.

Raymond watched with wide eyes as Sidney shoved Raymond's Glock and radio in the jacket pocket. Sidney was sorry these guys didn't carry Tasers, but the radio would help. After a second's hesitation, he reached over and pulled Raymond's cell phone out of his pants pocket.

As he stepped back, Raymond's foot connected with his damaged ankle, and Sidney almost passed out from the pain. He spun and slammed into Raymond's head with all the strength he could muster. The head snapped back and connected with the bench. This time, there was blood, and Raymond's eyes rolled to the back of his head. At least, he was breathing.

"Stupid *bastard*," Sidney spat through gritted teeth. "You brought it on yourself."

He felt the van slowing for the turn into the rest stop and positioned himself near the door, bracing himself against the built-in seat. If there was anyone at the rest stop, he was screwed, but all life was a risk. That's what made it fun.

Even though he couldn't run fast enough to get away from an eighty-year-old with a cane, let alone the rare healthy citizen willing to give chase, if he could disable Jake and get to the tree line without being caught, there was no stopping him. He knew the Florida underbrush.

Slower now. Sidney readied himself. He wasn't fast, but his good leg was stronger than two of anyone else's. That would serve him now.

As the door began to swing open, Sidney kicked out with all he had. Jake caught the full brunt of it in the face and dropped like a rock. For just an instant, Sidney thought he'd killed him. He crawled out of the van. No one around, thank God. Jake was breathing, although it looked like his nose might be broken. After gagging Jake, he grabbed his service revolver and tucked it in the back of his pants. Then, he rolled Jake over and snapped plastic restraints on his wrists and Jake's cuffs on his ankles before confiscating his radio and cell phone.

Now the tricky part. Good thing he was trained in these things. He got down and hoisted Jake in a firefighter's hold, bracing himself with his good leg. When the upper half of Jake's body was level with the van floor, Sidney dumped him inside and shoved in the rest of his body. He hated being so rough, but he was in a friggin' hurry. Once he locked the van tight, he was good to go. These vans were designed to hold prisoners; it should work for cops.

He limped across the asphalt lot toward the building, where he bought an assortment of high-energy snacks with the money he'd confiscated from Jake's and Raymond's pockets. Eighty-seven dollars. They didn't pay these guys enough. Still, it was cash, which would come in handy. Like now. He grinned as he stuffed the snacks into the jacket pocket.

He considered a quick visit to the john, but hell, the scrub and trees beyond the clearing were one big bathroom. Why waste the time?

His limp slowed him down some, but he was at the tree line in less than two minutes. Then, he heard a car. He ducked behind the nearest palmetto scrub as a car rolled into the rest stop. It slowed as it passed the transport van, then rolled on and stopped at the other end of the parking strip. Maybe they recognized it as a prisoner transport van, or maybe they were just antisocial. Either way, it worked for him. There was no way they could see or hear anything at that distance.

He pushed his way into the thicket, breathing in the rich loam of moist earth and rotting vegetation. He could hear rustling in the undergrowth— snakes and rats loved the palmettos—but it didn't bother him.

Ironic. It was the sheriff who taught him to conquer the outdoors. In his attempt to force the teenage Sidney to clean up his act, the sheriff dragged him to the Everglades for a week with only the clothes on their backs and a knife each. Sidney emerged from the ordeal with a sound knowledge of survival skills and a deep admira- tion for the sheriff.

And Sheriff Cord Arbutten had loved Sidney. Until Allie Grainger ruined everything.

He felt his gut twist. No time to worry about that now. He slipped deeper into the pines and undergrowth. They wouldn't find him now. Unless his luck ran out and some observant motorist heard noises from the van, he wouldn't be missed until he didn't appear for today's hearing. Then, they'd contact Seminole County before they began to trace the missing guards' route.

He had four—maybe five—hours to make it to Cocoa and get temporary wheels. Then, he'd drive to the Melbourne Airport and pick up something in the long-term lot. A quick plate switch and he was good for another couple of days at least. Once he had wheels, he'd find a flop. He might even visit his parents' house.

His uneven gait slowed as the idea blossomed.

Yeah, that's what he'd do. His mom always kept plenty of cash lying around, and unless the sheriff had confiscated them, his uniforms should be in the closet. He knew his mom would keep his room as if she expected him to come back home any day. Well, she'd get her wish, although she wouldn't know it.

Then, and only then, would he begin his campaign. He intended to destroy Allie Grainger's credibility and then her sanity before he finished her. He felt a little bubble of glee rise from his deepest recesses as he realized he'd done it. He was *free!* Christ, it was almost too easy, but he'd take easy for now. It would get difficult soon enough.

"I'm coming, Allie Grainger," he whispered to the forest, "and soon, you're going to know it."

Five

ALLIE PEERED AROUND THE ROOM as her eyes adjusted to the dim lights. Plenty of customers, but no Sheryl.

Lester's was a small bar in a strip mall on the 520 Causeway, the main drag from Cocoa Beach to the mainland. The causeway was comprised of a highway with elevated bridges that allowed free access for boat traffic on the Indian and Banana Rivers before the two rivers merged and dumped into the Atlantic Ocean thirty-five miles to the south.

Allie still shuddered when she remembered how near she came to plunging into that river when Sidney shot out her front tire and sent her careening into the bridge embankment.

When Allie initially returned to Cape Canaveral, Sheryl chose Lester's for them to meet on the premise that, because no cops frequented it, they could do some uninterrupted catching up. In reality, everyone found them there, from Joe before his death to Allie's ex-boyfriend Marc Frederick. These days, the bartender and Sheryl were dating. It had been going on for almost six months now, and Allie was beginning to suspect they were getting serious.

Sheryl and Del had founded their relationship on respect for each other's toughness—Del had belts in most martial arts, and he could disable a six-foot man just by squeezing a spot on his hand; Sheryl carried an unconcealed weapon, and she could freeze a man in his tracks with a look.

Not that Sheryl needed to be tough to do that. Her looks alone could—and often did—reduce the average man to a stammering mass of jelly, with her dark beauty and hour-glass figure. By contrast, Allie was a pale second, with straight blonde hair and freckles and a body that refused to put on weight in the right places. Although her ex-husband Garrison had tried to convince her otherwise, she now believed she looked good enough. Marc had thought so. And Rand certainly thought so.

Marc. She would have to call him and explain.

Several guys sitting at the bar also seemed to think she passed inspection. Allie ignored them and made her way down to the far end of the bar where she and Sheryl usually sat. Del was there before her.

"Long time no see, Allie. What'll it be?"

"Information."

"Huh?"

Allie laughed. "OK. A Diet Coke and information."

Del shuffled his feet. "Uh—Sheryl said I should give you regular Coke when you ordered Diet. You know, so you can put on weight. But, hey, if you want the Diet..." His voice trailed off as he looked around the room.

Allie smiled. That was so Sheryl. When Allie returned to Cape Canaveral, Sheryl had appointed herself Allie's protector, usually protecting Allie from herself. Sometimes, she even succeeded. "OK. Regular Coke and an order of fries. How's that?"

Del beamed. "Hey, that's good. She said I was to push the wings and fries on you. Wow! That's great."

He set a Coke in front of Allie and vanished into the back. Del was a good guy. Maybe not a scholar, but ambitious in his way. He was working at Lester's to save money to open his own dojo. In the meantime, he taught classes at half a dozen martial arts schools in the area. Allie wondered how he had the time to date Sheryl, but they managed. Allie knew Sheryl brought her room-mate Libby here often for dinner, and Del had completely won Libby over, a feat that earned him even higher marks in Sheryl's book.

And that reminded Allie why she was there. When Del came out of the kitchen, she motioned him over. "Have you seen Sheryl lately?"

Del frowned. "I was going to ask you the same thing, but I didn't want to pry. I called her a few times, but I didn't want to bug her or anything. I mean, if she's really busy. With work or whatever. I mean, it's not like she has to stop by or call me back." He wiped the clean bar, not meeting Allie's gaze. "So, you haven't seen her, either?"

Now Allie really was worried. She had assumed Sheryl was tied up in taking care of Libby or going hot and heavy with Del, but if neither was seeing much of her, where was she keeping herself?

She realized Del was waiting for an answer. The guy looked forlorn. Allie didn't have the heart to worry him more, but if she lied and told him she'd seen Sheryl, and Del hadn't, would that cause him to fear Sheryl was avoiding him? For all Allie knew, it might be true. She decided on a middle ground.

"Well, you know she's tied up with Libby, and work's always demanding. She keeps such crazy hours, especially since they've been training that new deputy to replace Sidney."

Del swiped at the bar, unhappy, but apparently resigned. "Yeah, that loser. What do you hear about him these days?"

"Not much. I know he's in some kind of mental facility pending trial."

"When's the trial set for?"

Allie snorted. "It's not. From what Sheryl tells me, his attorney keeps setting up hearings on pretrial motions. At this rate, he won't go to court for years, which is OK with me as long as he's safely locked up."

"That is one seriously bad dude."

"Don't I know it." It wasn't a question. Sidney had made two serious attempts on Allie's life. Both almost succeeded. Her nemesis of childhood had morphed into her nemesis of adulthood. It wasn't fair—which brought her thoughts back to J. Leonard Garrison, her other childhood nemesis.

She wanted to like her brother. After all, he was her only sibling, but early, the lines were drawn. Len belonged to her lawyer mother, and Allie belonged to her English professor father, at least, until she changed her major in college from English to Journalism and went to work with the *Atlanta Journal Constitution* after attaining a mere BA. Then, he'd pretty much washed his hands of her. Len, on the other hand, was his mother's rising star, a partner in Vivian Grainger's law firm. He possessed all the qualities her mother admired—a bent for the law, the gift of flattery, and unquestioning obedience.

"Your mother loves you, too, Allie. She even admires you in her own way. She just doesn't show it."

"You have to be kidding! She doesn't admire me."

"OK. Fears, then."

"Why in the world would she fear me? She has half the judges in Fulton County scared out of their britches. What's scary about me?"

"That's exactly what I mean. Don't you see, Allie? Vivian controls her world by inspiring fear in those around her. She's not the first person to use the technique, or the last. That's how she controls your brother. Len is terrified of her disapproval. You don't fear her or her disapproval, and that's what terrifies her. She can't control you."

"What a lovely thing to hear." But what kind of daughter wanted her mother afraid of her?

Del put a basket of fries—a double order, if Allie wasn't mistaken—in front of her, along with another Coke. He and Sheryl were serious about fattening her up. When she'd returned from Brussels at the end of her disastrous six-year marriage, she was a scarecrow, all in an attempt to please her impossible-to-please husband, who maintained she was chunky. She'd also high-lighted her blonde hair when he said it lacked luster and briefly considered colored contacts when he said her green eyes were drab. Grrrr...

"What's got you looking so mean?" Del asked, leaning against the bar.

Allie wasn't going to discuss Garrison with Del. Sheryl had probably already given Del a blow-by-blow of the marriage and breakup, but Allie didn't want to get into it. Besides, thoughts of Garrison weren't the only thing making her feel mean today.

"My brother showed up on my doorstep this morning."

"Hey, that's great."

Obviously, Sheryl hadn't shared Allie's opinion of her family with Del. "It's not *great*. It's *gall*. Len didn't come here because he wants to see me. He came here demanding his share of my inheritance from Aunt Lou. He's been after me to sell the house since I got it."

Del shrugged. "Well..."

Allie narrowed her eyes. "Don't even go there. If I decide to sell, it'll be my decision, not my brother's or my mother's or Myrna's."

"Who's Myrna?"

Allie waved the question away. "Someone I work with at the paper."

"Hey, I read all the articles you did on the sheriff. You did a real good job."

Allie looked up. The man was such a teddy bear. "Thanks, Del. You're a shot in the arm."

Allie heard loud noises at the other end of the bar. One guy shoved another against the bar. Before Allie could blink, Del had vaulted the bar, and he had one guy by the scruff of the neck. She couldn't hear what Del said, but she saw the guy hand Del some money before Del helped him out the door. Maybe not such a teddy bear after all.

Del took the more conventional way back behind the bar and came straight back to Allie. "So, is your brother gone?" he asked as if there'd been no break in the conversation.

It took Allie a second to focus. "Hardly. I sent him to the Hilton, but not before he threatened to take me to court. Like he has a leg to stand on. But he's a lawyer, and you know what they're like."

After a moment's silence, Del said, "You don't think he deserves any of the inheritance? After all, two million bucks—" He looked away, clearly embarrassed. Apparently, Sheryl had shared that bit of family history with him.

"It was two-point-three million, and I'll kill him before he'll get a red cent of it!"

Her words rang out in the quiet room. Allie looked up the bar to see every head turned in her direction. Her face burned crimson.

Del glared at them, and everyone returned to their beers. He turned back to Allie. "Hey, I know how you feel. Well, I don't know, but if you feel that way, I know you're right. You know what I mean?"

Allie reached over and touched his arm. "Yes, I do. You're loyal and trusting and Sheryl's lucky to have you."

He squirmed. "Except that she doesn't seem to want me. Not lately, anyway." He stared into the beer cooler for a long moment. "So, what are you going to do?"

"About what?"

Del grinned. "About your brother." His grin vanished. "I don't figure you can do anything about Sheryl."

Allie felt bad for him, but Del was right. She couldn't do a thing about Sheryl. "I'm going to ignore him until he goes away. He can't stay here forever. He has a thriving law practice in Atlanta. Mother won't let him be gone for long, and wimp that he is, he'll go running the minute she calls. I'm sure the only reason she let him come down here is because she was sure he could convince me to sell if he steamrolled me in person. But it isn't going to work. My days of being intimidated are over. From now on, *I* call the shots."

Again, her voice had risen, and she was getting some pointed looks. A couple of guys shook their heads and turned away. Even Del looked uncomfortable. Obviously, she wasn't fit to be in public. She pulled out her wallet to pay.

"Why don't you let me wrap these up?" Del asked, gesturing at the fries. "You can take them with you."

Allie shook her head. "You eat them, Del. I don't think I'm going to have much appetite for a while."

As she slid off the barstool and headed to the door, it swung open. Allie took a long step back when she saw who it was.

Six

ER BREATH CAUGHt in her throat. "*Marc.*"
Allie's voice came out a squeak. Marc Frederick. Her ex-boyfriend. Standing in the
doorway, framed by the afternoon sun, he reminded Allie of one thing that drew her to him in
the beginning—the man resembled an apparition
from Mount Olympus, with his white blonde hair
and tanned skin. Single. Successful. Overprotective.

They had a complicated history. A year before,
Marc had saved her life. Allie would always feel
gratitude for that. Lust between them was never
in question. A hot affair ensued, one that showed
Allie what she'd missed during the years with her
ex-husband, Garrison. Allie was satisfied with
what she and Marc shared. After her divorce, she
wasn't ready to jump into another skillet, but
Marc wanted more, like love and marriage. But
as he kept telling her, he was a patient man; and
so he was for six long months, until she almost
died trying to prove the sheriff hadn't murdered
his wife.

Sidney Finch thought she was attempting to
railroad the sheriff, and he appointed himself
executioner to make sure she didn't succeed. After
he shot out her tire and almost ran her off the

520-Causeway bridge, Marc made the mistake of telling Allie she brought it all on herself, the same words her mother used.

Six months ago on his last visit from Miami, Marc issued an ultimatum: "Quit your job and marry me, or it's over." Allie didn't do well with ultimatums. She called his bluff, and that was the last she saw of him. Until now.

Now, he stood in front of her. She knew it couldn't be coincidence. Marc knew Allie and Sheryl came here often. If he wanted to avoid her, he'd have picked another place to drink.

"What are you doing here?"

He didn't speak. He stared at her as if he were drinking in every detail. After a long moment, he reached out as if to touch her face. At the last moment, his hand drew back. "I wanted to see you. I've missed you."

Allie was aware that every eye in the bar was on them. She turned and retraced her tracks; only this time, she led Marc to a booth at the back of the room. Even before they were seated, Del was there.

He looked at Allie, his expression full of meaning. "You OK here?"

Allie nodded.

Del relaxed marginally. "What can I get you folks?" he asked, wiping the already clean table.

"Nothing," Allie said just as Marc said, "Two Cokes." Del looked at Allie, and she nodded almost imperceptibly.

When he was gone, Marc reached over and took Allie's hand. She pulled it away. "I didn't think I'd see you again after your last visit."

A sad smile played across Marc's lips. "No, Allie. *I* didn't think. I didn't think what I would lose when I tried to set the rules. I was wrong, and I'm sorry. I've missed you." The words poured from him as if he were anxious to get them all said before she could stop him. He reached over again for her hand.

Allie tucked it under the table. "It took you an awfully long time to realize it."

Marc sat back. "No, it didn't. I knew the day I drove out of here that I'd made a mistake. I missed you even before your house was out of sight in my rearview mirror." He leaned toward her, elbows on the table, his face earnest. "I had some heavy thinking to do, Allie. Remember what I said? That I had to decide what I could live with and you had to decide what you could live without. I really thought you got some kind of kick out of the excitement of going after bad guys."

He shook his head. "But you were right. You didn't bring a damn bit of that on yourself." He scowled. "Once I thought about it, I knew I was an idiot. I was an idiot to give you a take-it-or-leave-it. I know what a bad time you had with your husband. You didn't need the same kind of thing from me."

She could barely take her eyes off him, remembering the days and nights they'd spent together. Pure bliss, which is why it was so difficult when he walked away without a backward glance. Why should she believe it was any different now? When the next assignment threw her in danger's path, would he walk away again? Was she willing to take that chance? And what about Rand? The thought chilled her.

Marc stretched across the table, as close as he could get without touching her. "What do you say, Allie? Will you forgive me? Will you give us another chance? I know I was wrong. I'll never try to push you again."

Pretty words, but could he keep that vow? Did she even want him to?

Marc must have noticed something. He sat back. "Unless there's someone else. Is that it, Allie? Are you seeing someone else?"

"No." It was an honest answer, but it didn't feel honest. "Marc, I—I—" She cleared her throat and began again. "I don't know how the last six months have been for you, but they were hard for me. I—"

"Allie—"

She held up a hand. "Let me finish. Please." He nodded, and she continued. "When you walked out of my life, I was crushed. I had lost my marriage, my aunt, and my friend Joe. Then, you. The one thing that could have been prevented was you, but you chose to walk away. At first, I just felt betrayed. You couldn't accept who I was, so you left. Then, I began to question our feelings for each other. Could you really love me and want to marry me and walk away at that time in my life?"

"I didn't understand—"

"No, Marc. That's not the only thing I asked myself."

He watched her steadily.

"I had to wonder whether I could refuse to change something as simple as my profession if I truly loved you."

Marc averted his eyes. Finally, he looked back

at her. "And what did you decide?"

"I didn't. I don't have any answers." She laughed uncomfortably. "The jury is still out. I don't want to change professions, and not because I get high on danger. I *hate* danger, but it's part of what I do. Sometimes, I choose to put myself in risky positions to get to the truth, and sometimes, that makes people mad. That's just the way it is."

"I understand."

"I don't think you do. I'm not a shapeshifter, Marc. I can't turn myself into something you want in order to please you. Does that mean I don't love you? I don't know, but until I figure it out, well..." She spread her hands.

She knew him well enough to know how much her words hurt him. They hurt her, too, but she wouldn't take them back.

"Life is too short to compromise like that, Allie. Stick to your guns."

"You think I'm right to send Marc away?"

"I think you're right to put yourself and your feelings first."

"What if things don't work out with Rand? What if I lose them both?"

"Then, neither is the right one for you."

"That's pretty fatalistic, don't you think?"

"I think you owe yourself the best. That's what you deserve."

"Allie?"

She could tell he'd said it more than once.

"Where were you?"

She shook her head to clear it. "Nowhere. Here. Thinking."

"About us?"

"About—" She broke off, feeling someone at her elbow. She looked up and received the third shock of her day.

Sheriff Cord Arbutten stood beside her dressed in uniform, right down to the gun at his hip. "Allie," he said. Then, he nodded at Marc.

"Sheriff." Marc didn't offer his hand. He and the sheriff had never been comfortable with each other.

"Allie, may I have a minute of your time?"

Before she could answer, Del materialized. "Everything all right here, folks?" Del had been protective since the night Joe, in full uniform, had all but dragged her out of the bar, ostensibly to protect Allie from Sheryl and herself. Apparently, Del remembered too.

"Everything is fine, Del. Del Delaney, this is Sheriff Cord Arbutten. Sheryl's boss," she added pointedly.

Del's demeanor changed immediately, but not in the manner Allie expected. Del went white. "Has something happened? Is she OK?"

Cord blinked twice, and Allie would bet money he knew the whole scenario in the time it took to blink the first time. "Delaney." He nodded. "This doesn't concern Levine. As far as I know, she's fine."

Del took a step back and shrugged. "Hey, I was just worried." After a minute, he moved away.

Marc stood. "I'll give you two some privacy."

The sheriff motioned him back down. "You might want to hear this too."

He pulled over a chair from a nearby table and sat. "I've had some bad news this afternoon, Allie," he began.

Allie felt the blood rush from her head. Had
something happened to her mother or father?

He cleared his throat. "We got word that Sidney
Finch escaped during a routine transport from
Polk Correctional to the courthouse. He overcame
two armed guards while at a rest area near Cocoa
and vanished about five miles north of the Beeline."
The Beeline was Highway 528, connecting Cocoa
to Cape Canaveral.

"I thought he was in the hospital," she managed.

Cord nodded. "He was until a few weeks ago.
They moved him to protective custody in the
psychiatric facility."

Allie couldn't help it; her gaze went to the door.

"We're pretty sure he's headed out of state. He
took what cash the guards had on them. Not much,
but maybe enough to buy him a bus ticket somewhere. He's not likely to stay around here. He
knows what will happen to him if he's caught."

So did Allie. In Sidney's misguided attempt to
protect the Sheriff from Allie, Sidney had wounded
the man, a minor injury, but the other deputies
knew Sidney had fired the shot. They wouldn't give
him the benefit of the doubt if they caught him.

"I'm headed over to talk to his parents," Cord
said to Allie. "I don't think you have anything to
worry about, but I felt I ought to let you know.
I think if he'd be gunning for anyone, it would be
Levine."

Del appeared beside them. He must have been
hovering close enough to hear every word. "Does
she know?"

Cord didn't appear surprised. "It was on the
radio, and it'll be in the daily bulletin. She's not

likely to miss it. Don't worry," Cord said. "Levine knows how to take care of herself."

■ ■ ■

SHERYL LAY ON THE PRECINCT bathroom floor, spent and exhausted. God, what was wrong with her? She felt like she was dying—the violent bouts of nausea, the exhaustion, and it was getting worse. Had she poisoned herself, somehow? *For weeks?* Ridiculous. She'd never been sick a day in her life.

OK, there was the time she challenged a few guys to a beer-and-shot contest and heaved her guts out for two days afterward, but she won, damn it. And there was a reason for that sickness—alcohol poisoning, pure and simple. This was a fucking mystery. Fine one minute and on her knees the next.

How could she work like this? Jesus, if she went to the doctor, it'd be all over the department. Maybe she should see a doctor in Orlando. She had to use her real name—they checked photo IDs these days—but she could make her profession housewife or something. Waitress. Hairdresser. What the hell ever.

She heard the ladies' room door squeak open and lifted her burning face off the cold tile floor.

"Hey, Levine. You OK? Guys said you'd been gone a long time."

She pulled herself up on the toilet as footsteps started toward her. "Yeah. Fine. Just got the squirts. Musta been last night's tacos."

"That what Mrs. Odum's feeding you? With all her years cooking for Joe, you'd think she could do better than that."

"She does fine," Sheryl snapped. "I asked her to make them."

What a joke. She didn't eat dinner the night before; she was too sick. She told Jasper, her partner, she was eating at home, and she told Libby she and Jasper had grabbed a bite. Shit, she hated this lying, especially to Libby.

She wiped her mouth on the back of her hand. She knew Libby was beginning to suspect something. Another reason to see a doctor. Jesus, what if she was dying of something? Cancer or whatever? What would that do to Allie and Libby? Allie just lost Lou, and Libby lost both Joe and her husband. But at least, they'd have each other. Without her.

She rested her head against the metal stall wall and wept soundlessly.

Seven

A LLIE SLOWED as she passed Sheryl's house. Still no car. She slowed even more. Could that be what she was working? Sidney's disappearance? She shook her head. No. Sheryl had been scarce for weeks, and Sidney escaped only today.

Reflexively, she glanced behind her. No one following her. Not Marc. Not Sidney. Both had followed her around at one time, and she was getting pretty good at spotting a tail.

Marc. Oh, God, what was she going to do about Marc?

Nothing. That was the only answer she could come up with. Until she had a better handle on her emotions and his trustworthiness, she would play it by ear. One thing she knew. She wouldn't invest herself wholeheartedly in him again and have him walk away. Besides, there was Rand.

She pulled in her driveway and shut off the engine. Was that why she was so attracted to Rand? Because he was the polar opposite of Marc? Then, Rand's image and the memory of his words returned to her, and she knew it was more than that. Rand Arbutten made her feel like no man had in her life—petite and precious while, at the

49

same time, self-sufficient and capable.

She didn't know how he managed it, but that's what he did. She turned to jelly at the mere thought of him. And now, when would she see him again? Obviously, he thought Len was an old boyfriend back to stay. Why hadn't she said anything? Maybe because she was in shock and didn't snap out of it until Rand was gone. She couldn't blame him. She'd have done the same thing under similar circumstances.

She climbed out of the car but laughed this time at the catcalls coming from the construction site next door. Frank and his crew. Against all odds, since they were the ones destroying her little bit of paradise, they'd become friends. She waved up at them. "Hi, guys," she yelled. They were five floors up now, so they probably didn't hear her, but every man waved back.

Spook raced out to greet her as she stepped inside. She scooped him up and held him close to her face. "How's my fella? Are you hungry?"

Spook, at least at first, had been an unwelcome part of Allie's inheritance. The story was that her aunt had rescued the dog a few months before her death from Hodgkin's. They'd had a time getting used to each other, Allie and Spook, but now, she wouldn't take a million dollars for him.

As she flipped the deadbolt, the phone rang. When Allie saw who it was, she realized she'd expected the call.

"Hello, Mother."

Silence. "Why can't you answer the phone properly, Allison? I thought I taught you better manners than that."

Allie almost hung up, but she'd have to talk to the woman eventually. "Grainger residence. Allison Grainger, sole proprietor, speaking. May I help you?"

"Now, you're just being ridiculous. What do you mean, sole proprietor?"

Vivian was an attorney. Let her figure it out. "What can I do for you, Mother?"

Another protracted silence. Vivian Grainger wasn't used to having her questions ignored. Allie waited her out.

"I wanted to see if Len arrived there safely."

Allie seethed. Vivian wanted to know if Allie had already caved. "Is there some reason he wouldn't have? A plane crash or something?"

Allie could almost feel her mother's anger vibrate across the wires. "I do not appreciate your sarcasm," she said. "I asked a civil question. I don't think a correspondingly civil answer is too much to expect."

Allie rubbed her forehead. Her mother was right, much as it galled her to admit it. She didn't know why her mother—and her brother, come to think of it—always brought out the teenage rebel in her, but they did. Allie was getting too old for that knee-jerk reaction. Besides, she'd fought enough battles for one day.

"I'm sorry, Mother. Yes, Len arrived."

"That's better. Then, may I speak to him?"

"He's not here."

"Where is he?"

Exasperation reappeared in a heartbeat. "I don't know. I don't keep tabs on Len. Why don't you try the Hilton?"

"Why would he be at the Hilton?"

"Because that's where I sent him."

"I thought he was staying with you."

"Well, when the two of you made your plans, you forgot to mention it to *me*."

Silence. "Allison, are you drunk or on drugs or something?"

Allie gripped the phone so hard her hand cramped. "No, but drunk sounds really good right now. Look, Mother, I've had the day from hell. First, Len barged in and interrupted... something... and Sheryl is missing in action and Marc wants to reconcile and then the sheriff shows up to tell me Sidney escaped—"

Sharp indrawn breath. "Sidney Finch. That man who tried to kill you last year?"

Was that concern in her mother's voice? Allie felt herself soften just a bit. "The one and only."

"My God, Allison, he's a dangerous man. That's all the more reason you should let your brother stay with you. He could offer you some measure of protection."

So much for concern. And the thought of Len protecting her was ludicrous. He'd be more likely to offer her to Sidney on a silver salver. Allie went back to massaging her forehead. "I don't have room for Len here, Mother. I work from home. I have one bedroom and one office, and somehow, I can't see Len sleeping on anyone's couch."

"Well, if you'd move to a larger place..."

Allie barely resisted the urge to hurl the phone across the room. "I'm not having this conversation again. Not now." Not ever.

"Well, I think it's a sad day when you send your

only brother to a hotel. Totally unreasonable of you. Not that I'm surprised."

Exhaustion washed over Allie. "If you want to talk to Len, why don't you call him on his cell?"

"I suppose I'll have to, but—"

"Someone's at the door. I have to go." She wasn't surprised when the phone clicked loudly in her ear.

No one was at the door, but Allie couldn't bear another minute of listening to how unreasonable or selfish or cruel she was. Her family had always considered her lacking, but it wasn't until they learned she was Lou's only heir that the other epitaphs were added, maybe because until then, as with Lou, they merely scorned her. She was sick to death of them all.

She pulled a diet soda out of the refrigerator and tucked Spook under her arm. Her hand hesitated on the doorknob as she remembered Sidney had escaped, but then, she realized she was acting foolish. This was the last place Sidney would come. Allie was certain Clay would have someone watching the house, or at least driving by occasionally.

Besides, on the roof deck, she'd have the whole construction crew watching her. Now that highrise condos were going up on either side of her tiny beach cottage, privacy was a thing of the past. Sad. Even sadder, she knew she couldn't put off deciding about selling much longer. Once people lived in the buildings, her tiny stretch of beach would be littered with them, all their relatives, and their legion of friends. She knew she had to move. She tossed her head. She'd do it when she was damn well ready.

She waved at the guys hanging off the steel

girders as she put Spook on the lawn chair opposite hers. The roof deck wasn't glamorous. A set of spiral wrought-iron stairs led up to a flat gravel-covered asphalt surface. Low rails. Two lounge chairs and a table. Allie, Joe, and Sheryl used to camp up here when they were kids. A makeshift blanket tent and three sleeping bags were all it took to transport them to the wilds of Africa or Alaska, surrounded by crocodiles or ravenous wolves. She smiled at the thought.

"You kids were the highlight of my life. Well, one of the highlights."

Another was Sheriff Cord Arbutten. Cord and her aunt had loved one another for years. They hadn't acted on it because Cord was married. Now, he was a widower, and her aunt was gone.

"It's all right, Allie. The quality of love can't be measured by whether it is consummated. What we had was satisfying in its way."

"That's not the kind of satisfaction I'm looking for these days." She sat straight. Had she really said that to her aunt?

"I'm not a prude, Allie. I know all about sex. I know you're confused right now. And horny."

"I'm shocked!"

Allie heard a tinkle of laughter, or maybe it was her wind chime downstairs.

The breeze was rising as the day waned. Soon, it would be too chilly to stay up here. February in Central Florida, warm days and cool nights, ocean temperatures that remained above the air temperature thanks to an ever-cooperative Gulf Stream.

She watched as pelicans glided above her on

air currents she could only imagine. How did it feel to glide like that, weightless and unfettered? Had any human felt that way? Astronauts? Glider pilots? Didn't they take their earthbound baggage into the sky with them? Did pelicans have baggage?

She heard him before she saw him. So did Spook, who jumped from the chair next to her and huddled under hers. She didn't bother to open her eyes. His step was distinctive. As much as she hated the thought of confrontation, it was inevitable.

"Allie?"

She looked up. Against the setting sun, Marc again resembled a god from ancient Olympus. Apollo, perhaps, except Marc had broader shoulders. His sheer physical beauty took her breath away, but so had her ex-husband Garrison's at the time. Was she so shallow that a pretty face could sway her?

"You left without a word. I was worried about you."

She looked up, shielding her eyes. "I needed some time alone. Today has been a bit much."

"You mean Sidney." He sat on the lounge chair Spook had vacated. "That worries me, Allie. Sidney's a police officer. Despite what the sheriff says, I think you may be in danger."

Allie agreed. She didn't really believe Sidney was headed in another direction. He wasn't the type to skulk away and hide. Sidney would want to extract retribution and wouldn't stop until he did.

"Why don't you come back to Miami with me?

You're not working on anything right now, are you?"

She'd expected that. "I've just started a series about the people whose way of life is being destroyed by all this progress," she said, waving at the new construction around her. "I'm calling it 'Paradise Lost.'"

"That'll keep, won't it? At least until they catch him? It's not as if the construction is going to stop anytime soon."

"No, the construction isn't going anywhere. That's why I'm writing the piece."

"Then, come back to Miami with me. Just until they catch this guy."

Allie shook her head at the predictability of his words, but Marc misunderstood.

"OK, then I'll stay here."

"Marc—"

"I'll sleep on the couch if you want. It wouldn't be the first time."

Allie swung her feet to the floor and sat up. "No, it wouldn't, but if you sleep here again, it won't be on the couch."

Again, he misunderstood and smiled. "Well?"

She said nothing, and Marc's smile faded. "So, that's it? Go home, Marc, and let me put myself in danger again."

Allie jumped to her feet and stood over him, her fists clenched at her sides. "Do you hear yourself, Marc? Is it my fault again?"

"I didn't mean it that way."

Allie paced to the front of the deck and stood staring down until she got control of herself. Then, she came back. "But you did," she said, her voice lower. "And that's what it will always come to, won't it? If I don't live my life the way you think is right, and something happens to me, then it's my fault."

She sat back on the lawn chair and took his hands in hers. "Do you remember your ex-wife? You called her your little butterfly?"

Marc hung his head and didn't answer.

"You married Karen because she needed you. You *need* to be needed, Marc. It's as much a part of your makeup as being self-sufficient is mine. I don't *need* to need someone. I don't even want to need someone. When I have another relationship, it will be an equal partnership—or nothing."

Allie released his hands, and they dropped limply between his knees. He was silent for several moments. When he looked up at her, his eyes glistened with moisture. "I'm sorry, Allie, but I can't take that as a final no. I love you. I mean that. I told you once that I'm a very patient man. I'm also a determined man. I can't tie you to me, but I won't give up on us."

He reached over and brushed her hair back from her face. "Please think of what we had between us. It was too good to toss away without even trying."

Allie was near tears herself. She tried to speak, but he held a finger to her lips. "Please. Don't say anything now. Think about it. I won't push you anymore. I'll go back to Miami. All I ask is that you be careful. Sidney Finch is a lunatic. I don't want anything to happen to you."

Allie watched him descend the stairs. After a few minutes, she stood and walked to the edge of the deck where she could see the street. Marc's car was gone. Her shoulders sagged. Wasn't that what she wanted? Why could nothing in life be simple?

She came back and stretched in the recliner. The construction noise had stopped for the day. The air held a definite chill. She heard the waves crashing on the sand, rhythmically, endlessly. The one thing in life you could count on—the sea and its tides. Waves had rolled ashore pretty much since the beginning of time; they'd still be doing it long after everyone was gone. The thought was oddly comforting.

She pulled Spook up on her chest and buried her face in his fur. "Oh, little pup, what a rotten day this has been. Just be glad you're neutered."

■ ■ ■

SIDNEY KNEW HE WAS CRAZY to be here. Word had to be out by now about his escape, and the sheriff would have ordered drive-bys at least, but he couldn't resist.

He'd expected only to get a lay of the land, a visual picture to use in his planning stages, but then, she'd walked to the edge of the deck and looked down. Not at him. He couldn't tell what she was looking at. She only stood there a moment, but if he'd wanted to, he could have shot her without breaking a sweat. God, it was tempting.

Enough. He had what he needed. That deck might be useful. Construction on either side, which made visits difficult during daylight hours but good at night. Good visuals from above once construction stopped each day. Easy access from the beach or the construction sites. Probably lots of vehicles coming and going as future tenants checked out the area. Piece of cake.

Next, a quick visit to his folks' house to pick up some money and clothes. They always did dinner and a movie on Tuesday night. Home late. God, they were so fucking predictable. Then, on to a shopping trip at the airport long-term lot.

He started the car and eased off from the curb. This was going to be fun.

Eight

CORD PULLED THE CRUISER into the Finch driveway just as the couple was backing out of the garage. He tapped his horn, and they stopped.

Wally Finch rolled down his window as Cord approached. "Evening, Cord."

"Wally. Teresa." He nodded at Sidney's mother. "I'd like to talk to you both for a minute, if you can spare it."

Teresa Finch's lips thinned. It had been like that since Cord put Sidney behind bars, not that the three had ever been close.

"We're just leaving for dinner," she said with no pretense of cordiality. "Can't it wait?"

"Sorry, Teresa, but this is important. It'll only take a minute of your time."

"I don't see what could be so all fired important," she said. "You've already locked our son up in jail."

Cord watched Wally squirm in his car seat and wondered again how he could tolerate the woman.

"This is about Sidney."

She appeared to pale. "What about Sidney?"

Had the boy been here already? No. That was fear on her face, not guilt. "Can we talk in the house?"

Wally opened his car door and stepped out, but

Teresa beat him inside. She led Cord no farther than the kitchen and didn't offer him a seat.

"What is it?" she demanded.

"I got word this afternoon that Sidney overpowered his transport guards and escaped."

Teresa gasped, and Wally reached out to steady her. "Was anyone hurt?"

Cord nodded. "Both guards were injured, but neither of them critically."

"Thank God," Wally breathed.

"I suspect Sidney's headed the other way. I can't see him staying around here, but I wanted to alert you in case he decides to show up. It would be best for Sidney if you let me know if that happens." He spoke more to Teresa than her husband. "He's already in a lot of trouble, and now, there will be new charges against him, but it could be worse. It *will* be worse, if we don't catch him soon."

Teresa averted her eyes.

"I mean it, Teresa. If Sidney remains in the area, it can mean only one thing—that he's bent on revenge. He hasn't killed anyone yet, but if he does, don't forget that Florida has the death penalty." Tears sprang to the woman's eyes, and he moderated his tone. "That's why it's important we get him back behind bars before he does something really stupid."

Teresa pulled away from her husband. "You can say that after you ruined my baby's life? How dare you!"

Cord knew Sidney ruined his own life, had been hell-bent on ruining it since he was a boy, but he wasn't about to try to reason that with Teresa Finch. She had a blind spot where Sidney was concerned. Always had. According to her, Sidney could do no wrong. There'd never been any reasoning with her.

He looked at Wally. "For Sidney's sake, let me know if he shows up. He's injured three police officers now as well as several civilians. He's in enough trouble as it is. Don't let's compound that."

Wally nodded. He stood staring at his wife, his brow creased with worry, as Cord let himself out.

■ ■ ■

SIDNEY SLID DOWN in his seat as Cord Arbutten climbed into the cruiser. So, he'd already alerted them. That meant he'd probably alerted Allie too. So what? They'd never catch him.

What the hell were they doing home, anyway? They should be stuffing their faces at one of their favorite restaurants. How the hell was he going to get in the house if they were there? He kept his eyes on the house, hoping they'd head out now that the sheriff was gone, but no such luck. He looked at the clock on the car's dash. Seven-forty.

OK, change of plans. He'd hit the airport and then return here. He'd hoped to have his new threads before then, but no sweat. No one would look for him at the airport. They knew he didn't have money for plane fare. If everything went smoothly, he could be back about nine or ten o'clock. Perfect. His father would be sound asleep in his recliner by nine, and his mother would be sitting beside him, knitting or some other dumb-ass thing while she watched whatever soppy movie was on Lifetime.

He rubbed his forehead. Goddamn headaches. They had started after that Levine bitch rammed him with the cruiser, and they were getting worse. He'd take something for pain—he had a pocket full of pills—but he needed to be in control of all his faculties.

He pulled the car out and headed west.

■ ■ ■

ALLIE PEEKED OUT her front window. God, she hated this paranoia, except if Sidney was out there, it wasn't paranoia, was it?

Thank God. Sheryl's car was finally home. She snapped on Spook's leash and gave him his evening out on the way to Sheryl's house. Not much of a walk, but all he was going to get after dark until they caught Sidney. Allie knew he was around somewhere. She could *feel* it, just like she could feel it when they were kids and Sidney sneaked around. It made her skin crawl then, and it still did. She knew he was capable of murder. He had already tried to kill her twice. The phrase "three times a charm" sprang to mind, and she shoved it back into those deep recesses she rarely visited.

Libby answered the door, still using her walker. "Allie. How nice. Come on in. Have you had dinner? I cooked a pot roast, but Sheryl wasn't hungry so there's plenty left."

Had she eaten dinner? No. She didn't even have lunch. "I'm fine, Libby. I just came to see Sheryl for a minute." She looked around the room. No Sheryl. "I saw her car. Is she home?"

Libby bit her lip. "She's lying down. She was

real tired when she got home."

"Can I stick my head in? I won't wake her if she's asleep. I just want to say hello." And find out where the hell she's been for the last three weeks.

Libby stepped back, dragging her walker with her. "I suppose it'll be all right."

No light came from beneath the door. Allie almost turned around and left, but Libby seemed even more worried than before. She had to make sure Sheryl was all right.

She tapped lightly on the door.

"Huh?"

Allie opened the door and stepped inside.

The room was dark. Sheryl was stretched on the bed fully clothed. Her gun was on the bed beside her. Even in the dim light from the hall, she looked pale and haggard. "Oh, Allie. I thought you were Libby."

"May I come in?"

Sheryl raised her head before dropping it back on the pillow. "You're already in."

Allie smiled. That sounded more like her literal friend. "So, how are you doing? I haven't seen you for a while."

"Yeah, I've been pretty busy." She rolled over to face Allie. "So, how's it going?"

"OK. Uh—may I turn on the light?"

Sheryl reached over and switched on the bedside lamp. The bulb must have been a whole forty watts, but it was enough to show that Sheryl looked like hell. Her usually lustrous chestnut hair was dull and matted, and her skin had a sallow hue.

"You look *terrible*. What's the matter with you?"

"Thanks, Allie. I can always count on you to

cheer me up." She pushed herself to a sitting position and reached over to pet Spook. "Hey, little pup. Your mama taking care of you?" Spook licked her hand, and she turned to Allie. "I think I picked up a bug or something. I feel like shit."

"Libby said you didn't eat any dinner."

"What are you now—my second mother? If anyone needs to eat, it's you, beanpole." She poked Allie in the leg.

Allie wasn't fooled. She perched on the bed beside Sheryl. "Is there anything I can do? Anything I can get you?"

"Like what? A new stomach?" She waved her hand. "No, I—oh, shit!" She bolted off the bed and made a dash for the hallway.

Seconds later, Allie heard the sound of retching and then a toilet flush. These post-World War II houses weren't built for privacy. After a minute, Sheryl came back into the room, wiping her face with a wet rag. "Sorry. I told you. Virus."

"I'm so sorry. Are you sure I can't get you anything? Some ginger ale or something?"

"You want to make me barf again? I haven't drunk that shit since I was five years old. I don't imagine it's gotten any better."

Allie laughed. She reached over and squeezed Sheryl's arm. "If you're sure, I'll leave you alone to suffer in peace. But don't be a stranger, OK? I've missed you."

Sheryl stared at her for a long time without speaking. Allie could swear she saw fear in her normally fearless friend's eyes.

"Did you hear that Sidney escaped?" Allie asked.

Sheryl made a rude sound. "That little fucker.

That's another reason I want to get over this shit, whatever it is. I gotta be back on the streets. You and I know him. We know better than anyone else the kinds of stunts he'd pull." Her brow creased. "You be careful, will you? I don't like that you're unprotected. Why don't you go visit your parents for a while until we catch him?"

Allie couldn't understand it, but when Sheryl said it, it didn't sound patronizing. Marc had said pretty much the same thing, and she'd nearly taken off his head. "I think I'd rather have Sidney get me. No, not really," she said when Sheryl started to speak, "but I can't think of much worse." But she could. "Did you know Len showed up at my house this morning demanding half my inheritance?"

"Your brother Len? Jesus, Allie, what did you tell him?"

"I—" She broke off as Sheryl made another dash from the bed. Again, there was the sound of vomiting, a toilet flush, and Sheryl staggered back into the room. Clearly, Allie had overstayed her welcome.

She took the washcloth from the bedside table and wiped Sheryl's forehead. "I'll tell you all about it when you're feeling better." She stood. "You get well, and have Libby call me if you need anything."

"Why would Libby call you? I have my cell right here." She raised her head and looked around. "Oh, shit. I left it in the car."

"You don't need it. You're off duty, and you're sick. Libby can call me if you need me." Sheryl closed her eyes and nodded.

Allie pulled the bedroom door closed and stepped into the hall to see Libby, her face creased with worry, watching. "She said it's a virus."

Libby nodded, her eyes on the closed door. "That's what she told me."

When Allie reached her, she squeezed her thin shoulder. "Don't worry, Libby. Sheryl's tough. Just don't offer her any ginger ale."

Her eyes searched the shadows as she walked back home, and she breathed a deep sigh of relief as she stepped inside her front door and flipped the deadbolt.

She retrieved a diet soda from the refrigerator and settled on the couch with Spook close beside her. Sheryl really did look bad, worse than Allie had ever seen her. She'd never known Sheryl to be sick, even when they were growing up. Of course, Allie wasn't here year-round back then. But it still worried her. What if it wasn't a stomach virus? What if it was something more serious?

"Sheryl's going to be fine, Allie."

"How do you know? I thought you couldn't see into the future."

"Who says I'm looking into the future?"

"What's wrong with her, then? Is it just a stomach virus?"

"Oh, so now, I'm supposed to be your personal Ouija board?"

Allie buried her face in Spook's fur. "God, I miss you, Aunt Lou."

■ ■ ■

SIDNEY LOOKED AT HIS BARE wrist and then at the dashboard clock. Shit, he needed a watch. No sweat. There were bound to be several lying around the house.

Ten-thirty. The airport took longer than he expected because he wanted to find just the right
vehicle, but in the end, it was worth it—a nice,
nondescript, beige Lexus with the hood still warm.
You didn't park in long-term for an overnight trip
unless you were the world's biggest cheapskate,
and a cheapskate didn't buy a Lexus. He figured
he had three or four days, at least. Maybe more,
because he'd switched plates with a beige Taurus.
The coins he stole from Raymond made a nifty
screwdriver. Odds were the Taurus owner wouldn't
notice the plate change or report it missing for a
while.

He was parked a few doors down from his folks'
house, a boxy two-story clapboard in a quiet neighborhood. The living room light was still on. Sidney
wasn't surprised. His dad usually didn't wake
and head up the stairs until two a.m. or so, but
he was a heavy sleeper. No problem there. It was
dark upstairs, which meant his mom was dead to
the world. Even better. He'd wait another hour
or so, even though the old farts who lived in this
neighborhood usually hit the rack by nine o'clock.
He'd slipped out of Raymond's jacket at the airport
and reversed it so the fluorescent lettering was
inside. He'd be virtually invisible to any busybody
or restless insomniac who happened to glance out
the window.

The key was under the fake rock at the back
door. His parents had never installed an alarm
system even though he'd nagged them to do it.
Now he was glad.

The back door opened directly into the kitchen.

He could hear the drone of the television from the living room. Good. That would mask any noise he made. His mother kept her cash in a canister marked "Flour" in the walk-in pantry. He pulled out a wad of bills. *Jesus*! There must be almost a thousand bucks here. Why the hell wasn't this in the bank? Then, he smiled as he stuffed it into his pocket.

Now, the tricky part. He crept down the hallway toward the front of the house. As he neared the stairs, he saw his dad stretched out in the recliner, head resting against its back and snoring softly. Sidney couldn't count the number of times he'd sneaked out and in when he was a boy. Never once in all those years did they catch him, and he knew they wouldn't now. He knew exactly which steps squeaked and where. He didn't need a light. These people were dark phobic; there was a nightlight in what seemed like every other wall outlet.

He froze when he heard a creak from his parents' bedroom. If his mother got up now, there was nowhere to hide. He remained still until he heard her sigh, then go silent.

He tiptoed into his room, leaving the door open so he had the hall light. Christ, the place looked exactly as it did when he was arrested. Except cleaner. He smiled. His mom was a stickler for cleanliness and order, which was why she'd always cleaned his room. Back when he was a kid, he sometimes left little surprises for her, like a pair of girl's panties under his mattress or porno magazines in his closet, just to get her reaction, but she never called him on it. It was a disappointment, so after a while, he quit doing it.

He listened for a minute to make sure no noise other than the TV came from downstairs. Then, he crossed to the closet. When he opened the bi-fold, he almost gave a cheer. Pay dirt. His clothes. Old uniforms. He'd been afraid the sheriff would confiscate those after he was arrested, but they hung in a neat row. Even his personal weapon—a Glock 36 he'd taken off a drug head during a bust, untraceable to him if he had to use it—and four boxes of ammo on the closet shelf.

He grabbed the backpack off the closet floor and flipped it open. He wrapped his weapon and two boxes of ammo in an undershirt and stuffed it in the bottom of the backpack. As an afterthought, he pulled Raymond's firearm out of his jacket pocket and left it on the shelf with the other two boxes of ammunition in his stash. No one would notice he'd switched guns, which might be important if the sheriff decided to search his room.

Then, he eased a couple of uniforms off hangers and folded them carefully before putting them in the backpack. He didn't see any ironing days in his immediate future, and a wrinkled uniform would draw attention. Shirts, jeans, shoes, and socks. Underwear. Anything that wasn't a blue prison jumpsuit looked good to him.

He changed into black slacks with a real belt and a dark green turtleneck. Very respectable looking. He shoved Raymond's uniform under the bed. It didn't matter if his mother found it. She'd never turn him in. Civilian socks and shoes. God, it felt good to be dressed again. He looked around the room. What else?

He flattened himself against the wall at a sound

on the stairs. Shit! He was early. He reached over and eased the backpack toward him until it was out of sight. Nothing could be seen from the door. The bathroom door opened. The sound of a urine stream, then water running. Slow shuffling footsteps down the hall.

The door was mostly open, but Sidney could see through the doorjamb crack. His father stopped outside the door and stared inside. After a minute, he shook his head and moved off toward the master bedroom.

Something in the hopelessness of the gesture grabbed Sidney's gut, but he shook it off. What the hell difference did it make? His father gave up on him years ago, and vice versa. What could it matter now? Still, he didn't want to shoot him. He waited without moving until he heard his father snoring.

His last stop was the extra bedroom where his mother stored her memories. Back in her youth, Teresa Finch acted regularly in the Surfside Players productions in Cocoa Beach. She'd made many of her costumes, and she hung on to them. The closet and dresser were full of them. Costumes. Makeup. Wigs. Best of all, he and his mother were close to the same size. First time he'd ever been glad he was small.

He picked out a few things that might prove useful right away. Space in the backpack was limited, and he could always come back for more. Before he left the room, he slipped a short red wig and some costume jewelry in his pocket. A little makeup and a few other enhancements, and he could be Mary Lou Childers out for a late-night drive. Hell, dark as it was on this moonless night, he didn't even need the makeup.

As he slipped out of the house, he patted his pocket. He was flush, and he had most of the tools he'd need to begin waging his campaign. Now, he needed a place to stay, but that would have to wait until morning. There'd be a BOLO on him tonight. His height and limp he couldn't conceal. He knew a guy in Titusville who owed him a few favors. Tomorrow, he'd collect.

Nine

ALLIE'S SPIRITS PLUMMETED as she drove into the parking lot at the *Brevard Sun*. She had hoped to find Rand here. He still worked for the law firm in Orlando, fifty miles to the east, and only gave the newspaper a few days a month, but she hoped this was one of those days. She'd called and left a message on his cell phone telling him she wanted to talk to him, but she hadn't heard back. She knew his silence was intentional. Usually, he called back within five minutes.

Myrna was in the reception area with the telephone pressed to her ear when Allie entered. Fiftyish and comfortably overweight, Myrna ran the newspaper these days. Although technically the receptionist, she worked as the original owner's secretary for more than twenty years and knew the business stem to stern. After Cornelius Senior died and his son took over, Myrna stayed, although she detested Cornelius Junior, and with good reason—the man was insane.

Then, after Junior's death, a board of directors, who knew less about the business than Allie's dog did, ran the newspaper. It floundered until Myrna stepped in as unofficial acting editor and hired Rand part-time to schmooze the advertisers threatening to bail. She maintained he had all the assets she needed—he was a lawyer with tons of charisma, and he had a penis. Apparently, she was right. Rand charmed their advertisers into staying, and the paper was stable again.

Myrna could also be persuasive. She talked Allie into coming to work for the paper and then bribed her into serving as its only investigative reporter later when Allie wanted to quit. The promotion meant Allie could work out of her house and write what she wanted. Hard proposition to turn down. Overall, Myrna was a force to be reckoned with.

She wiggled her fingers at Allie as she made her polite goodbyes to whoever was on the other end of the line. "Jesus," she breathed, hanging up the receiver, "that woman can talk!"

"Who was it?"

"You don't know her. Gloria Jameson. She used to work here when Rupert was alive. She's sure the paper would benefit from a scandal column. Over my dead body." She pushed back from the desk. "Speaking of columns, how's your story coming?"

"Slowly. I've done a lot of research, but I haven't begun putting it together yet. I—" She broke off as Myrna stood.

"Let's go outside," Myrna said. "I'm dying for a cigarette."

Myrna was always dying for a cigarette. She was probably dying for a cigarette while she was smoking one. It was her trademark. Goodyear had the blimp; Myrna had her cigarettes.

Allie followed her outside to the four-by-four foot stretch of grass that was Myrna's smoking area.

When Cornelius number two died and Myrna took the reins, she'd had a crew jackhammer the concrete and put in sod. It was the only thing aesthetically pleasing about the low-slung, white building that more closely resembled a self-storage facility than a newspaper office.

Myrna already had a cigarette lit when she sat and motioned Allie to sit beside her. "So, what's the scoop on the construction industry?"

"Has Rand been here today?"

"Wasn't there some old philosopher who used to always answer a question with a question?"

"Socrates, and I don't think it's the same thing."

"Why are you looking for Rand?"

Allie considered concocting some fiction dealing with the newspaper, but Myrna would find out the truth eventually. She always did. "There was a misunderstanding at my house yesterday. Rand was visiting..." She looked over at Myrna.

"About damn time."

Allie felt the heat in her cheeks. "We were talking in the living room when my brother showed up unannounced. With his suitcase."

"He still pressuring you to sell the house?"

"And split the proceeds with him. Anyway, he told Rand I'd never mentioned him but forgot to add that he's my brother, and we don't speak. Rand took one look at the suitcase and left without another word."

"So, where is he now?"

"That's what I asked you."

"Not Rand. He isn't due back in town until Friday. I meant your brother."

Allie's shoulders sagged. "I sent him packing.

I could just kill him, Myrna. He threatened to take me to court. He says he's entitled to half what Aunt Lou left. It's not as if I need it all, but after the way he treated her, he doesn't deserve a dime."

Myrna took a drag off her cigarette and blew the smoke in the other direction. "He doesn't stand a prayer of breaking the will."

"Are you sure?" She shook herself. "That's not the point. Well, it is, but the main thing is that I don't need the grief."

"Not with Sidney Finch on the loose."

"You know about that?"

Myrna sat back. "Honey, I run the newspaper. Of course, I know about it. Sheriff asked me to keep it quiet, so I will. For now. But the sooner they catch him the better. You know he'll come gunning for you for turning his hero against him. I'd bet—"

Allie jumped to her feet as a car turned into the lot. It couldn't be. He wouldn't dare. Not here. She stood with her hands on her hips as he climbed out of the car and approached them.

Myrna was on her feet now. "Who is that hunk?" she whispered.

"That *hunk* is my brother, who has a hell of a lot of nerve showing up here."

Len stopped in front of them. "Good morning, Allie. I hope you don't mind my dropping by. I came by the house, but you'd left, so I thought I'd try here. I thought you said you worked from home."

"I do. Most of the time. Not that it's any business of yours where I work."

Len looked at Myrna and smiled. "Since my

sister obviously isn't going to introduce us, I'm Len Grainger, Allie's brother."

Myrna appeared mesmerized. Len had that effect on some women, with his you're-the-only-woman-in-the-world look. He practiced it on female jurors and probably his divorce clients—the women, at least.

"Allie's mentioned you," Myrna said, offering her hand.

Allie almost laughed. She'd mentioned Len all right. "I asked what you're doing here."

Len pulled his gaze from Myrna—an act, Allie knew—and looked at her. "I brought some papers for you."

Allie saw red. "What, a subpoena?"

Len smiled. "Of course not. Oh, Allie, you didn't take my teasing yesterday seriously, did you?" He didn't wait for an answer. "Can we go inside?" He addressed the last to Myrna.

Myrna seemed to come out of her stupor. "What? Sure. Yes."

Len took Myrna's arm, and Allie followed. She wouldn't have believed that even someone as crass as Len would have the effrontery to show up where she worked, but she'd underestimated him—and he was about to discover he'd underestimated her.

Once inside, she led him directly back to the newsroom. No way was she going to have a private tête-à-tête with him. Whatever he had to say to her, he could say in front of a room full of witnesses. *Teasing.* Right.

A couple of people nodded at Allie and looked at Len curiously. She stopped at the desk she used when she was in the office and spun on him. "Give me the papers."

Len looked at her outstretched hand, then back at her with amusement. He reached for an empty desk chair and pulled it over, sitting and resting his briefcase on his lap.

"I gathered some information I thought you might find helpful," he said, reaching into the case and pulling out a sheaf of handwritten pages. "I'd like to explain these calculations to you. They're pretty complicated."

Allie snatched them from his hand. "I'm fully capable of deciphering calculations." She spread the papers out on her desk. The squiggles that covered the sheets looked like hieroglyphics. "What are they?" She heard a titter of laughter from another desk and did a slow burn.

Len chuckled. He scooted forward on his chair and gestured to the first page. "These are computations of the value of Aunt Lou's house—"

"*My* house."

He ignored the interruption. "—as the market stands today. The housing market is on the rise, but it's still depressed. That won't affect the sale of Aunt Lou's property because it's in high demand, but it affects your purchasing power. Right now, it's a buyer's market. You could get an excellent property for about a tenth of what our aunt's house would go for. This second sheet—"

His voice went on, but she heard no more. It was all too much. First, he barged into her house and scared off Rand. Now, he was explaining how he could take advantage of her. Allie wasn't putting up with any more of it. She swept the papers to the floor. "What's the matter with you, Len?"

"With me? I'm just trying to help."

"Help me? *You* help *me*? What a *laugh*! You're just trying to help yourself, to weasel your way into half Aunt Lou's money, but you won't get a red cent."

With a sigh, Len bent and gathered the papers from the floor. Then, he shoved them in his brief-case. Rising, he looked down at Allie. The room was silent. Not a movement. Probably not a breath.

Len's Adam's apple bobbed, and he cleared his throat. His face was a mask of pain. In a whisper that easily carried into the far corners of the room, he said, "She was my aunt, too, Allie." After glancing around at all the faces turned their way, he left.

Only then, did Allie realize every eye was on her. "Can you believe that guy?" she said.

One by one, each of her coworkers looked away. Even Myrna, who had witnessed the whole thing, wouldn't meet Allie's eyes. What was wrong with these people? OK, she could understand the reporters' reactions; they didn't know about Allie and Len's history. But Myrna?

Defeat weighed heavily on her shoulders. It was her childhood all over again. No matter how crappy the stunt Len pulled on her, he always managed to make her the bad guy, to make her seem petty and unreasonable. She couldn't count the times her parents had looked at her, their faces drawn with disappointment. It wasn't fair. Damn it, it wasn't fair!

There wasn't a sound as she walked out of the newsroom. Noon, and her day was already going to hell in a handbasket. When she stepped out of the building, Len still stood beside his rental car, gloating over his morning's success, no doubt. Her heart gave a little thump when she saw Rand's car turning in to the lot. She could spot the exact second he saw Len. He braked and started to execute a U-turn. Allie wasn't having it. She'd had enough misunderstanding for one day. She stepped in front of his exiting car. When he came to a stop, she walked around to the driver's window.

"I need to talk to you," she said as he rolled down his window.

His face wore no expression. "I don't know if today—"

"Please, Rand. It won't take long."

After a long hesitation, he put the car in reverse and backed into a nearby space.

Allie awaited him at the building entrance. She ignored Len's cordial wave as he drove out of the lot. When Rand reached her, she turned and led the way into the newspaper's only conference room, closing the door behind her. This was one conversation she wanted kept private. She didn't know why Rand was avoiding her to this extent, but she knew she didn't want the newspaper staff to find out at the same time she did.

She turned and faced him, her arms folded across her chest. "Did you get my message?"

He crossed his arms in a mirror image of hers and leaned against the conference table. "I did."

"Why didn't you call me back?"

"I've been pretty busy—"

"That won't wash, Rand. You've always called me back. Even when you were tied up in court, you sent a text message to say you'd call later."

He shrugged. "I didn't think there was any hurry."

"That's not how you felt yesterday before Len showed up."

He pinned her with his eyes. "Exactly. What was the point?"

Allie was beginning to enjoy herself. "Do you want to know more about Len?"

"I know he was here a minute ago. Why would I want to know more?"

"I've known him—"

"I don't want to hear this." He turned away.

"Since I was born. He's my brother, Rand. My big, obnoxious brother."

It took a moment for her words to sink in. When they did, he turned back, a broad smile starting on his face. "Your brother?"

"Uh-huh."

His eyes lit up like New York at dusk. "Why didn't you tell me?"

Allie took a step toward him. "When? You were out of there so fast—"

"I thought..." He stepped nearer.

"You thought what?" Another step. "That he was an old boyfriend?"

"Hell, no. I wouldn't have left for an old boyfriend."

"Then, who?"

He moved a step closer. "I thought he was your ex-husband."

"*Garrison*? Why would you think it was Garrison?"

He shrugged, stepping closer. "The suitcase. I didn't figure you'd welcome an old boyfriend with a suitcase. An ex? Marriages and divorces are complicated."

"Garrison is in Brussels. Besides, if he showed up on my doorstep, I'd send him packing even faster than I did Len."

There were mere inches separating them now. Rand looked down at her. "You sent Len packing?"

She nodded. "To the Hilton, although he can go to perdition for all I care."

"So, let me get this straight. There's no one staying at your house, but you?"

"And my dog."

"And your cute little non-watchdog. Seems almost too good an opportunity—"

"To let go to waste. My thinking exactly."

Both had lowered their arms. They were touching now, chest to chest, so close that her breath stirred the fine hairs at his temple. Rand reached over and outlined her face with his fingertips. Allie felt the heat of the contact sear her. Another minute and they'd be on the conference table.

Just as Rand pulled her closer with his other arm, the door opened, and Allie jumped away.

Myrna stuck her head in. "Hey, you two OK in here? It's awfully quiet."

"We were doing fine," Rand answered, a suggestive smile on his lips, "although maybe here isn't the best place for us to... do fine."

"Maybe not. We have a staff meeting in here in fifteen minutes. You two coming?"

"Not to the staff meeting," Rand said, his eyes still on Allie. "Next time, maybe. Right now, we have another engagement."

■ ■ ■

SIDNEY HELD UP THE BLANK clipboard as if checking the address. The magnetic door sign he'd stolen off a parked delivery vehicle—City Courier—gave him credibility if anyone missed the significance of the clipboard. He reached in the back seat and retrieved the gaily wrapped package. He was especially proud of the bow. Bright yellow. It coordinated nicely with the contents of the box. He wished he'd had time to get her something more special, but once he got settled in his new trailer in Cocoa, there'd be plenty of time. He could let his imagination go wild... and he would.

Carrying the clipboard under one arm and moving slowly to hide his limp, he walked across the lawn to the front door. He knew she wasn't there—no car.

He made a big show of knocking. Then, he studied the clipboard again. After making a check in an imaginary box, he placed the package on the front stoop and walked back to his car, whistling.

He hoped no neighbors noticed he was driving a Lexus. He hadn't thought of that when he made his snatch. Still, if he had to be on the run, it was better to ride in luxury.

He whistled as he opened the car door and slipped inside. He hoped Allie Grainger enjoyed her little gift.

Ten

RAND WAS RIGHT BEHIND HER when she pulled in her driveway. Neither spoke as they made their hurried way into the house. With the door barely closed behind them, Rand pulled her into his arms. There was no caution this time, no let's wait for later, no wine, and who the hell needed it anyway? Not she.

She ran her hands up and down his back. His muscles felt so solid, so... male. She wanted to eat him alive. He brought his mouth down on hers, and she plunged into the kiss with all the enthusiasm of a woman long denied. She nibbled his lips, his chin, trailed her tongue to his ear as his hands traced her outline.

His breathing was ragged. He eased her backward toward the couch. Good enough. Who needed a bed? Allie heard a moan and wasn't sure if it was her or Rand. Or both.

They fell the final two feet to the sofa cushion. She barely noticed. She couldn't get enough of him. Her hands moved of their own volition—arms, shoulders, neck, back, legs. His were just as busy, caressing her, tracing each inch.

As he moved over her, the front door slammed open. Sheryl stood in the doorway, a wrapped package clutched in her hand and her mouth open in shock. "Uh—I—uh…"

Allie sat up, pulling her clothing right. Rand remained where he was, sprawled on the couch, a look of tolerant amusement on his face. "Deputy Levine, how are you?"

"Jeez, guys, I'm sorry. I didn't think. I—"

"Didn't knock," Allie finished for her. "Come on in, and shut the door. Will you never learn to enter a room like a normal human being?"

Sheryl looked sheepish. "I guess not."

"It would be good to see you again, Levine, if this was any other time," Rand said, still smiling.

"Back atcha, bud," Sheryl said with a smile. "I need Allie."

He nodded. "I find myself in the same situation. You can't have her."

"Who says?"

"Hey, people," Allie said, waving her arms. "I'll decide who can and can't have me, if you don't mind." Her face burned as she realized what she'd said. She looked at the package in Sheryl's hand. "What's that?"

Sheryl looked at the box as if just remembering it. "Uh—beats me. It was on your doorstep."

"I didn't notice," Allie said, brushing the hair back from her face.

Sheryl gave Rand the once-over and smirked. "I'm not surprised."

Rand grinned and looked at the package Sheryl held. "A secret admirer?"

"God, I hope not." Allie took the box and tore off the bow and ribbon. When she saw what was inside, she gagged and dropped the box.

Rand and Sheryl were at her side in an instant. "What is it?"

Sheryl pulled a pen out of her pocket and stuck it in the mass of goo that had spilled out of the box. A quick sniff and a scowl. "It's shit. Jesus, who would send you shit?"

"I don't—" Then, she remembered Len saying he'd come by the house looking for her. But was Len low enough to pull a stunt like this?

"What?" Rand and Sheryl asked in unison.

"My brother," Allie spat. "He said he came by this morning. Now, I know why."

"You really think your brother would do something like this?" Rand asked, looking down at the brown mess with distaste.

"Do I think he's mean enough to do it? Yes. Would I have credited him with more imagination and taste? Yes, but maybe he was short of time." She stalked around the small room, raking her fingers through her hair. "God, I don't know. I don't want to think Len would do something like this, but after he threatened me—"

"Threatened how?" Rand asked, his voice a razor.

"Not like that. Not a physical threat. He threatened to take me to court about my inheritance. He's convinced he's entitled to half of that and half the proceeds of the sale of the house."

"You're selling the house?" Sheryl asked.

"*No.* I mean, yes. Probably. Eventually." She looked at Sheryl. "Can you really see me living between two high-rises?"

"Mid-rises," Rand corrected.

"*Whatever.* Who cares? I'm still the proverbial

toadstool among the redwoods. I know I'll have to sell eventually, but Len came to my office today to quote me property values. He wanted to show me how I could sell, share with him, and still make money." She sank into a chair and dropped her head into her hands.

Rand came to stand behind her and began to massage her neck. Allie looked up gratefully.

"Len just doesn't get it," she said. "It's not about the money. It's about fairness, about how he and my whole family treated Aunt Lou. She specifically said in her last letter to me that I wasn't to let any of my family bully me out of my inheritance."

"Do you still have the letter?" Rand asked.

"Of course. I've never thrown away anything from Aunt Lou. Why?"

"Just thinking ahead. In case he goes forward with his threat."

Allie shook her head. "You lawyers..."

"Hey, don't pigeonhole me with your brother. I just want to make sure you're protected legally."

Allie reached up and squeezed his hand. "I'd never pigeonhole you with Len. He's a shyster. You're a man of the law." It was on the tip of her tongue to add "like your father," but she wasn't sure Rand was ready to hear that yet. Someday.

"It might not be Len," Sheryl said, her voice low.

Allie spun toward her. "You think Sidney was here?"

"Isn't he still in Polk?" Rand asked.

"He escaped yesterday," Sheryl said. "Sheriff's convinced he's headed in the other direction, but he doesn't—" Suddenly, she paled and raced toward the bathroom. It was a replay of the night before.

"What's wrong with her?" Rand asked, staring after her.

Allie bit her lip. "I don't know, and it has me worried sick. She said a virus, but it's been going on too long."

"Has she seen a doctor?"

"That's why I'm here," Sheryl said, coming back in the room with a washcloth fisted in her hand. "Allie, I need you to go to Orlando with me. No questions asked."

"Why aren't you seeing a local doctor?"

Sheryl closed her eyes. "That was a question." She looked at Allie. "I wouldn't ask you, but if I get sick while I'm driving, it could be dangerous. Libby can't drive. I don't want any nosy deputy tagging along with me, and that leaves you."

Allie's lips twitched. "I'm flattered."

She looked at Rand, who shrugged. He leaned over Allie's shoulder and whispered, "Our day will come." He slipped back into his shoes—when had they come off? —and with a brief salute at Sheryl, headed out the door.

Allie reached for her purse. "What kind of doctor are you seeing?"

"That's another question. Please, Allie. Tell me if you can't do this. I can probably drive myself, but..."

Allie wanted to be with Sheryl when she learned what was wrong with her, especially if it was something serious. "One rule," she said pulling her keys out of her purse. "I drive."

■ ■ ■

ORLANDO WAS FIFTY easy miles west of Cape Canaveral, and they made it in less than an hour. The trip was mostly silent. Allie knew Sheryl talked nonstop when she was nervous, so what she was feeling went way beyond nerves. Could it be fear? In all their years together, Allie had never seen Sheryl afraid, so she had nothing to gauge by.

When they reached Orlando, Sheryl directed her from a piece of paper she clutched in her hand. It looked like handwritten notes. Soon, they were near the heart of downtown.

Sheryl motioned Allie into a covered parking deck. When Allie took the ticket and pulled into the first available spot, Sheryl snapped off her seatbelt and turned to face her. "I want you to stay here and wait for me. I shouldn't be very long, and it's not hot or anything."

"But, Sheryl—"

"Please, Allie. You probably think I ask a lot of you, but I need this one more favor."

Allie shook her head in exasperation. Sheryl asked hardly anything for herself, and she gave nonstop without ever expecting anything in return. As desperately as Allie wanted to know what was going on, she knew she had to honor this request—at least to a point.

"OK. I'll wait for you." She held up her cell phone. "Call me if you need me to come inside or anything, OK?"

She could see Sheryl go limp with relief. "Sure. Will do."

Sheryl's hand shook as she released her seatbelt and opened the car door. She walked toward the multistory across the street with the enthusiasm of a doomed man approaching the gallows. It took all of Allie's control not to run after her. If anyone ever needed a friend, it was Sheryl—which was the reason she didn't chase after her. Sheryl needed a friend she could trust.

She, however, had not promised to wait in the car. Allie watched Sheryl's progress in the rear-view mirror. A few moments after Sheryl entered a massive pair of glass doors, Allie slipped out of the car and started across the street. The sign she'd missed when she turned into the parking deck read "Orlando Regional Medical Center." Why a medical center instead of a doctor's office? When Allie drew closer, she realized the doors Sheryl used led to the Oncology Department. Oncology? Wasn't that cancer?

She stepped back, feeling the blood leave her head. Impossible! Sheryl was too young. Thirty, the same age as Allie. Cancer didn't happen to thirty-year-olds, except Allie knew it did. Had Sheryl already been diagnosed, or was she in there having some test right now? If so, Allie intended to be with her, no matter what she had promised.

She pushed through the double doors and stared in confusion. Corridors branched off in four directions: Oncology, Radiology, Women's Center, and Outpatient Surgery.

She headed toward Oncology because it was the closest. Nearly every chair was filled. Half the people appeared frail, most wearing some kind of scarf or something over their heads. One man in a wheelchair looked almost beyond medical help. Allie repressed a shiver, and she was disgusted by her faintheartedness. They were in groups of two or more. Patients and their caregivers?

She didn't see Sheryl in the waiting room. A receptionist sat behind a glass partition. Allie tapped the glass. When the woman slid it open, she said, "I'm meeting my friend here after her appointment. Sheryl Levine. Do you know how long she'll be?"

The woman checked the computer screen. "I don't see her here. Are you sure you have the right day?"

Allie didn't have to try to look uncomfortable. Everyone in the waiting room watched her. "Uh—maybe she said tomorrow. I'll—uh—call her. Thank you."

She repeated the process at radiology and out-patient surgery with minor adjustments to her spiel. At the Women's Center, she hit paydirt.

"Mrs. Levine. Yes, here she is." She checked the clock on the wall. "I think she just left. You can probably catch her if you hurry."

Allie sprinted out of the office taking several wrong turns before she again found the entrance. From where she stood, she could see there was no Sheryl crossing the street, no Sheryl standing by the car, and because Allie had the keys in her hand, she knew Sheryl wasn't inside the car. She turned and retraced her tracks. As she passed the ladies' room, Sheryl stepped into the hall, her face the color of unleavened dough.

She stopped when she saw Allie, then she brushed past her and hurried toward the exit. Allie had to run to catch her.

"Sheryl, wait!" Sheryl's cop stride was worth three of Allie's normal steps. They were in the middle of the street before Allie caught her. She reached for Sheryl's arm, but Sheryl shook her off. Allie stayed a step behind her all the way to the car. When she clicked the remote, Sheryl climbed in the car and clicked her seatbelt, then sat staring straight ahead.

Allie climbed in the car. "Sheryl, whatever it is—"

"Just drive. Please."

"Honey, you have to talk—" She broke off as Sheryl unsnapped her seatbelt and jumped out of the car.

Allie caught up with her on the sidewalk. "Where are you going?"

"I'll catch a ride. You can go on back by yourself."

Allie's concern turned to irritation in a flash. "Bullshit. Get back in the car. I brought you. I'll drive you home."

Sheryl looked at her for the first time. Her eyes were red; her face appeared cadaverous. "No questions."

"Not if you don't want—"

"No conversation."

OK, so Sheryl intended to shut her out completely. Allie could work on that later. Right now, she just needed to get Sheryl back in the car. "Agreed."

After several moments of searching Allie's face, Sheryl spun and headed back to the car. Allie didn't let out her breath until Sheryl was safely snapped in her seatbelt.

It was a long ride back. Allie kept her promise only because she was afraid Sheryl would jump out of the moving vehicle if she spoke. She turned the radio to an easy-listening station, only to have

Sheryl reach over and snap it off.

This was a completely new person in the car with Allie. Sheryl kept her face averted, but occasionally, Allie saw her reach up and swipe at her eyes. Sheryl wasn't a crier, but Allie would bet her friend's eyes weren't dry once in the forty-five minutes it took them to get to the Coast.

When they reached the intersection of 520 and A1A, Sheryl spoke for the first time, her voice raspy. "Take a right, will you?"

A left turn took them home. "Sure. Where to?"

"Just..." She motioned toward the south.

Allie drove. She went through Cocoa Beach, Satellite Beach, and Indialantic. Only then, did she have a clue. "Sebastian Inlet?"

Sheryl gave a short nod.

Another fifteen miles of two-lane road landed them at Sebastian Inlet State Park. Until 1965, A1A had ended at the inlet, only to pick up again in Vero Beach, a few miles south. Then, the state hired Cleary Brothers Construction to build a fifteen-hundred-foot, concrete arch bridge to span the Inlet. Much of the area was already designated as wildlife preservation areas, but Florida turned the land at either end of the bridge into a state park, complete with lots of rules, and built a long fishing pier over the original jetty. But even that couldn't spoil the natural beauty.

A narrow two-lane road led to the parking area. Sand and sea and scrub palmetto. Who could ask for more? It had always been one of Allie's favorite places, but she and Sheryl had never been there together.

Allie barely had the Jeep in park when Sheryl

jumped out and headed toward the fishing pier. Allie took off after her. Was that why they were here? Did Sheryl intend to throw herself off the end of the pier? Whatever she intended, her footsteps slowed as she neared the end. She stopped and leaned her forearms on the iron railings, staring out to sea.

Allie looked around as she caught her breath. On weekends, the pier was a madhouse of crazed anglers, many with several fishing lines in the water. Today, it was nearly deserted. A few hearty souls in wetsuits challenged the surf on bright-colored boards. The wind off the water was cold. Well, cold for Florida, she amended.

She didn't dare speak. Instead, she joined Sheryl at the rail and watched her watch the water. The currents here were treacherous. Waves slammed against the stone jetty, throwing spray head high. Allie was already wet and freezing, but Sheryl seemed oblivious to the elements. Just when Allie was about to cry uncle, Sheryl turned and looked at her.

"I'm sorry."

"For what?"

"For dragging you here. For being such a bitch in Orlando. For everything."

Before Allie could tell her it was OK, Sheryl said, "I need to talk to you and Libby. Together. Do you have some time?"

Allie felt her chest constrict. Together? Not good. "Of course. I have all the time you need. When?"

"Now. I mean, as soon as we can get home." She turned and headed back toward the parking lot, her steps slow now, as if she were slogging through deep beach sand.

Allie tried to inject a playful note in her voice. "I don't suppose you want to give me a hint, I mean, because I'm such a good friend and all?"

Sheryl stopped and looked at her. "This is serious, Allie. I need to talk to both of you at one time. OK?"

What could Allie say?

Eleven

EVER SINCE THE SHERIFF told them of Sidney's escape, Teresa Finch had expected him to show up at the house. She knew he wouldn't come when his father was home. Wally had never understood Sidney, which was probably one reason the boy had problems. Every child needed parents who loved him unconditionally. Her parents had criticized everything she and her sisters did, and Teresa decided early that she wouldn't raise her children that way. She'd hoped for a houseful, but she had some problems with Sidney's birth that ended her childbearing years. It didn't matter. Sidney was enough for her.

Teresa wasn't a fool; she knew Sidney had problems, but so did most high-spirited youngsters. Wally accused her of sparing the rod to Sidney's detriment, but she told him Sidney needed love and understanding, not the strap. She wouldn't let Wally break Sidney's spirit, and she certainly wasn't going to do it. Wally never really came round to her way of thinking—they didn't talk much about Sidney—but he eventually quit insisting she punish the boy.

Now, Sidney was running from the law. It was ridiculous. She'd heard the story of what happened, and all this because Sidney was trying to protect the sheriff, who was not only Sidney's boss, but also the one man who'd made an effort to help Sidney. Teresa remembered when the sheriff dragged Sidney off to the Everglades to "make a man of him," as Cord said. For a full week, Teresa waited for the call telling her that they were sick, injured, or worse. Instead, Sidney returned a changed boy. From then on, Sheriff Cord Arbutten was Sidney's guiding light. Now...

She sighed and turned from the window. Watching the street wouldn't make him come any sooner, and Wally was due home soon. Sidney knew Wally's schedule as well as she did. Wednesday and Friday afternoons at the firehouse. Wally retired a few years back, but he still liked to spend time with the men. Teresa was just glad to have him out of the house some.

Time to start thinking about dinner. As she stepped into the pantry, she noticed the lid on her mad-money canister was partway open. Had Wally borrowed some? Occasionally, he took a five or a ten when he didn't want to go to the bank, but he always put it back. She stood on tiptoe to reach the top shelf. When she opened the canister, she gasped.

Gone. More than a thousand dollars. Wally wouldn't take that much, not without telling her. She slumped against the wall. Sidney would, though. It wouldn't be the first time. Of course, he always said he didn't take it, but Teresa knew, just as she knew now. Her baby had been in the house, and she didn't get to see him. It made her want to cry, but it meant he was around, and he was all right. She didn't care about the money. Not if he needed it. Was it enough? What if he needed more? That would mean he'd come back, and maybe she would see him this time.

She stuck the canister back on the shelf and then hurried into the bedroom and snatched her purse. Not quite two hundred dollars in her wallet. It wasn't much, but it would do until she could get to the bank. Tomorrow. She'd make a special trip tomorrow. And she'd have to think of something to tell Wally.

Back to the pantry. As she started to lift the canister down to put the money inside, Wally stuck his head in the door.

Teresa let out a small scream. "Wally, you *scared* me!"

"Sorry. Here, let me help you." He reached up and pulled the canister down. "I was coming to put back the ten I borrowed the other day."

She tried to take it from him. "No, I..."

Wally opened the canister and looked inside. He looked at the money in her hand and back at the empty canister. "Tessie? You want to tell me where all that money went?"

"I—I—"

He waited. When she said nothing more, he turned and walked out without a word.

■ ■ ■

SIDNEY HAD PARKED two doors down and had watched Allie's house for most of the morning. He saw her leave with Levine. He didn't know how long she'd be gone, but he had to make his move now, while the construction workers were sitting down on the beach eating lunch. He probably had half an hour tops.

He was a redhead today, dressed in jeans and a T-shirt, which his strap-on boobs filled out nicely, if he did say so himself. He sauntered as well as he could with a fucked-up leg and foot along the walk to the front door. After slipping on surgical gloves, he pulled the little leather case out of the purse hanging from his shoulder. It only took him about ten seconds to get past the deadbolt. The fools paid six ninety-five for a piece of metal he could probably pop with his foot and considered themselves safe. The only thing that kept a house safe was a dog.

And speaking of dogs. He saw the little mutt run down the hallway as he opened the door. Some watchdog.

Sidney closed the door behind him and crossed the living room in four strides, in time to see the pooch run into some kind of home office. He pulled the door closed. There, that took care of the dog— for now. And it altered his plan. What would cause Allie Grainger the most grief? He hesitated only a minute. He had a lot to do, and he had to do it fast. He was only sorry he wouldn't be here to see her reaction.

Back at the car, he rummaged in the trunk. Fortunately, he'd stored some of his future surprises in here. He was afraid to leave it in the trailer in case that sleazeball who'd loaned it to him decided to poke around while he was gone. He grinned when he uncovered the glass jar.

Twenty minutes later, he was leaving when a

thought struck him. He crossed to the back door and opened it several inches, pulling off his red stained gloves before he slipped out.

The construction workers were back at work when he rounded the house to the front. He got a few catcalls, so he tried to inject a little wiggle in his walk. Apparently, his disguise was effective.

As he climbed behind the wheel of his latest vehicle, he saw a car pull up in front of her house. A tall guy got out and strode to the door as if he owned the place. Sidney watched as he rang the doorbell. Then, he knocked. And again. Finally, he propped an envelope up against the door before he got back into his car and drove away. After a brief hesitation, Sidney put the car in gear and followed him.

■ ■ ■

"COME IN WITH ME," Sheryl said as they neared the house. They were the first words out of her mouth since they'd left the Inlet.

"OK. Let me walk Spook and—"

"Now." Her eyes cut over at Allie. "Please. Spook can wait. I mean, if you were writing, he'd have to wait, right?"

This new Sheryl was scaring her. "Right."

Allie pulled into Sheryl's driveway instead of her own. The houses were less than a block apart, squat cinderblock structures from about WWII, with small sandy front yards and patchy vegetation. The difference was that Allie's was directly on the beach; Sheryl's across the street and three doors down.

This time, Sheryl didn't bolt from the car. Instead, she sat for several minutes staring at nothing. The front curtain twitched. With a sigh that sounded like resignation, Sheryl unsnapped her seatbelt and climbed out of the car.

Allie followed a few paces behind. She didn't want to hear what Sheryl had to say. It couldn't be good, not if Sheryl was this upset. She'd considered half a dozen diseases, with cancer being at the top of the list. Allie knew Sheryl couldn't have children; that's what had broken up her marriage. Could the problem be related to that?

Libby was ensconced on the chair nearest the window, her walker to the side. When they entered, Libby tried, but failed to paste on a smile. Her gaze went from Sheryl's blotchy face and red eyes to Allie's face. Her brow creased as she looked back at Sheryl. "Are you all right?"

Sheryl sank on the sofa. She didn't speak until Allie sat. "No," she said, staring at the floor. "I—" She cleared her throat and began again. "I went to the doctor and—"

Allie was holding her breath, and she knew Libby was too.

"I thought something had to be really wrong with me. I mean, I've been sick for so long. So, I called a doctor in Orlando."

"Why Orlando? Why not someone local?" Allie didn't know why she asked the question. Maybe to stall off whatever Sheryl was going to tell them.

It didn't work. Sheryl ignored the interruption. She looked from Allie to Libby and then back down at the floor. "He told me—I'm pregnant."

Allie and Libby both gasped. Libby spoke first. "Still?"

Sheryl looked at her. "What do you mean, 'still'?"

Libby blushed prettily. "Well, honey, I knew you were pregnant. When you didn't tell me and then made that doctor appointment, well, I thought—"

Allie finished for her. "That she was going to get an abortion?"

Now, Sheryl gasped. "You knew? You both knew?"

"Not me," Allie said, her head still spinning from the news. "I thought you were dying of cancer or something."

Sheryl turned to Libby. "How—I mean—when..."

Libby reached over and clutched Sheryl's hand. "I only had one pregnancy, but the symptoms were obvious. The nausea. The exhaustion. Crying at the drop of a hat. It might have been thirty years ago, but I'll never forget those early weeks. Do you mean you never suspected?"

"Why would I? The doctor told me I couldn't have children." She glanced at Allie. "I thought I was dying too."

Libby's face was alight, her eyes sparkling. "A baby in the house. How wonderful! Now, I have a reason to work even harder on my walking. I can't take care of a baby and drag a walker around, can I?"

Allie was still in shock. "I don't understand. How could the doctors have been wrong? I mean, didn't they perform tests?"

"Yeah. Sure. Lots of tests. He said the results weren't conclusive, but when I didn't get pregnant, well, we assumed..."

"Ernie assumed," Allie said. She knew about Sheryl's devastation when Ernie dumped her to move on to more fertile ground. Now, he was a couple of years into his second marriage with no little Ernie clone bouncing on his lap. Allie wondered what he'd say when he heard Sheryl was pregnant—because he'd hear. Sheryl's parents had stayed in touch with the creep, determined that he and Sheryl would get back together one day.

"Have you told Del you might be in a family way?" Libby ventured tentatively.

Allie hadn't even thought of that. Of course Del was the father. How would he take the news?

"I can't," Sheryl said, shaking her head violently. "We talked about it a bunch of times. He said he doesn't want kids. I told him I couldn't have kids, so we didn't use anything. He's going to think I laid a trap for him. He'll hate me. Oh, *God*, what am I going to do?" She looked from Libby to Allie, her eyes filled with tears. "And how can I still be a cop and have a kid?"

"The same way the other female officers do," Libby said. "I'm sure the department has a maternity leave policy. And you have me as a built-in babysitter. Oh!" she clapped her hands together, grinning. "I couldn't be more pleased for you."

Allie felt a smile begin to form on her face. "And a built-in honorary aunt across the street. Oh, Sheryl, do you know how wonderful this is? You can have children."

The tears in her eyes spilled over. "But—but what if it isn't OK? I mean, kids are born with birth defects and stuff like that. What if it dies? What if I die in childbirth?"

Allie and Libby laughed.

Sheryl swiped at her tears and glared at them. "And what if Del doesn't want the baby?" The laughter died.

"Then, he's a complete fool," Libby said abruptly, "and I don't think Del's a fool."

Sheryl looked at her gratefully. Then, she turned to Allie. "Will you come with me to tell him? I can't—"

Allie reached out and took Sheryl's free hand. "Sure, and if he isn't happy, I'll help you beat the hell out of him."

Sheryl smiled for the first time. "Oh, I'd like to see that. Mr. Black Belt would have you on the floor in two seconds." She looked back at Libby and seemed to be struggling. "You don't mind? I mean, that it's not Joe's?"

This time, Libby had tears in her eyes. "Of course, I don't mind. Well, you know how much I'd love to have Joe's child, but honey, a baby's a baby. They're all precious." She wiped her eyes. "I don't think I've ever been happier."

Sheryl looked as if she was on the verge of tears again, and Allie felt her eyes sting. "Come on," she said, standing. "Let's go walk Spook, and we'll go tell Del."

■ ■ ■

SHE SAW THE ENVELOPE propped against her front door as soon as she neared the house, her name scrawled across the front.

Sheryl walked up behind her. "Another present?"

"God, I hope not." Anger caused Allie to rip the envelope open without caution. Irritation followed close on its heels when she pulled out the sheets of paper and realized what she was holding—quotes from property developers on what she could get for the house, flyers from new condo developments in the area. Len had been here again.

She jammed her key in the deadbolt. "That bastard. You grab Spook while I throw this trash away," she said over her shoulder as she headed into the kitchen.

She was headed back to the living room when Sheryl said, "Allie?"

Something in her voice was wrong. Allie hurried across the room.

Sheryl was staring down the hall.

"What's wrong?"

Sheryl held up one hand. "Stay there," she said, moving slowly down the hallway.

Allie did as she was told. That's when she noticed the back door was ajar. "Someone's been in here."

"Tell me about it." Sheryl was headed back in her direction, already dialing her cell phone. She mumbled a few words and snapped the phone closed. She looked around. "Where's Spook?"

Only then, did Allie realize the significance of the open back door. But maybe... "Spook!" She looked behind the couch. No dog. She raced across the room toward the hallway. When she stepped into the hall, she froze.

Blood. Bloody handprints and smears on the bathroom door. Then, she realized there was a trail of blood from the bathroom into the living room and the kitchen. Her stomach lurched. "*Spook!*" She started down the hall.

Sheryl grabbed her hand and pulled her back.

"Allie, stop. Stay out of there. It's a crime scene."

Allie felt the floor sway under her feet. "Spook?"

"I don't know. I didn't open the bathroom door. We'll have to wait until the techs get here."

She led Allie to the couch and pushed her down. "Stay here."

Allie was too stunned even to cry. Spook? Who would hurt Spook? Could Len do something like this? He didn't like dogs, but would he...

She shook her head. But if it wasn't Spook, then who—

She felt the room start to go dark and felt her head pushed between her knees.

"Breathe," Sheryl barked. "Take deep breaths."

■ ■ ■

WITHIN MINUTES, Allie heard sirens screaming in the distance. Suddenly, the room was full of officers, a couple pulling on gloves as they headed toward the bathroom. She couldn't cry; she couldn't think. Only then, did she realize she still clutched the envelope from Len in her hand.

No, he couldn't have. No matter how desperate, Len couldn't have done something like this. And if he had, would he have left a calling card on the front porch? Oh, God, had someone hurt Spook? She, the girl who'd never wanted the dog, who'd bought into all her mother told her about them being dirty and insect-ridden. She'd die if someone had hurt Spook. She'd kill whoever it was with her bare hands.

Twelve

ALLIE FELT A PRESENCE at her elbow and looked up. Sheryl.

"Spook's not in the bathroom."

"Who then?"

"No one. They don't think it's real blood. It looks like that crap you concoct out of corn syrup and food coloring."

Allie couldn't get her head around it. "Then, why? And where's Spook?"

She heard a soft whimper coming from the hallway, jumped up, and headed in that direction. It was coming from her office. She eased the door open, terrified of what she'd find, and there he was, cowering against her desk.

"Oh, *Spook*." Allie dropped to the floor and pulled him into her arms. The strain of the last few hours overwhelmed her, and tears fell like a Florida cloudburst. She didn't realize she was squeezing the puppy too hard until he yelped. She loosened her grip, but didn't let go.

She felt hands pulling her to her feet. "Come on, Allie. Let's get you out of here and let the guys do their work."

She used the tissues Sheryl thrust into her hand to dry her eyes.

"We'll be at Lester's if you need us," Sheryl said over her shoulder as she hustled Allie out of the house. Apparently, their secret place wasn't secret anymore.

After giving Spook to Libby with only the briefest explanation for all the police cars, Sheryl ushered Allie into her CRV.

"Won't they have questions?" Allie asked as Sheryl put the car in gear.

"Not many. I told them you'd been with me all day, filled them in on Len's presents. They'll lift some prints—if there are any. They can check for a match. I told them he threatened you."

"Not threatened... exactly. Besides, I can't believe Len would do something like this. If that blood is fake, Len wouldn't know how to make it. And how would he get in the house?"

"Are you sure of that? Of any of it? Because I don't think you've spent enough time around your brother to make that call."

"But why leave the envelope propped against the front door to draw attention that he'd been there?"

"Could be a message for you. Here's what I can do if you don't sell and move."

Allie shook her head. "I still can't see Len pulling a stunt like that."

Sheryl pulled into a space at Lester's. "If not Len, then who?"

They met each other's gaze. "It's exactly like something Sidney would do," Allie said.

"The sheriff's convinced he's not in the area."

"And you? Are you convinced?"

Sheryl's expression was her answer. "Jesus, I need a drink! Let's go inside."

As she walked through the front door, Sheryl seemed to recall why they were there. During Allie's crisis, it was as if nothing else was in her head. Now, Allie could see it all come rushing back—in her posture that sagged as if she'd aged in the space of a blink, in her step that slowed to the pace of a snail crossing quicksand.

Del was behind the bar. When he saw Sheryl and Allie, his face brightened, but when he saw Sheryl look away, he seemed to regroup. He rolled his shoulders back as if gearing up for a physical blow. "Ladies," he said, stepping over to them. He looked at Sheryl. "Long time no see."

Sheryl's gaze swept the room, landing on nothing. "Well, you know. Work."

Del studied her expression. "Yeah. I know work. That the only problem here?"

Sheryl blanched, and Del appeared to take a mental step backward. Allie could see the hurt on his face.

"So, what brings you here today?"

Sheryl looked at Allie, who said, "Starvation. Can we have two menus?"

Del turned his back on them for a minute. Allie thought he was reaching for menus, but when he turned back, his hands were empty, and his face a thundercloud aimed directly at Allie. "I know I said I hadn't seen her for a while, but that didn't mean I wanted you to drag her here against her damn will. If she's done with me, then she's done with me. I'm not going to go begging her to come back—"

"She didn't drag me here."

Del ignored her. "So, if she doesn't want to be

here, why don't you just—"

Sheryl grabbed his waving hand. "Why don't you talk to me?"

"Because I don't need any more grief," he said, not meeting Sheryl's eyes. "Look, I know how things go. You go at it hot and heavy for a while, and then it's over. Goodbye. Don't let the door hit you and all that." He pulled his hand away and turned to leave.

"I'm pregnant." Sheryl blurted out.

Del stood with his back to them for a long moment. Then, he slowly turned, his expression unreadable. "What'd you say?"

Sheryl squirmed on her barstool. "I said I'm pregnant. Listen, I'm not trying to make it your problem. You don't owe me anything. I'm a big girl, and I got myself into this. I'll handle it. I don't need your help."

Del didn't seem to hear a word she said. He pointed his finger at her, and then at himself, his face flushed. Sheryl nodded.

For a moment, it was a frozen tableau. Then, Del swung his bar towel up in the air and shouted, "I'm going to be a daddy! Hey, everyone, I'm gonna be a papa!"

All eyes were on them as Del jumped over the bar and grabbed Sheryl off her stool. "Jeez, honey, why didn't you tell me?"

"I just found out—"

"I thought you couldn't have kids."

"You said you didn't want kids."

"I lied, honey. I mean, I didn't want you to worry about it. I figured after we got married—"

"*Married!*"

"I figured we could adopt a half-dozen or so."
He pulled her to him and wrapped her tightly in
his arms, burying his face in her hair. "My God,
I thought you came here today to blow me off. I
thought..." His voice trailed off.

Sheryl wriggled out of his grip. "Wait just a
minute, buddy. We never discussed marriage.
What makes you think—?"

"Hey, you're having my baby." He looked at Allie
in appeal.

"It's her hormones," Allie said, grinning. "Give
her a few minutes to get used to the idea."

Del hesitated before sinking on one beefy knee.
"Marry me, Sheryl. I love you. You have to marry
me. You're pregnant, for God's sake." He said the
words with reverence.

Sheryl scowled down at him, but then a smile
played across her mouth. "Get up, you idiot," she
hissed. "Everyone's watching."

"Not until you say yes."

"Get up," she said again. "I'll think about it."

Del jumped to his feet with the grace of a profes-
sional martial artist. "What do you mean, you'll
think about it?" He pointed to her belly. "That's
our baby growing in there, and he'll need his
father."

Sheryl looked bemused. "Maybe he—or she—
will, some day, but right now, junior only needs
me." At Del's crestfallen look, she seemed to relent.
"I said I'd think about it."

Del pulled her back into his arms. "This is one
time when I won't take no for an answer. God,
girl, my head is reeling. I knew we'd eventually
get married, but I never thought I'd be a dad. This

is the coolest thing that's ever happened to me."

Sheryl pulled away. "Yeah, that's because you're not barfing up your guts every day. Now, why don't you be a good little daddy and get me some wings and a bloody Mary?"

Del looked stunned. "You can't drink alcohol. It could hurt the baby. And you need something healthier than chicken wings. I'll fix you a hamburger with LT. No fries. They're too fatty. Maybe a side salad..." He was still mumbling as he made his way around the bar and into the kitchen.

Sheryl sat back down on her stool and looked at Allie. "I guess he's OK with the idea of the baby." Her eyes glistened, but the smile on her face told it all.

"I think he is."

Sheryl shook her head. "I hope he's not going to be like this the whole nine months. I mean, about the booze and eating healthy and shit."

Allie grinned. "I think he is," she repeated.

■ ■ ■

SIDNEY SAT PARKED in the Hilton parking lot and struggled to take off his fake boobs, laying odds this joker would be more comfortable talking to a strange man in a bar than talking to a woman. He couldn't get the hooks to open. Jesus, how did women deal with these things? He'd seen his mother reach behind her and have it undone in a flash, slip the straps down her arms still fully clothed, and be out of the goddamn contraption within seconds. It must be something women were born knowing.

Finally, with a curse, he ripped his T-shirt over his head and took off the bra. Thank God, the hotel parking lot was deserted.

Again dressed, this time as a guy with horn-rimmed glasses, he entered the hotel. He didn't know who the guy at Allie Grainger's house was or what he was doing here at the hotel—hell, he could be a courier, for all Sidney knew—but maybe he'd get lucky and stumble on to something. It was worth a try, and what the hell else did he have to do?

He heard the clatter of dishes and muted conversations from the restaurant and headed in that direction with purpose. Lo and behold, his target was ensconced on a barstool with a beer in front of him, staring in the mirror as if it were a television. Sidney took a stool two seats away and ordered a draft, and then sat patiently waiting for his chance. He had no doubt one would present itself.

The guy was halfway through his second beer when Sidney heard him mutter something.

"Sorry?" Sidney said, turning to the guy. "Did you say something?"

The guy looked surprised to find someone else at the bar with him. "Just talking to myself," he said.

Sidney nodded. "Work or women?"

"I beg your pardon."

"When a man starts talking to himself, it's usually one or the other." He turned on his stool and held out his hand. "Stan Falstaff," he said and wondered where the name came from.

The man shook his hand. "Len Grainger."

Sidney sat back. It was taking a chance, but

it was the only way to find out. "Grainger? Any relation to Allie Grainger?"

"You know her?"

"Not well, but our paths have crossed." He wondered just how close Allie and this brother were. "Do you live around here? I don't remember seeing you before."

Len turned on his stool. "I'm visiting from Atlanta."

"Staying long?"

The guy's face shut down, maybe questioning the wisdom of talking to a stranger in a bar. "As long as my business keeps me here," he said, reaching for his wallet.

So, their bullshit session was over. Still, he'd just met Allie Grainger's brother. He might be able to use that.

"Good talking to you," Sidney said, holding out his hand again. "Maybe I'll see you around again."

"Same to you," the guy said, dropping a twenty on his bar tab.

Sidney sat back, nursing his brew. Well, waddaya know. He'd just introduced himself to Allie Grainger's brother. He wasn't sure what he could do with that, but he was equally sure something would come up.

Thirteen

THE NEXT MORNING, Allie sat on the living room sofa with Spook curled on her lap, her unread article notes beside her. The night had been uneventful—thank the powers that be— but she awoke thinking about her brother. The more she thought about it, the more this thing with Len bothered her. She knew greed was a natural human emotion, one they looked at first in murder cases, but she still couldn't figure out why he was so intent on getting money from her. Why now? He hadn't made that big a stink when her inheritance came through. Her mother made all the noise back then. Len blew it off with a "you always were her pet." Was this escalation of his determination her mother's doing? She knew they wanted her to sell—

She heard a scraping at her front-door lock. Someone was trying to get into the house. To finish what they started? There was nowhere to go, except to run out the back. She could wave her arms, and the construction workers would see her. Before she had a second to react, the door flew open. Allie clutched her throat.

"They didn't find a damn thing," Sheryl said, stomping in. "The blood was fake, just like I

115

thought. No fingerprints." She seemed to notice Allie's expression for the first time. "What?"

"You scared the hell out of me." She let go of her death grip on Spook, who ran over to Sheryl, wiggling in excitement. The traitor. "Why didn't you knock?"

"I didn't want to disturb you if you were working. What's the big deal?"

"Sidney's on the loose, and you ask what's the big deal? What if that had been him? What could I have done?"

Sheryl perched on the arm of a chair. "That's something to think about. What would you have done?"

Allie wasn't ready to let it rest. "Knock next time. If I'm working, I'll ignore you. Then, you can use the key and scare the hell out of me."

"All right, already. Give it a break. Next time I'll knock. Probably."

Allie shot her a dirty look, but Sheryl had a valid question. "I was going to run out the back door and yell so the construction workers would see me."

Sheryl thought for a minute. "Not bad, but no defense against a gun. You'd never have made it that far."

"Comforting thought."

"Realistic."

"Don't you think the construction workers would hear the shot and come running?"

Sheryl made a scoffing sound. "Over all that noise? They'd probably think it was a backfire. And even if they recognized it as a gunshot, they couldn't make the ground in time to catch him.

Don't forget. Sidney has nothing to lose. He couldn't outrun them, but if he made it to his car, he'd be home free."

An even more depressing thought. "How is his leg? Is he fully mobile?" She and Sheryl had not once discussed Sidney since Sheryl rammed him with the police cruiser. Allie hadn't pushed for information because she didn't want to know anything about Sidney Finch. Now, she'd better learn as much as possible.

"Depends on what you call fully." She reached down and picked up Spook, who squirmed with pleasure. "Sheriff's kept in touch with Polk. They say Sidney can walk, but with a pronounced limp. That's more because of his foot than his leg. A lot of bones were crushed beyond repair. They say he's usually in a lot of pain."

"Good."

"Damn straight. But I'll bet that doesn't improve his temper. He'll be out gunning for you, and knowing Sidney, I mean that literally. He's just playing with you now—"

Playing. "If it's Sidney who is playing these pranks." She shuddered. The fake blood hadn't felt like a prank.

"You really think your brother would do this kind of crap. He has too much—oops!" She covered her hands with her mouth and raced to the bathroom.

Allie heard the now familiar sounds of retching and flushing, then water running in the sink. She was surprised when Sheryl walked back into the room smiling. She raised her eyebrows.

Sheryl shrugged. "It's different now that I know what's causing it. Besides, Libby says it'll end soon."

She leaned against the sofa. "Back to Sidney."

Allie groaned.

"He's a problem that won't go away... for either of us, but at least I have some training and carry a weapon. You, on the other hand, are a civilian wimp."

"Thanks a lot."

"Truth hurts. It'll hurt more if he gets hold of you." She straightened. "I have to get to work, but think about it. I could teach you to handle a gun, and Del could show you some nifty self-defense moves. At least, you wouldn't be completely un-protected."

When Sheryl was gone, Allie thought about it. She'd never had any dealings with guns other than as someone's target, but Sheryl had a point. If she was going to continue in her line of work, she'd better think seriously about learning some self-defense techniques.

She resolved to go talk to Del about taking some classes. And she could own a gun. It wouldn't kill her. Hopefully, it wouldn't kill anyone else, either.

■ ■ ■

SIDNEY SMILED AS HE SLIPPED his clipboard under his arm and headed back to his car. He didn't care if the construction workers saw him. He was dressed as a middle-aged guy. He'd added heft to his upper body with a down vest under his jacket and sprayed silver in his hair. Just to be safe, he'd also added a few pounds to his face with his mother's stage makeup, noticeable bags under his eyes, and topped it all off with a crepe hair mustache. Those were the things people noticed, not hands or ear shape. In fact, few people ever noticed shit.

Speaking of which, he hoped Allie liked her new present. He'd intended to leave it for her overnight when he was less likely to be noticed, but with no car in her driveway, it was irresistible. Why put off until tomorrow fear she could feel today.

He chuckled as he climbed into the innocuous blue Ford he stole that morning from his long-term shopping lot. He'd returned the other two vehicles to the airport without a hitch, wiping them clean before slipping on winter gloves to drive them back. It might be Florida, but it was damn cold, at least by his standards; gloves would be unremarkable. And they wouldn't notice their cars had been used until they realized they had the wrong plates. Then, what would they do? It was a schoolboy prank. No one would link it to him.

OK. So Allie Grainger wasn't home. Where was she?

He spotted her Jeep as he drove past Lester's parking lot. She was so stupidly predictable. This was where she'd come every time she spotted him following her. He hesitated for only a moment before turning into the lot. He was going in. He wanted to see who she was with and what she was doing. The risk only enhanced his excitement. Still, disguise or not, he'd have to move carefully or his limp would give him away.

He stepped in the door and quickly moved to the bar, not even giving his eyes a chance to adjust to the gloomy interior. The fewer people who noticed him, the better. The place was packed, at least for Thursday lunchtime. Either people were getting a head start on the weekend, or the food was damn good. He didn't care. It provided him much-needed cover. He edged between two guys watching television and ordered a beer. As he waited, he watched the bar mirror.

There she was at the end of the bar, hunched over in conversation with a guy who looked like a tank. Jesus, Sidney wouldn't want to tangle with him. Hands like hams, shoulders he probably had to turn sidewise to get into a door. If this were her current boyfriend, Sidney would give him a wide berth.

He took his beer and was about to make a move down the bar when the outside door swung open. Sidney chanced a quick peek and almost pissed his pants. *Levine.* Shit, if she spotted him, he was a dead man. She passed without a glance in his direction and headed straight for the other end of the bar. When she got there, the tank guy wrapped his arms around her and swung her in the air. Sidney expected her to punch the guy's lights out; instead, she grinned like an idiot. Interesting.

Sidney decided to take a chance. None of them even looked his way as he moved toward them. The jostling from the crowd hid his limp. When he was close enough to hear, he again slipped between two men at the bar until he was invisible.

"...telling Del I want to take some classes from him. You know, basic self-defense," Allie said. "With Sidney on the loose, it wouldn't hurt."

Sidney sputtered in his beer. What an idiot! Did she think a few self-defense courses could protect her from a trained law enforcement officer? What the hell. Let her think it. False confidence could be a killer.

"Did you give any thought to buying a gun?" Levine asked. "I could give you lessons."

"That too," Allie said. "I'm going to need all the help I can get with two men after me."

Two men?

Now, the tank piped up. "You don't think your brother would do anything to harm you, do you? I mean physically."

When Allie turned to the tank, her gaze passed right over him without recognition. "Who knows? He's making threats. He even showed up where I work, trying to make me look like the heavy. He's good at that. And I know Len. He never gives up. He'll keep it up until he gets his share of the inheritance, and I'll tell you, I'll kill him before he sees a dime of Aunt Lou's money."

Her voice had risen, and a couple of people turned around to look. Apparently, the tank noticed. "So you've said before, but you want to watch that kind of talk in public. Folks might get the wrong idea."

Allie dropped her head in her hands. "You know I don't mean it. It's just so frustrating. He's always done this kind of thing. I was in trouble half my childhood because Len made everything look as if it was my fault. Then, if I called him on it, he'd play the poor injured party. I just wish he'd go home and leave me alone."

The tank started to say something when the other bartender called, "Hey, lover boy, you wanna give me a hand? I'm drowning here." That got him on his feet.

Allie and Sheryl continued to talk, their heads

close together, but it didn't matter. Sidney had heard enough. Plenty. He began to work his way back down the bar. So, the brother and sister were at odds, and she'd been threatening him in public. Poor stupid Allie Grainger. She didn't know it, but she'd handed him the weapon he needed. Now, he just had to load it and fire.

■ ■ ■

ALLIE SPOTTED THE WRAPPED package on her doorstep before she even turned into her driveway and felt a little twist in her belly that might have been fear; but before she defined it, anger swept it out of the way. She was tired of these childish pranks. She refused to be intimidated by a little dog poop. At least, she hoped the last package had been dog poop. For just an instant, she considered calling Sheryl, but that was ridiculous. They hadn't found prints on the last box or wrapping or in her house after the break-in. There was no reason to think her secret admirer had gotten careless this time.

She slammed out of the Jeep and headed for her front door, ignoring the greetings Frank and his crew called down. When she reached the box, she hesitated again. What if it was a bomb of some kind? A bomb? Was she crazy? Sidney wouldn't blow her up unless he was there to watch, and Len—well, maybe, if he thought he was her heir. What was she thinking? Len wasn't a killer. A bully, yes, and good at it, but not a killer.

Fury at being the butt of these ongoing pranks overrode caution. She snatched up the box, tearing at the wrappings, ripped off the lid—and screamed.

Fourteen

ALLIE FLUNG THE BOX AWAY FROM HER, but it was too late. They were on her, in her clothes, everywhere. She screamed again, beating at her body and tearing at her clothes. "Get them off me. Oh, God!"

Suddenly, Frank Gray was at her elbow, his son Bobby on his heels. "What is it? What's on you?"

"*Roaches*. Oh, God, *roaches*! They're all over me. Help me get them off. *Hurry!*"

She saw the men exchange glances as she yanked her top over her head. Two black palmetto bugs crawled away as it hit the ground. Frank stomped them before pulling off his jacket and wrapping it around her. She kicked off her shoes and ripped off her pants, sending another half-dozen bugs scurrying for protection. She shook her hair and dug her fingers through it.

When she heard Frank say, "They're only bugs," she realized what she'd done. She was standing on her front stoop wearing only her panties and bra and Frank's jacket. She was sure her remaining neighbors were staring out their windows at her, not to mention the entire construction crew

She pulled Frank's jacket around her and tried to shove her key in her front-door lock, but her hands shook too badly. "Help me get inside," she begged. She handed her keys to Frank.

He unlocked the door and swung it wide for her to enter.

"I'm sorry," she told the men who stood staring at her as if she'd lost her mind. "Wait here for a minute. Please."

In her bedroom, she stripped off Frank's jacket, then her underwear, and checked every inch of her body. Nothing. They were gone. Thank God, they were gone. She could still feel them crawling on her, but it was her imagination. They were gone.

She slipped on a bathrobe and went back into the living room, her face burning in shame. She handed Frank his jacket. "I'm sorry. I'm so sorry. It's a fear. Irrational, I know, but I can't stand them."

"No problem," Frank said, his voice gruff. "My wife's the same way."

"Did you see who left the box on my doorstep?" She looked from one man to the other, not really expecting that they had.

"Not the same guy who left the first package," Bobby said.

Allie looked at him, surprised, and he colored. "I'm not being nosy or anything, but the present was hard to miss, all wrapped up in pretty paper and a bow. I thought that maybe you had a secret admirer. Courier delivered it."

"What did he look like?"

Bobby piped up. "Skinny guy. Dark hair. Carrying a clipboard or something."

"What about today?" his dad asked. "Same guy?"

Bobby shook his head. "No, today's guy was

different. Older. Kind of chunky, if you know what I mean." He scratched his head. "And it was a different car. Blue Ford Taurus. New. The last one was a Lexus. I remember thinking it was a pretty nice car for a courier. City Courier. You might call them and see if they can tell you who ordered the delivery."

Allie stared at him. "That's amazing."

Frank beamed on his son with pride. "Bobby notices everything. He's going to college at night. Majoring in Criminal Justice. He just made the Dean's List."

"I'm only a sophomore," Bobby said, blushing scarlet. "I hear it gets harder as you go along."

"Well, when you get to be a senior, let me know," Allie said. "I have a lot of connections with the Sheriff's Office, and I'll be glad to put in a good word for you."

She let Frank and a grinning Bobby out and locked the front door after them. After scrubbing for fifteen minutes in a scalding shower—she could still feel the hideous roaches crawling all over her—she called Sheryl. Then, she did something she rarely did at home, especially in the daytime. She had a drink.

■ ■ ■

"IT HAD TO BE SIDNEY," Allie said, sipping her rum and Coke.

Sheryl had laughed at her, calling it the training bra for drinkers, but it was all Allie had in the house, a leftover from her Aunt Lou. Training bra or not, it had the desired effect; she could now get the glass to her mouth without spilling half.

"How do you figure?"

"Don't you remember? He did the same thing to us when we were fifteen. It didn't bother you, but it scared me to death."

"I'd forgotten all about that. Yeah, I remember. But what's the big deal? They're just bugs."

Allie shuddered. "To you, maybe, but they terrify me."

"They can't bite you or anything."

"I *know* they can't bite me," Allie said sharply. Then she blew out a breath. "I know my fear's irrational, but I've always been terrified of them, and Sidney knows that."

"What about Len?"

Allie laughed. "Len's even more scared of them than I am, if that's possible. There's no way he could have put them in the box, and it's not the kind of thing you go out and buy, even on eBay." She shook her head. "No, it's Sidney, which means he's been around all the time."

Sheryl scuffed her boot on the carpet. "We have to involve the sheriff."

Allie was beyond trying to protect anyone but herself. "By all means. Involve the whole department. If Sidney's around, I need all the help I can get." She took a sip of her drink and made a face. "This is disgusting."

"Told you."

"Anyway, you should have seen me standing out there, ripping off my clothes, and screaming. God, how humiliating!"

"Bet the neighbors got an eyeful."

"And all Frank's crew. And probably Sidney, if

he was anywhere around." She could feel her face burn. "Oh, God, Sheryl, I hope he wasn't. I'd die if he saw how well he succeeded in terrifying me."

■ ■ ■

SIDNEY SAT AT THE HILTON bar, nursing his beer and basking in the glow of his success. Jesus, she went crazy! It was better than he expected. He never in his wildest dreams—and he had some wild ones—imagined her tearing off her clothes like that. He squirmed on his stool. Not a bad body, if a little skinny. Nice ass, though. He wondered if she always wore those tiny little bikini panties.

He shook himself. Enough of that. He didn't need the distraction. What he needed was a break. His plan was set. The sooner he pulled it off, the better. He'd sit glued to this stool every day if he had to, but he was counting on a bit of luck. Her brother was here at the hotel. Sidney had checked, and his car was in the parking lot. What the hell could he be doing up in his hotel room? He chuckled as a few possibilities crossed his mind. Whatever. Sidney was willing to wait. Minus his weapon, he was in uniform this time. What better to inspire trust? Even the bartender treated him more nicely once Sidney told him he was off duty. The disguise this time was blonde hair and his favorite mustache with horn-rimmed glasses. Nerd, intellectual, Scandinavian cop.

The place was nearly deserted. Two business types in dark suits sat at the far end of the bar, making multimillion deals, maybe. Or swapping sports scores. Who gave a shit? A horny couple crawled all over each other in a booth in the corner. If Sidney had been the bartender, he'd have told them to take it upstairs.

He'd just ordered his second beer when his break came. He watched Allie's brother enter the room, take in the businessmen and the couple, and then perch on a stool one down from Sidney. Sidney ignored him. Let the man come to him this time. The guy ordered a Manhattan—fucking sissy drink—and ate the cherry when it arrived. What a pussy. Then he tipped the drink off in one big swallow. When he didn't fall off his stool, Sidney reconsidered, and smiled. Maybe a drunk pussy. The brother ordered a beer, and Sidney did a mental cheer. One beer should do the trick, but again he'd underestimated him.

It wasn't until two beers later that he began to look around. He saw Sidney and frowned, trying to jar his memory, no doubt. After a minute, his brow cleared. "Hey, again," he said, holding out his hand.

Sidney shook it but feigned confusion for just a minute. Then, "Oh, hi, I remember you. You're Allie Grainger's brother."

His words had the desired effect; the guy reared back on his stool, almost losing his balance. "Don't even say her name around me."

"Family trouble, huh?"

"She's a bitch."

Sidney scooted over next to him. In a low voice, he said, "I wasn't going to say anything, you being her brother and all, but she's not very popular with the local cops."

Len looked again at his uniform. "You a police

officer?"

Sidney nodded, assuming the guy wouldn't know the area well enough to tell the difference between a city uniform and county. "She's all cozied up with the sheriff, but we're keeping an eye on her."

"What for?" the dude asked, scowling.

"Nothing big," Sidney said hastily. He couldn't blow it now, not when he was so close. He remembered what she'd said about her inheritance. "Talk is she's ripped off a couple of contractors. Had them do the work and then reneged on the bill. That kind of thing."

Len scowled. "Sounds like her. She's the greediest woman alive." He finished his second beer, and Sidney held up two fingers to the bartender. "But she'll be sorry," Len said.

"You think so? What can an honest man like you do against someone like her? We've been watching her for months without a break. All we have are their allegations."

Len looked at the fresh beer the bartender placed in front of him. "Did I order that?"

"I did," Sidney said. "Figured you deserved at least a drink."

Len excused himself, staggering slightly as he headed toward the men's room.

The bartender made his way down to where Sidney sat. "Your friend OK?" he asked, nodding at Len.

"He's OK," Sidney said. "Just having women trouble. Better to let him spill his guts."

"Should I take that?" The bartender started to reach for Len's beer.

Sidney intercepted it. "Nah, let him get drunk. That way, he'll hate himself more than he hates her, and that'll be the end of it." When the bartender looked skeptical, he said, "He's staying here at the hotel. If I have to, I'll take him upstairs and pour him in bed."

The business guys waved their check in the air, and the bartender moved off to take their money. While his back was turned, Sidney stirred three of his sleeping bombs from the hospital into his beer. He'd switched the glasses by the time Len returned.

Len looked at the new beer on the bar and reached for his wallet.

Sidney held up a hand. "Mind if I ask you a few questions about your sister before you go? Anyone as greedy as her should get what she deserves."

When Len hesitated, Sidney almost groaned aloud. *No.* Not when he was so close. He didn't want to use physical violence. That wouldn't stop him, but it was riskier that way. He breathed a sigh of relief when Len took his seat, but he made no move toward his beer.

"I don't know what I can tell you. We rarely even see each other. She wasn't this way before she inherited all that money. You know about the money?"

"I heard something, but why don't you tell me about it?"

Almost a half-hour later, Sidney saw the changes begin. He'd drunk the whole fucking beer. The man must have the constitution of a horse. Finally, his eyelids began to droop, and his speech took on a pronounced slur. Sidney hoped it didn't kill him, but then, he reconsidered. That might be OK, too, as long as it couldn't be pinned on him.

He picked Len's key card off the bar. The room number was scrawled on the strip of plastic with a magic marker. Convenient. He needed to get him out of here before he lost consciousness altogether. Dead weight was a pain in the ass.

Len didn't even notice when Sidney reached in his back pocket and took his wallet. He pulled out three twenties and laid them on the bar. With a friendly wave at the bartender, he pulled Len off his stool. When the bartender approached, Sidney said, "Nighty-night time for my friend here."

The bartender looked worried. "You need any help?"

He almost said, "I won't if you'll shut your fucking mouth and get lost." "No, I have him. He just needs to sleep it off."

Len's legs didn't give out until right outside his room. Sidney opened the door and dragged him the rest of the way. He glanced around. Nice room. Shame they couldn't stay. Housekeeping had already been in, which meant they wouldn't be back until tomorrow. Sidney didn't know how long the pills would work. One knocked Sidney out for eight hours, which is why he started pocketing them. It didn't do to be unconscious for long periods, even in a medical facility. Not when you'd shot a cop. Of course, this guy was a lot heavier, but the alcohol would double their effect. Sidney smiled. Anyone with any sense knew not to mix alcohol and drugs.

Just to be on the safe side, he muscled Len onto a bed before cuffing his wrists and securing his

LIVE in Person

ankles. He used a clean pair of socks from the open suitcase as a gag. After he retrieved an extra blanket out of the closet, he rolled Len over, so he faced away from the door, and tossed the blanket over him, covering everything but the top of his head. Hopefully, that would hold him until Sidney got back.

■ ■ ■

HE HADN'T HAD THIS MUCH fun since he was a kid. After ditching the guy's rental car in a secure cruise-line parking lot at Port Canaveral, Sidney called a cab. It cost Len twenty-three fifty to get Sidney back to the hotel. After the driver dropped him off under the front portico, Sidney crossed the lot and climbed in Len's rental car. It was hotter than a bitch. Winter in Florida. Maybe when all this was over, he'd move north. Might as well. His days in this county were over, like his career in law enforcement. His face burned.

He drove around to the loading dock but parked a little ways away. It wouldn't do to arouse suspicion.

Still in uniform—people tended to mind their own business around cops—he prowled the halls until he found a linen cart in an unlocked main-floor closet. This was the tricky part—a cop pushing around a linen cart would look suspicious to anyone.

He didn't meet a soul. Housekeeping seemed finished for the day or at least working on a different floor. He felt like doing a happy dance as he pushed the cart into the room, letting the door click shut behind him.

After checking to make sure Len was still out—he was—he retrieved his duffel bag from the cart and went into the bathroom to change. When he emerged, he was dressed all in white. He didn't have a tag that read linen service, but who the hell else would wear white overalls?

Getting the unconscious man into the linen cart was tricky, but Sidney ended up laying the cart on its side on the floor. Then, he rolled the guy off the bed and into the cart. Piece of cake. He gathered all the linens he could find without stripping the beds—the towels from the bathroom, the blanket he'd used to cover him, and another one from the closet—and threw them over Len. Then, he pulled the cart out in the hall.

He felt a little thrill of excitement as he realized he had little chance of making it. Someone was bound to see him, to notice an unscheduled linen pickup in the middle of the day or to see his dumping the body in the trunk of the car.

He knew at that moment he was cut out for this life. Not protecting citizens from the ordinary scum, but pitting his wits against all obstacles. No drug had ever given him a rush like this. Setting himself against impossible odds using only his superior intelligence, training, and determination—that's what he was about. Why hadn't he realized it before? It was because of the sheriff. Sidney had been such a wuss back then, so desperate for someone to like him that he'd tried to become what the sheriff wanted him to be, but that wasn't him. *This* was him.

The elevator button dinged, and Sidney felt his

heart lurch. If it was one of the maids, he was blown. Jeez, he'd hate to have to take her out.

It was a guest in a bikini with a bad sunburn. She glanced at Sidney and then the cart before starting down the hall. With a silent laugh, he pushed the cart down the hall until he found the freight elevator. The next tricky part. If anyone was around, he or she might challenge him. He knew he could subdue whoever it was, but that could cause problems... and he didn't need any problems. Not now.

When the elevator stopped at the loading dock, he peeked around before stepping out, dragging the cart behind him. Almost home.

He had the cart at the edge of the loading dock when his luck failed. He heard voices getting closer. Sidney quickly sat down on the edge of the loading dock, swinging his feet as if he didn't have a care in the world.

One guy glanced over, but didn't approach. "Just waiting for my truck," Sidney said, gesturing at the cart. "You got a cigarette?"

The guys shook their heads and moved away, like Sidney figured they would. When they were gone, he backed the car up to the loading dock, opened the trunk, and rolled Len inside. Sidney heard his head crack against the edge of the trunk and winced. A quick check showed he was still alive. The head wound was superficial, but head wounds bleed like a bitch. All the better.

Seconds later, he was Cocoa-bound with his cargo, a treasure beyond measure. He laughed at the rhyme. And soon, Allie Grainger would be up to her bleached blonde roots in trouble.

Fifteen

"I**T HAD TO BE** S**IDNEY**," Allie insisted. "No one else knew about my fear of roaches."

Cord still looked skeptical. Allie had filled him in on everything that happened since the first "gift" appeared on her doorstep. As much as she hated to acknowledge it, the sheriff still had a bit of a blind spot where Sidney was concerned. She didn't know what else to do to convince him.

"Sheriff—" Sheryl put a hand on Allie's arm.

Cord cleared his throat to speak. "All right. For the sake of argument, let's say it is Sidney pulling these pranks. Where did he get any of this? The boxes. The... gifts. Where is he hiding that he's eluding all the law enforcement officers in the area? How is he getting around? No cars have been reported stolen in the last few days. For that matter, where is he staying, and how is he paying for it all?"

"But—"

"I'm not saying you're wrong, Allie," Cord said, his face troubled. "I'm just saying it's a stretch. If it's Sidney, we'll catch him."

"That's not good enough." Allie's words surprised her almost as much as the sheriff.

She jumped up from the sofa and went to stand

behind a chair. "I'm sorry, but it sounds like something you'd tell a child to get her to take her medicine. 'It'll be OK.' Well, it's not OK. Sidney's pulling pranks now, but who knows what it'll be next. Snakes, maybe."

"Now, Allie—"

"He did it before."

Cord looked at Sheryl, who nodded. Cord rubbed his forehead.

Allie hated to bring more pain to the man, but damn it, she was tired of no one believing her. Understandably, Len might be trying to make her look bad, but Sidney was a known felon. She groaned. God, she sounded like Sheryl.

Cord sat forward, resting his forearms on his thighs. "I don't mean to condescend to you, Allie, but if Sidney's doing these things... well, he has to have help. Lodging, vehicle, money." He motioned toward the construction site. "And your friend over there said two couriers in two different vehicles delivered the packages. You heard him. One was young and thin and the other a hefty older man. I don't see how—" Cord broke off, sitting back against the sofa.

"What?" Allie and Sheryl asked, almost in unison.

It was a long moment before Cord answered. "I might be wrong." He looked from Allie to Sheryl. "I just remembered that Sidney's mother used to be big in the Cocoa Players."

"What—"

"Local theatre," Sheryl answered, her gaze on Cord.

"If Sidney was disguised—" He looked up. "It's a long shot, but if he was disguised, he might have gotten what he needed from Teresa. Without her knowing, I hope. There's a chance he could have gotten money..." His voice trailed off.

Neither Sheryl nor Allie spoke. They'd told Cord everything they knew. At first, his disbelief was palpable. If he was coming to their side, Allie wasn't going to blow it by opening her big mouth.

Finally, Cord stood. He looked at Allie. "You wouldn't consider going somewhere else until—"

"No."

He nodded. "That's what I figured. Probably better. At least law enforcement here knows him and has an idea of what to expect. If it is him."

Allie didn't say a word. Denial, as she well knew, died hard.

■ ■ ■

TERESA SLIPPED THE TWO thousand dollars out of her wallet. She didn't care what anyone said. If her boy needed something—food or medicine—she was going to see he had it or at least the means to get it. It was risky. She knew Wally was keeping an eye on her. She couldn't walk into another room without his following a minute later. He'd even curtailed his visits to the firehouse. She finally sent him to the store on a fool's errand just to get him out of the house. She didn't have long. The Publix where they shopped was only a mile or so away, and it wouldn't be difficult to get the things on her list.

She tiptoed down the stairs as if he were in the house, feeling like a criminal. It was an awful feeling. How could her poor boy stand it?

The house was quiet. Too quiet. Every step she took pounded in her ears—or was that her heart? This was going to be the death of her. She knew it, but she'd willingly die for her son. What kind of parent wouldn't?

The kitchen was empty. She knew that, but she still breathed more easily. She slowly opened the pantry door, wincing when it squeaked. She needed to get Wally to oil those hinges. When the door was open wide enough, she stepped in. And hit something.

She squealed as the pantry light switched on. Wally stood there, his face looking like a Florida summer thundercloud. In his hand was the flour canister that still held the two hundred dollars she'd put in earlier. His gaze held hers for a long moment before it trailed to the wad of bills in her hand. Gingerly, he reached over and took the money from her. "I won't let you do it, Teresa."

"Do what?" Wally's face looked sad—and old, Teresa realized with a start.

"I won't let you give him money."

"He's our *son!*"

Wally didn't raise his voice. "He's a criminal."

"How can you say that about your own son? You know none of this was his fault. If that woman—"

"It wasn't any woman, damn it. Can't you see that? It was Sidney. Sidney fired those shots at the innocent motorists. Sidney almost ran Allie Grainger off the bridge. What if he had succeeded? Did you think of that? What if she had died?"

"He did it to protect his boss."

"That's fiction." He scrubbed his face with his hand. "All right. Maybe he thought he did it to

138

protect his boss, but he thought he was protecting him from discovery. He was covering up what he thought was a crime, which would have made him accessory to murder. Can't you see that?"

Teresa looked at her husband. Instead of being angry with him, she pitied him. Wally looked old and tired. It wasn't his fault he couldn't love his son the way Sidney deserved. It was sad. Wally would never know the kind of selfless love she felt for their only child. It was his loss.

They were coming out of the pantry when the doorbell rang. Teresa stayed where she was while Wally went to answer it. She heard Cord Arbutten's voice and almost went upstairs, but it wouldn't do any good. She'd have to face him eventually.

The men were on the way to the kitchen when Teresa intercepted them. She ushered them back into the living room, intent on keeping this a formal, and not a social, occasion.

■ ■ ■

SIDNEY WATCHED AS THE SLOW, painful awareness of his circumstances washed over Len. He was still bound, tethered to Sidney's bed, his wrists and ankles still in restraints. Sidney sat across the room, again the fat man but wearing the fright wig and mask. He first assumed the disguise when he was trying to scare Allie Grainger off, before she forced him to use stronger measures. This was a different set—orange hair and a cannibal mask, complete with bloody teeth. Judging by Len's reaction, it was a shame he hadn't tried this one on Allie. For twenty-five bucks, he'd picked up a voice-altering microphone at a kid's store. Amazing what kids could buy these days.

He spoke into the microphone. "If you're calm and do what you're told, you'll be OK. Don't try to move. Don't try to identify me, or I won't be able to let you live."

Len blinked several times, as if trying to focus his vision. "What happened? Where am I?"

"Don't ask questions. If you behave, you'll be my guest here for a few days. If you screw up, you'll be dead. Your choice."

Len tried to struggle to a sitting position. He fell back against the pillow.

"That's better," Sidney said into the mike. "I don't want to harm you, but I will if I have to. I will feed you. Don't drink much water, or you'll have a problem. I have food for you now. Do you want it?"

Len shook his head, his eyes riveted on Sidney.

"Some water, then. You must be thirsty."

Len shook his head again. Then, he nodded.

"Water?"

He nodded. Then, harder.

"All right. Don't try anything stupid, or you'll pay."

He put the microphone down and crossed to the bed, the glass already in his hand. He held Len's head up so he could swallow without choking. Len took about half the glass without trouble. Then, he tried to swing his cuffed hands over to hit Sidney. Sidney jumped back out of reach, but it pissed him off. He drew back and hit the asshole in the jaw, not enough to knock him out, but enough to hurt plenty, judging by the groan. Then, he held Len's nose until he opened his mouth, and dumped the rest of the water in it.

As Len gagged and sputtered, Sidney went back over and picked up the mike. "Don't try that again or I'll kill you. I have nothing to lose. Your death is meaningless to me." The fear in Len's eyes was gratifying.

Back in the living room of the trailer, Sidney picked through the contents of Len's pockets. Less than a hundred bucks. Disappointing, but he was sure his mom had refilled his personal cookie jar by now. Keys to Len's car that Sidney had left at Port Canaveral after bringing Len here and tying him to the bed. The blood in the trunk should lead them on a merry chase. He'd picked up a new car on the off chance anyone had seen him deliver that second package to Allie. Cruise-line parking lots were almost as good as airports. Maybe better. Cruises tended to be longer than out-of-town business trips, and the same ticket that got him into the lot got him out. Len was only seven dollars poorer. A bargain any way you looked at it.

Cell phone. Now, that was interesting. Sidney scrolled through the contacts. Mostly 404 area codes. Sidney knew Allie was from Atlanta. He called information and asked for the courthouse in Atlanta. As soon as the mechanical voice intoned 4-0-4, he hung up. When he came on the ICE—in case of emergency—listing, he mentally forged the next link in the hang-Allie-Grainger chain.

He pressed TALK. Then, he listened to the female voice say, "Hello? Hello? Len, is that you? Hello?" before he punched the end button.

Well, shucks. Soon, everyone who mattered would know that Allie Grainger's brother was missing.

■ ■ ■

SHERYL WAS GONE. Allie tried to make up for lost time, but her notes about construction overtaking private ownership of beach property were meaningless. How could she worry about property loss when she was in very real danger of losing her life?

She was about to head up to the deck when the phone rang. When she saw the number, she considered ignoring it, but she was tired of being a coward.

"Grainger residence," she said in her good little girl voice. "Allie speaking."

"Don't pretend you don't know it's me, Allison. I know you have caller ID."

"I'm just doing as ordered when you called last time, Mother. It seems I'm damned if I don't and damned if I do."

That prompted a long moment of silence.

"Is—uh—your brother there?"

Allie wouldn't rub her nose in it. "No, I haven't seen Len since yesterday." When he came to the paper and made her look like an ass. "Have you tried his cell?"

"Of course, I've tried his cell," Vivian snapped. Allie heard her take a deep breath. "The thing is I got a call from his cell a while ago. When I answered, no one spoke." There was a little hitch in her voice. "I'm worried. It's not like Len to—well, to do something like that. He knows I'd worry. I'm afraid something might have happened to him."

For just an instant, Allie wondered if her mother would feel the same if she called and didn't speak. Unworthy, but just the same... "Have you tried his hotel?"

"Yes, I tried several times. And I've called his cell repeatedly with no results. I'm really worried, Allie." It was the first time Vivian Grainger had called her that since her twelfth birthday. She really was worried. "I know it's a lot to ask, but... could you go to his hotel and check? Is it far?"

Allie felt something inside her melt. "No, it's not far. I'll be glad to check. Don't worry. I'm sure Len is fine."

There was a long silence on the line. Allie tried to imagine her mother wherever she was—she always used her cell, so it was hard to tell—but she couldn't. Vivian Grainger as a frantic mother was something outside her experience.

"Thank you, Allison," she said, her voice barely audible.

So, their Allie moment was over. She couldn't even resent it.

■ ■ ■

CORD PERCHED UNEASILY on one of Teresa's living room wing chairs. He didn't know why women even had these chairs in their homes. His wife had been the same, saying the chair lent an air of elegance to the décor. Who would notice? Cord could count on one hand the number of times he'd sat in his living room. Same here. The furniture looked unused, and Wally appeared to be as uncomfortable as Cord.

"What brings you to see us, Cord?" Wally asked. He looked strained to Cord, not as affable as usual. Teresa sat rigid, looking at neither of them.

"I have reason to believe Sidney might still be in the area," Cord said, not willing to sugarcoat it.

"What reason?" Teresa demanded.

Cord noticed she didn't seem surprised. For that matter, neither did Wally, although he seemed worried. "A number of incidents have occurred that can possibly be traced to Sidney."

"Has anyone been hurt?" Wally asked.

"Not yet," Cord said. "Terrified, but not physically injured. But it's only a matter of time. I think we all know that. I wondered whether either of you knew anything about his whereabouts."

The room was deathly silent. Cord heard the hum of a lawn mower nearby. A dog barked in the distance. The air hung heavy with unspoken words.

"He's appeared in a number of disguises," Cord said, and Teresa gasped. "I wondered if we could look around and see if anything's missing. I'd like to check his old bedroom, too, if I may."

"You don't have a search warrant," Teresa shot out, her chin lifting in belligerence.

"Teresa, for God's sake," Wally growled. He turned to Cord. "Of course, you can. If there's anything missing, we'd like to know as well."

"There's nothing missing," Teresa said as she followed them up the stairs. "I'm the one who cleans this house, and I would know."

Both men ignored her. First, they went into the spare bedroom. The box where Teresa kept her theatrical makeup was open, half its contents strewn on the floor.

"I was looking for something," she said. "I didn't have a chance to put it all away."

Cord and Wally exchanged glances, but neither said anything. It was obvious Wally had no idea what should be there, and if anything was missing, Teresa wasn't going to tell them.

Next, they went into Sidney's bedroom. The room appeared as it might have looked when Sidney was arrested. It made Cord sad to see that Teresa had turned it into some kind of shrine.

He looked around the room. If anything was missing, he had no way of knowing. On a whim, he knelt and looked under the bed. There was something dark there, something fabric. He pulled it out. A prison uniform and Raymond's missing jacket, if his guess was right.

Teresa gasped, her hands flying to her mouth.

"He's been here," Cord said unnecessarily. "Did you see him?" he asked Teresa.

"No."

"Do you know when he was here?"

"No."

"Teresa," Wally said.

"I *don't*," she cried. "Why don't you both quit hounding him?" She spun on Cord. "He didn't mean to shoot you. He was trying to stop that woman from ruining you. Why can't you just leave him alone?"

"Because he's a dangerous man," Cord answered quietly. "He's not your little boy anymore, Teresa. He's a grown man, and he's shot a lot of people. You could cost your son his life by trying to protect him."

"And you could end his life trying to catch him," she said, tears starting down her face. "If you'd all just leave him alone—" She spun on her heel and ran from the room.

Cord and Wally looked after her. "I'm sorry," Cord said.

Wally shook his head. "No, I'm sorry. She's never been rational where that boy is concerned."

"Except that he's not a boy anymore."

Wally said nothing.

After a minute, Cord said, "OK if I look in his closet?"

"Sure. I'm not sure what should be in there."

Cord pulled open the closet door. The first thing he saw was one of Sidney's uniforms hanging neatly in the middle. All his deputies had several uniforms. Cord motioned at the uniform. "Any idea where the rest of his uniforms are?"

"Not a clue, really. Teresa has always been the one to clean this room. I don't think I've ever seen inside his closet."

Cord nodded. He spotted the gun on the top closet shelf. "Is this Sidney's?" he asked, motioning at the pistol.

Wally's face sagged. "I didn't know he had a gun in the house. I know he's an officer and all, but I've never held with having weapons around."

"May I take it?"

Wally nodded without speaking.

Cord pulled a tissue out of the box on the dresser and lifted the gun by the barrel. Then, the two boxes of ammunition. "I don't suppose—"

"I have a bag in the kitchen."

Cord could hear Teresa banging pots in the kitchen as they descended the stairs. He waited in the hall until Wally returned carrying a Ziploc bag.

Wally walked him to the door. Cord stopped and turned to the man. "If you can get her to tell you about anything that might be missing, it might help us catch him before he does something we can't help him with."

"I'll try, but you know Teresa."

When Cord climbed in his cruiser, he studied the neighborhood. Sidney had been here in the last couple of days. He'd been in his parents' house without being seen. At least from Teresa's shock at seeing the navy jumper, he assumed she hadn't seen him. But she knew he'd been there. So did Wally. He couldn't see Wally protecting Sidney, not when he knew what his son had done. He might protect his wife, though. And he knew Teresa would protect Sidney with her last breath. If she kept it up, it might also be her son's last breath.

Sixteen

ONVERSATION STOPPED WHEN Allie entered the newsroom. The place wasn't crowded, just a few reporters who glanced up and then immediately away. Allie had stopped by hoping Rand had made it back to town, but Myrna said she didn't expect him until the next day. For the first time since Allie had known her, Myrna didn't invite her outside for a cigarette pow wow. She didn't know whether Len had been back to cause more trouble or if this was residual damage from his first visit, and she wasn't about to ask.

She'd gone by the hotel the evening before, honoring her promise to her mother. One desk clerk—a young attractive woman, not surprisingly—confirmed that she'd seen Len go into the bar a little after noon, but she didn't see him come out. The bartender said he'd just come on duty. She'd have to ask the day bartender. She would have gone up to Len's room, but they wouldn't tell her which room was his, not even when she pulled out her driver's license to prove relationship. No wonder. What if she was a wife checking on her husband? They did ring his room and let her leave a message on his voice mail. "Call Mother," she said.

All this she dutifully reported to Vivian Grainger, who seemed to think Allie hadn't done enough, even though when pressed, her mother couldn't suggest another course of action. She got in one stab about Allie's job. "You're supposed to be an investigative reporter. Why don't you investigate?"

Len was probably out to dinner, Allie suggested. Maybe he had butt-dialed Vivian, which earned her a reprimand for her crudeness. Maybe his cell phone battery was dead, and he couldn't get to his charger. Maybe the charger was broken. There were a hundred reasons her mother shouldn't worry, and none made a bit of difference. Allie was supposed to keep trying to find him. Sure. When pigs sprouted fluffy pink wings. She had another man on her mind, and since he was MIA as well, she decided to see if she could dispel some hard feelings Len had caused.

Her first targets were Holly Miller and Tommy Saers, both new kids on the block at the paper like Allie herself. Both were fresh out of college. Tommy was still battling a moderate case of acne, and Holly looked like the sweet blonde cheerleader next door. She fairly exuded innocence. Allie liked them both a lot. They'd been her staunchest supporters at the newspaper, except for Myrna. She'd hate to lose their friendship over a misunderstanding caused by her jerk of a brother.

She didn't see Tommy, but Holly was at her desk. Allie sidled over and leaned on the corner of the next desk. "How's it going?" she asked.

"OK," Holly said, her face troubled. "How about you?"

"I've been better," Allie said truthfully. "You

know Sidney Finch escaped."

Holly nodded. "I heard."

"It's not for public broadcast, but we think he's still in the area. In fact, he's been pulling some nasty pranks on me."

Holly's mouth dropped open. "You're kidding! Aren't you scared?"

"Terrified. I'm jumping at shadows. Who knows what he'll do next?"

The look Holly gave her now was sympathetic. "No wonder you were so upset with your brother. Under all that tension."

Allie knew she could go two ways. She could let Holly assume that Sidney had turned her into a bitch, or she could do it the difficult way. Typically, she chose the difficult way. "That's not why, Holly. Listen." She pulled up a chair and sat. "You don't know Len. He's not what he seems."

Holly averted her eyes. "He seems nice."

"That's what I mean. He seems nice, he looks nice, and to some people, especially those who can further his career, he probably is nice. But to me…" How to convince her. "You know he was talking about my Aunt Lou?"

"His aunt, too, he said." The temperature in the room dropped ten degrees.

"Yes, his aunt, too," Allie agreed. "He knows how much I loved her, but he hated her. No, that's not true. What he said was he didn't care enough to hate her. He said he scorned her. He said she was a step above trailer trash."

"That's *awful*! Why would he say such a thing?"

"To hurt me. Don't you see? Len knew it was a way to get to me, just like he knew coming here and embarrassing me in front of everyone I work with would get to me. He's always been that way."

Holly frowned at her desk. "He didn't seem that way."

"It was an act. He's a lawyer. They're all actors. I think they practice in front of mirrors."

A little smile lit Holly's face. "Not Rand."

Allie smiled back, a goofy smile, she imagined. "Not like Rand at all. Unless he has me completely fooled. Rand is honest. He's... sincere." She could feel her face heat up.

Holly was smiling at her openly now. Allie decided to press her advantage. "Tell the others, will you? If you get a chance. I'm not a monster out to cheat my brother out of his rightful share of my inheritance."

Holly's face shut down. "What would it hurt to share with him? I mean, he was her family too."

Wasn't the girl listening to her? "Aunt Lou left it to me. She specifically told me not to let my family bully me out of it."

Allie waited for Holly's response. Finally, Holly shrugged. "Money does funny things to people," was all she said before turning back to her computer.

Allie waited for a moment. It was too late. Hurricane Len had been through. The damage was done, and Allie didn't know when or how the cleaning up and rebuilding would begin. Clearly not today.

After bidding Holly and then Myrna a brief goodbye, which either barely returned, Allie left.

Her next stop was Lester's, where she learned Del was teaching at one of his jobs. Allie had seen the place in passing, so she pointed her car in that direction.

■ ■ ■

No ONE WAS IN THE RECEPTION area when she entered, but she heard a soft chime echo in the back. The space was Spartan to the point of ugliness—a Formica counter and little else. A large glass window divided the front from what she assumed was the studio or whatever they called it. Through it, she could see a dozen students in pajama-like uniforms going through a strange series of moves. As she watched, they all moved in unison, kneeling down first on one knee, then the other, before sitting on their legs. It looked painful to Allie. Del stood poised like a white-draped statue of Atlas in the front of the room.

She didn't want to interrupt the class, but she needed to know how long she would have to wait. A plain burlap curtain hung in the doorway to the studio. As Allie reached out to pull it aside, a young man slipped through.

He smiled up at Allie and executed a little bow. "May I help you?"

Allie stepped back. What a pretty child. Slight, dressed in a loose uniform thing like the rest of the students, with his long black hair caught up in multiple bands. "Uh—I'm looking for Del. Del Delaney."

"Sensei is with students now, but the class is almost over. May I tell him your name?"

Hadn't the child heard her? "Who's Sensei?"

His smile widened. "*Sensei* means teacher."

Allie felt her face burn. "Oh, it's Allie. Allie Grainger."

"Please wait here." As he walked away, Allie realized his feet were bare. That's how he'd crept up so soundlessly. Glancing back through the window, she saw that everyone was barefooted, even Del. She watched as the boy slipped back into some formation. The students' concentration was absolute. At a word from Del, they bowed low, then scooted around in another direction and bowed again. They began an exchange in a language Allie didn't understand.

She could hardly take her eyes off Del. Before, she'd only seen him as a bartender, friendly and big. Here, even barefooted and dressed in his pajama-like uniform, he exuded authority. Allie had often wondered what her militaristic friend Sheryl saw in the easygoing, genial bartender. Now, she knew. Allie had known that Del was a martial arts instructor in several disciplines, but knowing and seeing were two different things.

As Allie watched, the students crossed their hands. Then, Del said something like *Mosquito!* and they each slashed their hands to the sides. The suddenness of the move startled Allie, and she stepped back, feeling like a voyeur.

Moments later, the students began to emerge. As she watched, they transformed from a precision machine into young boys and girls, laughing and giggling as they crossed the room to retrieve their shoes from a shelving unit against the wall, punching each other's shoulders and jostling as they went. She got curious looks as they filed out the front door in twos and threes. No wonder. She had to seem old and decrepit to these babies.

Allie was about to pull aside the curtain when Del came through. "Allie," he said, giving her a hug that threatened to crush her bones. "I didn't know you were coming."

"I didn't, either," she said, extricating herself from his bearlike embrace. "I stopped by Lester's, and they said you were here teaching. I thought I'd stop by and see the place."

He grinned. "What do you think?"

"I think I'm overwhelmed. It's all so... so different and... and ritualized. You don't expect me to learn all that stuff you were doing in there, do you?"

Del laughed aloud. "Not unless you want to. Sheryl told me to show you some down-and-dirty street-fighting tricks. Ready?"

"*Now*?"

"Why not? I have almost an hour until my next class. We could at least get started."

"But—I—" She looked down at her clothes.

"Don't worry. We probably have some extra gi. We loan 'em to the kids who can't afford uniforms.

"What's a gee?"

"It's what you wear so you don't tear your flimsy clothes. Come on back."

As they stepped in the studio, Del stopped so suddenly that Allie ran into his back. "Shoes," he said, looking down at her feet. "No shoes in the dojo." Humbled, Allie kicked off her shoes and followed Del.

Just through the door was a storage unit. Del pulled open the door, and Allie stared. She expected the usual locker-room clutter. Instead, she saw uniforms, mats, blocks of wood, towels, and several things she didn't recognize, all lined up with prefect precision.

Del handed her a uniform. "There's a bathroom over there," he said motioning to the far corner of the room. "But hurry. We don't want to waste a minute."

Allie wasn't sure about not wasting a minute, but if Del was nice enough to help her, she would comply. She struggled out of her work clothes and into the coarse garment Del had furnished her. It hung off her like moss off an oak. She felt ridiculous as she stepped into the dojo. "I don't think it fits," she told Del.

He grinned and handed her a cloth belt. "It fits fine. It's supposed to be loose so you can move without resistance. Tie the sash around your waist. Next time you come, wear something spandex. You might be more comfortable."

The next hour flew by. Allie had expected a few tips and tricks, but Del took his self-defense seriously. "It begins with mental and physical discipline," he told Allie.

"Do I have time for that stuff?" she asked.

"It's essential."

He explained that she needed to begin to work out. "You need to be in decent physical shape to defend yourself. Nothing elaborate—a daily run on the beach, a couple hours in a gym a few days a week."

Allie turned away before she rolled her eyes.

"Mental discipline is even more important," Del explained. "You have to be mentally ready to defend yourself with any part of you. Once you're attacked, you need to turn into a fighting machine. Don't be afraid to hurt your assailant. That's the goal. Go for the eyes, the throat, whatever you can get to, and give it all you have. You want to disable your attacker, not just piss him off. And use your voice. Growl. Cuss. Scream your head off. Women, especially, are afraid to use their voices, but it's an effective weapon. Your attacker won't expect it. It could throw him off guard. Scream like you're furious, like you've gone crazy." He paused. "Go ahead. Do it."

Allie looked around. "You mean now? Here?"

Del nodded.

"I can't scream now. I'd feel silly."

Del looked at her.

Allie drew in a deep breath and prepared to scream. What came out was more a wheeze.

"Pitiful," Del said, shaking his head. "OK. We'll make it more real. I'm going to attack you with the intent to kill. Screaming is the only thing that will save you. Give it everything you have." He spun and stalked a short distance away. He stood there staring at her for a long moment as his face transformed itself into a hideous scowl. Then, he lunged.

Allie gasped. It was like being in the path of a speeding locomotive. She let out what she thought was a respectable scream as she hunched and turned away to lessen the inevitable pain. Nothing happened. When she turned back, Del was grinning at her, poised on his toes mere inches from her.

"Good instincts," he said. "Bad scream. Practice in the car. Roll up your windows, and scream your head off until it feels natural." He came down off his toes. "Now, about your stance. Don't hunch over. It's an instinctive reaction because you're protecting your body, but that enlarges the target. You want to minimize the target area. And speaking of instincts, it's human instinct to protect the face and head. If you jab at someone's face, he's going to try to block it. That could open a vulnerable spot. Another thing to remember is always go for your attacker's weak point." Following Allie's gaze, he said, "Not a guy's balls. He's going to protect them first. Whatever's his weakest point. Backs of knees. Eyes. Be ready to gouge your attacker's eyes out if you have to." When Allie made a face, he said, "It's him or you."

Allie thought of Sidney Finch. "I could hurt him."

"Don't kid yourself. Your fight-or-flight instinct will kick in, and you'll want to opt for flight. Train yourself to think fight. Think about it. Envision it. Daydream about it. Imagine what he's going to do to you if you don't stop him. He won't be satisfied with killing you. Not from what Sheryl's told me about him." His eyes softened when he said Sheryl's name before turning to ice again. "He wants to make you pay, and he's going to do it in the ugliest way he can imagine. And from what Sheryl tells me, he has a real ugly imagination."

■ ■ ■

SIDNEY WATCHED ALLIE climb into her Jeep and smiled. So, she was really trying to learn to defend herself. What a laugh.

He'd followed her to Lester's and was just about

to climb out of his ride when she came back out. Scared the piss out of him. She'd glanced at him sitting in his car, but she'd seen a perky smiling redhead checking her makeup in the rearview mirror. No recognition. God, he was good.

She put the car into drive and pulled away. He looked in the backseat at the things he'd taken from her house that morning. She'd never know he'd been there. No sign of forced entry. Not since he'd left one of her office windows unlocked that last time he'd been there. You'd have thought she would have double-checked, but not his girl Allie. Dumb as a stump.

He couldn't wait to give her the next surprise, but he had a few preparations to make first. Soon, though. Very soon.

Seventeen

ALLIE WAS SURPRISED TO SEE CORD'S cruiser in front of her house as she pulled into the driveway. Something about Sidney?

She jumped out of the Jeep and met him halfway across the yard. "Did they catch him?"

Cord shook his head. "Not yet. We've stepped up the search, though, now that we think he may still be in the area." He looked uncomfortable. "Can we talk inside for a minute?"

Allie frowned. "Sure." She hesitated as she approached her front stoop.

"I heard about the palmetto bugs," Cord said.

There was nothing waiting for her outside. Remembering the blood, she wasn't sure if that was good or bad.

Cord apparently sensed her discomfort. "Let me go in first," he said.

Allie was inches behind him. Everything appeared the same as she'd left it. She checked the back door. Still locked. She breathed out. Then, she looked over her shoulder at Cord. "Coffee?"

"No, thanks," he said. "I don't have long, but I wanted to update you. Can we sit down?"

"Just let me check..." She crossed to the sofa and looked behind it. Spook looked up at her, his little tail thumping the wall.

"OK."

She perched on the edge of a cushion. Cord took the chair opposite. "I visited Wally and Teresa Finch," he said. "It appears Sidney's been there, although they both indicate they don't know when. He took some of his old clothes—" He paused when Allie groaned, then went on. "There was a weapon in the shelf of his closet, so he might be unarmed."

"Small comfort," Allie muttered.

"I'm not sure, but he might have stolen some of his mother's costumes and makeup from her days in the theatre. She was unwilling to confirm or deny what was missing."

"I know Teresa Finch," Allie said. "She's not going to help us."

Cord nodded. "The possibility of a disguise or several disguises makes it a lot more complicated. We're checking with the Cocoa Players to see if they keep old playbills. If we can get a list of parts she played back when she was active, we might have a better idea of what we're looking for. In the meantime, our best means of identification is the limp. According to the doctors at Polk, it's pronounced. He'd have trouble hiding it."

Allie stared at the floor, trying to imagine Sidney disguised. He could look like anyone. Man. Woman. How in the world would they ever catch him? She realized Cord had fallen silent. She looked up.

"There's one more thing," Cord said. "I—um—got a call. From your mother."

"*What?*"

Cord nodded. "She's worried about your brother.

Apparently, he's never been out of touch this long. She wants me to look into it."

Allie jumped to her feet. "Of all the ridiculous, stupid..." She trailed off, sputtering.

"Now, Allie, I know it might be a little pre-mature—"

"*Premature?* You'd think Len was six years old instead of thirty-six. It's been what? Two days? And she's calling the police? She's insane!"

Cord stood. "Well, insane or not, we're obliged to check on him. She's filed a missing person report. She said she asked you to look into it, but she hasn't heard back from you."

Allie could feel her face burn scarlet. "I *looked* into it. I went to the hotel and talked to the desk clerks and the bartender. I called her back and told her what I found out, which was nothing. What else was I supposed to do?" She could feel tears of frustration threaten, and she blinked them back.

Cord squirmed. "You did what you could. Now, we'll take a look into it. It's our job, Allie. Let us check it out for her."

When Cord was gone, Allie reached behind the sofa and picked up Spook, carrying him over to a chair. As she buried her face in his fur, tears began to slip down her face. It was just like when she was a kid. She couldn't do anything right. If she made a "B" in school, it should have been an "A." If she got a part in the school play, it should have been the lead. She wasn't pretty enough. She wasn't popular enough. Not like Len. She wasn't aggressive enough to suit her mother. She hadn't been scholarly enough to satisfy her father. She knew she was being childish, but it didn't matter. She knew she was wallowing in self-pity, but she didn't care.

She hadn't seen Len three times since her marriage. Now, he was back in her life—uninvited—and again, she was a lesser mortal. She hadn't satisfied her mother, so Vivian called the police. She didn't find Len, so Cord was going to do it. She had felt this way her whole damn childhood. Not good enough.

No, that wasn't true. Not when she was with Lou. Lou made her feel intelligent and like she was capable of accomplishing anything.

"You are, sweetheart."

"So you've always said, but apparently, I'm not. Not capable enough for mother. Not when her precious son goes missing for two whole days. If I were missing for a month, she wouldn't turn a hair."

"That's not true, Allie. Why do you think she calls you every few days?"

"To torture me. To belittle me."

"To check on you to make sure you're all right."

"You don't know that."

Silence.

"Does she really worry about me?"

"Of course, she does. That's the real reason she's pressuring you to move back to Atlanta. So she can keep an eye on you. One of the reasons, anyway."

"And so I won't become independent like you."

"That's another."

"Well, too bad. You're one of the most amazing women I ever met. I want to be just like you."

"And I want you to be just like you."

Her tears had dried. Spook reached up and licked her salty face. "What about that, puppy? She said my mother worries about me. What do you think about that?"

Spook whimpered and buried his face in her hair.

■ ■ ■

ALLIE WAS WORKING in her office that night when she felt a presence behind her. She had moved her desk so it was in front of the window, and she could see Sheryl's reflection in the glass. She spun off her chair and caught Sheryl in the midsection with her open hand. Sheryl fell backward, and her butt hit the carpet.

"Not bad," Sheryl said, getting back to her feet. "I told you Del's a hell of a teacher."

"One class," Allie said. "One class and I'm thinking like a warrior."

"What kind of shit did he put in your head? You caught me off guard because I know what a wimp you are. Were," she said, rubbing her stomach.

Allie felt all the blood drain out of her head. She stumbled to her feet. "Oh, my God, I'm so sorry. I forgot. Did I hurt you? Did I hurt the baby?"

Sheryl laughed, pointing to her pelvic area. "The baby's down here, dipshit. He's going to have to grow a whole hell of a lot before he's up there."

"He?"

"Figure of speech. Can't call it an 'it.' Besides, Del's determined it's a boy. It'll serve him right if it's a girl. I already told him whatever happens, it's his sperm's fault."

"Is he still as excited about the baby?"

"He's wacko about it. Already buying baby clothes and toys. He found this little gi—" She broke off. "That's a—"

"A uniform you wear for martial arts. It's made out of coarse fabric so it can take a beating."

"Damn, you're a good student. That's what Del said." She looked at Allie out of the corner of her eye. "And that you squeal like a pussy."

"I do not!"

"Prove it. Scream."

Allie hesitated. Then, she let out a scream that hurt her ears.

"*Jesus!*" Sheryl said.

"I've been practicing," Allie said, grinning. "Now, you'd better go tell Frank and the boys that you're not killing me."

"Hell, they knocked off hours ago."

Allie stared at her, then at her dark window. "What time is it?"

"Eight o'clock. You that involved in that Paradise Lost article?"

Allie stepped in front of her computer. "I'm kind of working on something else."

"What?"

"Well... it's a story about—about Sidney. About what made him what he is."

"Fuck! What a depressing subject."

"Not really. It's fascinating. I've been researching what makes a criminal a criminal. How they start in that direction. What influences shape them."

"All I want to know about Sidney is that he's behind bars. Or dead."

Allie winced, even though she felt the same way.

"Cord said he might be wearing disguises."

Sheryl nodded. "He alerted the department. We could be looking for anyone."

Neither spoke for a moment. Then, Sheryl said, "Which is what brought me here."

Allie realized Sheryl was in uniform. "Are you on duty?"

"Just got off. I wanted to bring you a present. And you owe me seven hundred dollars and sixty-eight cents."

"What kind of present costs me seven hundred dollars?"

"And sixty-eight cents. Come in the living room."

Allie followed her. Sheryl picked up a black box from the coffee table and held it out to Allie.

"It's too big for jewelry," Allie said.

"Ha, ha. Open it."

Allie opened it. She reached in and pulled out the gun. "It's cute," she said, surprised. "Cute and expensive."

"You can afford it," Sheryl said, taking the gun from her. "It's a Glock 26 Gen4. Subcompact. Small grip. Perfect for your hand. Takes nine-millimeter ammo. Ten- or fifteen-round cartridges. It comes with three tens, but I bought extra."

"More than thirty bullets? I'm not planning to go on a shooting spree."

"You have to practice, dumbass. You need to go down tomorrow and apply for a carry-concealed permit. Takes about twenty days, which we might not have, so I'm giving it to you now. Try not to shoot anyone with it unless you have to. I'd hate to waste a night bailing your ass out of jail."

Allie softened. It was all bluff. She knew Sheryl

would take the responsibility for Allie having an illegal gun. She'd probably take a bullet to protect her best friend. "If I blow Sidney away, I'll take full responsibility. No bail required."

"Sure. You say that now, but if you were behind bars, I think you'd sing a different song. Anyway, down and dirty. It has three safeties that all release when you pull the trigger. Ammo loads like this." She reached in the box, pulled out what Allie assumed was a cartridge, and snapped it in to the handle. "Pop it out like this." She released it and then pushed it back in. "Don't pull the trigger unless you mean to kill."

That was sobering, but Allie took the gun from her.

"We'll get into the details later. Now, I have a late date with my honey. We plan to fool around for a while, so don't be calling me on my cell if you shoot yourself in the foot."

Allie laughed. "Don't forget to use protection."

Sheryl grinned. "You know, I'm kind of glad I didn't."

When Sheryl was gone, Allie went back into her office. The gun was on her desk, and she picked it up. It really was somewhat cute if you didn't think of it as a deadly weapon, and it felt good in her hand. Not heavy at all. If she had to own a gun—and she was now convinced she did—this one might be just right. Trust Sheryl to find the perfect match.

Spook was under her desk chair, his usual spot when she was working. Now, he made a sound low in his throat. He crept out from under the chair and turned toward the window, the sound getting louder. Then, he barked.

The unaccustomed sound scared Allie so much she almost dropped the gun. She looked. The vision staring back at her through the glass was hideous. Distorted features. Blood dripping from its mouth. She screamed and raised the gun.

Then, it was chaos. She heard footsteps running across the yard. Spook barked nonstop. Allie felt as if she was going to black out. What was that horrible thing? Then, she heard a car start in the distance and tires squeal as it sped away.

A mask. It had to be. No creature on this Earth looked like that. Not unless it'd been dead and buried for six months. And a mask meant Sidney. It was almost his trademark. He'd worn one months ago when he was trying to scare Allie into dropping her investigation of Jean Arbutten's death. A different one, not nearly as frightening. Knowing it was Sidney didn't help a bit; it made it worse.

That's when she realized the window lock was disengaged, and she gasped. God, he could have come right in. When did she forget to lock it? She shook her head. She hadn't. She kept the windows locked all the time. Which meant Sidney must have left it unlocked the last time he was in her house. What if she hadn't noticed it was unlocked. She could have been sleeping in her bed... She shivered as she reached over and twisted the lock, yanking the curtains closed.

She put the gun down on her desk and picked up Spook. "Good dog. Good dog, Spook," she murmured. "It's OK. It's gone, baby. The bad man is gone. It's OK."

She hoped her words calmed Spook, because

they weren't doing a damn thing to calm her.

■ ■ ■

SIDNEY TOOK DEEP BREATHS as he drove. Jesus, was he stupid? He almost got his fucking head blown off because of pure carelessness. Who coulda known the bitch would have a weapon? Most broads didn't like guns. This had to be Levine's doing.

He'd only meant to freak her out, a little something to get her in the right frame of mind for tomorrow night. Once she saw him, he was going to creep away, and he would have if that little dog hadn't barked.

Hell, he couldn't blame the dog. It was just doing its job, the same way Sidney had always tried to do his job. Besides, the dog had never barked before. Not in all the times Sidney had broken in. Was it mad at him for locking it in the office? Jeez. He'd had to do that. Otherwise, it might have gotten outside and gotten run over or something. But how did you explain something like that to a pup?

He ripped off the mask and wig and stuffed them in his duffle bag on the passenger seat. He needed to check on his prisoner. Even though Sidney kept him drugged, it didn't do to leave him unattended for too long, but he needed funds. That meant another trip to his parents' house. And he had to get rid of this car. He'd been driving it for twenty-four hours. Long enough.

He started to head for Melbourne Airport, but changed his mind. That would take over an hour round trip. He had too much to do and too little time, and this goddamn headache was killing him. He didn't dare take anything for it. The only thing that touched the pain was narcotics, and he couldn't afford to be drugged out. Things were heating up. He had to be alert. If only his head didn't hurt so bad.

OK, he'd go back to Port Canaveral. There were plenty of cars there, and it was only five minutes away. Sure, this one would be reported missing, but big deal. How long would it take them to find it wedged in among two or three hundred other cars?

■ ■ ■

THE SWITCH WAS EASY. The port parking lots had twenty-four-hour security, but how much coverage could two Rent-a-Cops provide for a five-acre lot?

This bozo actually had a spare key in a metal box under the driver side running board, which saved Sidney the trouble of hot-wiring it. And bozo had left his parking ticket wedged in his sun visor. Better and better. Sidney happily paid the $23.50 to exit the lot. Money well spent.

He made a quick trip to Cocoa to check on his guest. The guy was out cold. If Sidney had calculated right, he probably had three or four hours to visit his folks.

It was almost ten o'clock when he switched off his car lights and glided to the curb several houses down. No lights were on at his parents' house, but that didn't mean one still wasn't awake. He'd give it another hour or so. Then, he'd make his move.

■ ■ ■

TERESA KNEW WALLY was still downstairs, even though she could see from the top of the stairs that the lower floor was dark. He was avoiding her. He hadn't spoken a word since the sheriff's visit, hadn't come to bed. Why couldn't Cord Arbutten leave her and her family alone? Why wasn't he out chasing dangerous criminals instead of hounding her? That was what she paid taxes for—to pay his salary. She had half a mind to file a complaint against him for harassment if he didn't leave them alone.

She had tried to sleep. It was after eleven, and she was exhausted, but sleep wouldn't come. She'd tried to slip in the pantry several times to put money in the canister, but Wally was always there before she had a chance. She knew better than to go downstairs now. Wally would want to know why, and what could she say? But what if Sidney needed money for something? Where else might he look?

Her purse. If she could get her purse downstairs, he'd see it if he came in the house. He knew she always carried money with her. He'd helped himself to it enough times. But how could she do it without Wally suspecting?

Then, she had an idea. She picked up her purse and headed downstairs.

Wally sat in the living room in the dark. He glanced up when Teresa came down the stairs, but said nothing. Maybe he wouldn't. Maybe he was so angry with her that he would leave her alone.

That hope was dashed when she switched on the kitchen light. The pantry door was ajar. Either Wally had been in there again, or—or Sidney had been. Was she too late?

She jumped when Wally walked up behind her. "What are you doing up?"

"I need to take a pill. I can't sleep."

Wally glanced at her purse, then back at her. "You had to bring the whole purse downstairs? Why didn't you just bring the pill bottle? Or why didn't you get some water in the bathroom upstairs?"

He remained rigid for a full minute before his posture sagged. "What are you doing, Teresa? Isn't the boy in enough trouble? Don't you realize that helping him will only make it worse—for all of us?"

She was so angry, she was trembling. "I know you don't care about him. You never have—"

"That's not true."

"But I love him. What if he needs money for medicine—?"

"Or booze or drugs or bullets—"

"Or food. Would you let your own flesh and blood starve? Is that what kind of father you are?"

Teresa saw Wally's face go red. His breathing was audible. "All right, goddamn it. Is that what you want? You want him free long enough to commit a crime that will get him hung, fine. By all means, let's help him. Then, when he's shot to death trying to avoid capture, it'll all be on you."

He reached in her purse and snatched her wallet. He started to pull out the cash, but then he snapped it closed. "Why just give him cash? Why not give him all your credit cards? Then, he can have a good run for his money before he's caught."

He stomped to the pantry and swung the door wide. He turned back to say something but stopped. He must have seen the shock on her face.

Sidney. Dressed in black sweats.

171

Wally remained frozen, but Teresa stepped forward, "Sidney. Oh, sweetheart, I knew you'd come."

He barely spared her a glance. His eyes were on his father. The wallet. His father's face. He reached out and snatched the wallet before Wally could react. "Don't try to stop me," he said, heading toward the back door.

Teresa was horrified when Wally stepped between Sidney and the door. "I have to, Son. You're making a big mistake. If you aren't careful, you're going to get yourself killed. Think what that'll do to your mother."

"But not you," Sidney sneered. "You can go fuck yourself. And get out of my way."

As he tried to brush past, Wally shoved him back and reached for his cell phone. Before Teresa could blink, Sidney's fist shot out, catching Wally along the side of his head. Wally went down, his head hitting the floor with a sickening crack. Blood poured from the opening.

Sidney's mouth fell open. He hesitated slightly. Then, he clutched the wallet to his body and ran out the back door.

Teresa went after him, but he vanished. Back inside, she knelt on the floor beside her husband. She could see he was breathing. She picked up his cell phone from where he'd dropped it and started to dial 911. Then, she put the phone down as sorrow as profound as any she'd ever felt washed through her.

This is what they had driven Sidney to. All of them. Cord. Wally. All those people who turned their backs on him once he was in trouble. Where would he go now? And what in God's name was going to happen next?

Eighteen

"TRY POINTING AT THE TARGET," Sheryl said, her voice heavy with sarcasm.

"I *am* pointing at the target," Allie said for what she knew was the hundredth time. "The gun keeps jumping."

Sheryl pulled off her headgear. "It's called recoil, and you're supposed to compensate for that. Aim lower. If you shoot any higher, you're going to start bringing down birds."

Allie pulled out her earplugs, which weren't helping much anyway. "I give up. No," she said when Sheryl started to speak. "Not forever. For today. My eyes burn, and my back hurts, and I think I'm getting a blister."

Sheryl made a face. "You are such a wimp. What's a blister? Christ, you probably have to go to bed for a week for a hangnail."

"And take a Darvon," Allie agreed as they put away their gear. This shooting a gun was a whole lot more difficult than it looked. She wasn't kidding about having a blister. It had popped about an hour ago, and it was probably infected by now.

They walked in companionable silence to Sheryl's car. Typically, Allie would have insisted on driving— Sheryl drove like Evel Knievel on steroids—but

Sheryl knew the way to the range. It was Allie's first time, but not, she vowed, her last. She'd enjoyed the first hour, but Sheryl seemed determined to render her an accomplished sharpshooter in one day.

"Lester's?" Sheryl asked as she slid behind the wheel.

"And step on it."

Allie regretted her words the minute they were out of the parking lot. Sheryl wove in and out of traffic like an EMT with a free bleeder in the back. If Allie weren't so starved, she might have told her to slow down. Not that it would have done any good, but if they had an accident, the blame would rest squarely on Sheryl's shoulders. Not that they were likely to survive a crash at this speed.

Twenty minutes later, they bellied up to the bar at Lester's. As usual, their drinks were waiting for them. Sheryl's, these days, was a cola.

Allie looked at the Bloody Mary with double celery. "How did you know I was hungry?" she asked Del.

"Sheryl said she was taking you to the range. It always gives her an appetite. I figured you'd be no different."

"You wouldn't say that if you saw her fire a gun," Sheryl said. "You'd better teach her a lot of hand-to-hand, because if she has to defend herself with a gun, she's dead."

"Stop picking on me," Allie said, punching Sheryl's arm. "I'm doing the best I can. How good were you when you started?"

Sheryl started to answer, and then stopped. "OK, you have a point, but I had weeks to improve. I doubt you do."

"Thanks for planting that thought in my head."
She turned to Del. "I want a hamburger with
everything and a large fries."

"You are hungry. How about you, honey."

"I want two beers and some wings."

"OK. A grilled chicken sandwich on wheat and
another Coke. Back shortly."

When he was gone, Allie looked at Sheryl. "I
can't believe how well you're taking this whole
thing."

Sheryl smiled, and it transformed her whole
face. She looked softer—and happier than Allie
had ever seen her. "I think it's kind of cute, you
know? I've never had anyone who wanted to take
care of me before. I kind of like it."

Allie's experience was the opposite. Other than
her mother, everyone she came across wanted to
take care of her, and she hated it. "Is Libby still
as pleased as she was about the baby?"

Sheryl snorted, sounding more like herself.
"She's in heaven. It's all she talks about. She's
doubling her physical therapy so she'll be fully
mobile by the time little Rocco here comes." She
patted her middle.

"Rocco?"

"That's what Del wants to name him."

"What if he's a she?"

Sheryl stared at her for a minute and then
grinned. "Rockette?"

They were still laughing when Del returned
with their food.

■ ■ ■

SIDNEY SQUIRMED IN HIS BOOTH. The fucking bitches. Laughing their asses off. Well, let them. They wouldn't be laughing long.

He thought back to the night before, and his eyes stung. Man, he hoped his dad was OK. He'd only meant to graze his chin. Just enough to distract him. Fuck, what if he'd killed him? He hadn't dared hang around to see if an ambulance showed up. He knew the minute his dad came around, he'd call the sheriff. Then Cord would know for sure that Sidney was in town. Sidney had hoped to keep him in the dark a little longer. Well, whatever. It was too late now.

He turned as the door opened, and he almost fell out of his seat. Christ. The sheriff. What the hell was he doing here?

Sidney scrunched lower in the booth as he waited for the sheriff to spot him, but he continued down to the far end of the bar. Sidney wanted to hear what he said to them, but he didn't dare walk. The place wasn't crowded, and they'd spot his limp for sure. Goddamn this foot. And it was Allie Grainger's fault. Every bit of it.

He could make out every third word or so. Not enough to make sense of what the sheriff was saying. He fumed.

■ ■ ■

"...A RUCKUS AT THE FINCH'S house last night. Apparently, Sidney paid them a visit. Wally tried to stop him from leaving, and Sidney knocked him out. Wally split his head when he came down."

"Is he OK?" Allie asked.

"He'll be fine, no thanks to Teresa. She didn't call the paramedics until half an hour after Sidney left. Wally could have bled to death. It took a dozen stitches to close his scalp. He'll have quite a scar to remind him."

"Sidney's out of control," Sheryl said.

Cord nodded his agreement. "But that's not what brings me here." He turned to Allie. "Your brother's car was located at the Port Canaveral lot. They do a license plate check every few days to make sure no cars are abandoned there. Check them against their records. They realized it was a rental and called the rental agency. They identified it as registered to Leonard Grainger."

Allie could barely breathe. Her heart threatened to burst out of her chest. "Len?" She felt Sheryl's arm go around her. Allie barely noticed.

"No, the car was empty. Wiped clean of prints." He looked around and lowered his voice. "There is what looks like blood in the trunk."

Allie gasped.

"The lab is processing it. Could be it's animal blood or something else altogether. We're not sure. I have to call your mother—"

"Oh, my God," Allie said, dropping her head in her hands. "This is a nightmare."

"Don't jump to conclusions," Cord said, his voice gentle. "We don't know for sure he's a victim of foul play."

Allie's head snapped up. "What else could it be? Do you think he cut himself and bled in the trunk and then hopped a cruise ship?" At Cord's wounded look, she relented. "I'm sorry. I just can't believe all this is happening. First, Sidney escapes and comes gunning for me, and now, Len disappears..."

She looked at Sheryl. "You don't think—"

"He wouldn't dare. That's kidnapping."

"So what? He's already facing attempted murder."

"But why would he snatch Len? And where's the ransom note?"

"It's only been two days. Maybe he hasn't had time to deliver it yet. Or... what if it's not ransom he's after?"

"What then?"

"Revenge. The same thing he's been after since he got out. If he knows how Len and I feel about each other, what better way to make me look bad than to have Len disappear?"

"How would Sidney know you hate each other?"

"We know he's been in my house. Maybe he's been other places and overheard me talking."

"Sidney's not that smart. Or that resourceful," Sheryl shot back. Then, she hesitated. "OK. Maybe he is, but where would he keep him?"

"Wherever he's staying. He has to be sleeping somewhere. If Len is still—" She couldn't say the word.

Cord held up a hand. "Wait just a minute, both of you. You're going off the deep end." He turned to Allie. "We have no reason to suspect Sidney had any part in your brother's disappearance. The two situations could be totally unrelated. We're going to proceed on the assumption that they are until we have reason to suspect otherwise."

He looked at Sheryl. "Levine, I don't want this supposition bandied around. It could take the focus off the separate investigations. If we find any connection at all, we'll proceed differently at that time, but not until then. Do you understand?"

Sheryl nodded. "Yes, sir."

Cord looked back at Allie. "I'll let you know what your mother says when I call her."

"Do you have to tell her about the blood in the trunk? She's going to be frantic."

"No, I'm not going to tell her about the substance we found in the trunk until we've confirmed what it is. We don't know that it's blood. I'm going to tell her we located his car and that there seems to be no indication of violence—which is true at the moment. I'm also going to tell her we have officers questioning the staff at the Hilton and that we'll let her know as soon as we learn anything."

"Don't forget, she's an attorney."

"I deal with attorneys every day, Allie."

"Not attorneys like my mother, you don't."

■ ■ ■

ALLIE HEARD THE TELEPHONE ringing when she let herself in the front door. One glance at caller ID had her heading in the other direction. She was not ready to talk to her mother. She had reached the bedroom when she heard the answering machine kick in.

"Allison, I know you're there. Don't be such a coward that you hide from a simple telephone call. I spoke with that sheriff down there, and he told me he'd talked to you. You know they found Len's car. Despite all that nonsense that sheriff was spouting, I know something's happened to Len. No one parks their car in a cruise line parking lot and

walks away. If that incompetent police department down there doesn't do something about it,
I plan to take matters in my own hands. I'll hire
an investigator of my own if I have to, since you
apparently don't want to help. This is all your
fault, Allison. If you'd shared Lou's inheritance
with your brother in the first place, he wouldn't
have come down there."

Vivian took a shaky breath. "I know you're there.
If you don't pick up this phone immediately, I'm
going to be on the next plane..."

That did it. Allie ran across the room and snatched
up the phone. "Mother? Is that you? I just walked
in the door."

"Of course, you did. You are such a poor liar,
Allison. What have you heard about your brother?"

"Nothing other than what the sheriff told you.
I know they've put on extra deputies to help in
the search." Two lies, but this was an emergency.

"What are you going to do? I mean you personally. This is your fault, you know."

Allie held the phone away from her ear as her
mother ranted. The hell of it was if Sidney had
snatched Len, it truly was her fault.

■ ■ ■

ALLIE WAS STRETCHED OUT face down on the sofa two
hours later when she heard a knock at her front
door. She almost ignored it. She wanted to bury
her head under a pillow and not come out until
all this was over.

She didn't see an outline through the frosted
jalousies, so she peeked out the window. Rand

was heading back to his car. Should she let him? She was in no mood for company tonight, not even his. At the last minute, she yanked open the door.

"Rand!"

He turned, and a smile split his face. It remained in place until he was halfway across the yard. Then, he hurried his steps.

"What is it?" he asked when he reached her.

Allie couldn't talk to him in the yard, not with the eyes of all the neighbors and possibly Sidney on her. "Come inside."

"You've been crying," he said as she shut the door behind him and flipped the deadbolt.

"For hours," she agreed. Then, she began to fill him in on what had happened in the past week. Somewhere during her recital, he went in the kitchen and returned carrying two glasses of wine, the wine Allie had put in the refrigerator in anticipation of their first night—years ago, it seemed.

Several glasses later, she was huddled against Rand with her head on his shoulder, the empty bottle of wine on the table before them.

"What a hell of a mess," Rand said.

Allie nodded. "And I'm convinced Sidney has him, and your father's convinced it's unrelated."

"He's always had a blind spot where Sidney's concerned."

Although Allie had said the same words, she wasn't convinced that was what was going on here. "I think he knows I'll go to pieces if I think Sidney has Len. Which I did, of course. I think he's trying to protect me."

"Hmmm."

Allie wasn't going to push it. "I'm convinced

when we find Sidney, we'll find Len."

Rand frowned. "I hope you're right. I don't think Sidney would kill him. They'd fry him for that in a heartbeat."

"That's what I'm hoping he's thinking. But in the meantime, what's happening to Len?"

Nineteen

"YOU'D BETTER EAT WHILE you have a chance," Sidney said into the microphone.

He'd waited until they all left Lester's before dropping a bill on his tab and heading out the door. That bull boyfriend of Levine's gave him a funny look, but he didn't say anything.

Now, Sidney was determined to get some nourishment in his prisoner, but the stupid bastard refused to eat. Every time Sidney got the spoon close to his mouth, he clamped it shut. How the hell was he going to get the drugs in him if he didn't eat? It hadn't worked in the water. The asshole spit it on the floor.

"You're drugging the food," Len said as if he heard Sidney's thoughts.

"You'd better be glad I'm putting them in your food. There are a lot worse ways to get them in you. Besides, what the hell do you care? You don't have any appointments."

"How long have I been here?"

Sidney didn't answer. He had blacked out the trailer's windows as soon as he moved in. Easier and more efficient than buying curtains.

"They'll be looking for me," Len said. "As soon as my family realizes I'm gone, they'll be looking."

"You went on a cruise," Sidney said. He laughed. "That's where they'll find your car."

"No one will believe that. I'm an attorney. They know I wouldn't just walk away from my practice without telling anyone."

Sidney didn't answer.

"Why am I here? Is it money? If it is, I don't have any."

"So what? Your mother does. Your sister sure as hell does."

"How do you know so much about my family?"

Silence.

"Don't bother trying to get money out of my sister. She'd rather see me dead."

Sidney couldn't help it. He chuckled.

"You know about that?" He struggled against his restraints. "Who are you? What do you want?"

Sidney hit him on the knee, not enough to damage it, but enough to hurt, and he was gratified when Len cried out in pain. "You ask too many questions," he growled into the mike. "Don't try my patience, or you'll regret it. And you'd better eat this food. I'm going to get the drugs into you one way or another."

"No."

"I hear they're just as effective if they're delivered anally."

Len's eyes widened. "You wouldn't."

Sidney reached over and picked up a pair of surgical gloves, dangling them in front of Len. "You don't think so? Why don't you just roll over and try me."

Len stared at him for a long time. Then, he opened his mouth.

■ ■ ■

As TERESA PUSHED OPEN the door with her foot, the tray she was carrying threatened to spill its contents on the bedroom carpet. "I brought you something to eat."

Wally looked from her face to the tray before turning his face to the wall. "No, thank you."

"Please, Wally, you have to eat. You haven't had a thing all day. You'll get sick."

"I said no. Thank you."

Teresa put the tray on the bedside table and turned on the lamp before sitting on the edge of the bed. Wally scooted over as if he couldn't bear to be near her. "You can't go on like this," she said. "I know your head hurts, but it won't help to starve yourself."

"My head is fine."

"It's *not* fine. It's swollen, and you lost a lot of blood. You have to keep your strength up. You have to eat."

Wally turned back toward her. "Why did I lose a lot of blood, Teresa?"

She looked away.

"Maybe because you were willing to let your husband lie on the floor and bleed to death so your criminal son had a chance to get away. What if I had died? How would you feel then?"

"I knew you weren't going to die. I know how much head wounds bleed. Sidney had enough of them when he was a kid."

"So did I during my years as a firefighter. So did some of my buddies, and some of them died. You didn't know if there was intracranial bleeding."

"I—I—"

"You would have let me die to protect Sidney.

That's the bottom line."

She jumped up from the bed. "Well, someone has to protect him. All the rest of you are trying to—to—"

"To stop a criminal." Wally pushed himself up on his elbows. "I've done a lot of thinking, Teresa. I've put up with a lot over the years in the name of Sidney, but I'm done with that."

Her breath hitched. "What do you mean?"

"I'm leaving. I'm leaving you, and I'm leaving here. I'll make sure you're taken care of financially, but I don't want to be with you anymore. I'll move out as soon as I can find a place."

"You don't mean that. You *can't*. We've been married almost forty years, Wally. I love you. You *can't* leave me."

"You say you love me. Those are words. Actions speak a whole lot louder." He lowered himself back to the pillow. "Will you please turn out the light? It's hurting my eyes."

Teresa switched off the lamp and walked blindly down the stairs. Wally didn't mean it. He'd change his mind tomorrow when his head wasn't hurting so badly. He couldn't leave. What would she do without him?

She started into the kitchen, but then she turned and went into Wally's study. It was really a downstairs bedroom he converted years ago. It was a nice room. He'd lined the walls with book-shelves and installed a desk and a recliner, and there was even a little television in the corner.

Teresa headed to the desk and switched on the computer. She clicked the icon for her bank and typed in her password. And smiled.

Gas charges, two of them. Charges from Winn Dixie, so he was eating. She felt tears start to her eyes, and she blinked them away. One charge at a motorcycle shop for a helmet. Was he riding a motorcycle? They were *so* dangerous. She hoped he'd be careful.

Satisfied, she logged out and switched off the computer. It was such a relief to know he was all right.

■ ■ ■

RAND HAD OFFERED to leave, but Allie didn't want to be alone, so they went out to dinner. The world had gone crazy, and Allie feared she might join it if she weren't careful. What she wanted was an element of normalcy in her life.

Dinner was wonderful. They were at the Heidelberg in Cocoa Beach. It was one of the places her Aunt Lou used to take her when she was a girl. The owners were transplants from Germany. If you didn't know from the beer, the food would convince you of its authenticity. Allie managed a few bites, even though her heart wasn't in it. It was with Len, wherever he was. It was one thing for siblings to fight, but it was quite another when that sibling was in danger, as Allie was finding out.

She didn't doubt Len was in danger, any more than she doubted Sidney had him. Sidney Finch was a dangerous man. Crazy. He wouldn't stop at childish pranks, and who knew what he'd do next? It might be good that Sidney thought Allie hated Len. That might be the only protection Len had.

She rubbed her forehead. How could she ever

have believed she hated Len? Resented, maybe, and with good reason. But hate? He was her brother, her only sibling. If anything happened to him because of her, she'd never forgive herself. Maybe that was what family was all about; you drove each other crazy, but in the clinches, you stood together.

"Allie? Are you all right?"

Rand watched her, his forehead creased with worry. Allie reached across the table and took his hand. "I'm sorry. I can't get Len off my mind."

"Do you want me to take you home? I could stay with Dad tonight if you'd rather."

Allie gripped his hand harder. "I want you to take me home, but I don't want you to leave. I don't know if—if—but I don't want to be alone. I know that's selfish, but I'm afraid to be alone."

Rand reached over and stroked her arm. "It's not selfish. Of course, I'll stay." A smile played across his lips. "Even if we don't, although I can't promise you I won't try. You can only ask so much of a man."

Allie huddled near the restaurant door while Rand paid the check. She could feel Sidney's eyes on her. For once, she welcomed the sensation. If he was here watching her, he couldn't be where Len was, doing whatever he was doing to Len.

They drove back to Allie's house in relative silence, with only soft music to accompany their breathing. Traffic was heavy. Friday night in a beach town. Pedestrians clogged the sidewalks, much as cars, creeping along as their occupants took in the sights, clogged the roads. Garish neon lighting blocked out any view they might have had of the stars overhead, especially as they neared Highway 520, where blinking signs advertised everything from bathing suits and beach toys to motels and bars.

Cheap and touristy. Those words sprang to mind. But people loved it. They flocked from hundreds of miles away to be part of the action. Lou had told Allie about when Cocoa Beach was a sleepy little town; when the behemoth Ron Jon Surf Shop complex was a wooden shack in a strip mall; when the only nighttime traffic consisted of exhausted workers from Cape Canaveral bellying up to the counter at Wolfie's, only to fall asleep over their pastrami sandwiches. That was before Disney World came to Orlando, before all the cruise lines invaded Port Canaveral. Allie had seen pictures, and she longed to go back in time and experience that Cocoa Beach.

"You would have loved it, Allie. That was before I went to work for the Sheriff's Office. I worked at Wolfie's as a waitress. They had the best food south of New York City."

"I wish I could have been there with you."

"There are good things about every time, things we look back on later and long for."

"What's all that special about now? What will I look back on?"

"Lots of things. Your house before the construction. Lester's. Sheryl and Joe and the years you shared. The man sitting beside you."

"I'll look back on him?"

"I didn't mean that literally. I was talking about moments and things you'll treasure in the future."

"Will we have future years?"

"The Ouija board is closed for the night."

"Is Len OK? At least tell me that. Is he OK?

Silence. Then, *"He's OK. For now."*

Tears sprang to her eyes. She blinked rapidly as they pulled in her drive behind her Jeep.

Rand put his car in park and turned to her. When he saw her tears, he reached over and pulled her into his arms. "What is it, Allie?"

A sob choked her. "Len."

"I know—"

"No." She pulled back. "He's OK. Aunt Lou said he's OK... for now."

"She told you that?"

Again, Allie waited for the skepticism, for the derision. There was none.

"Thank God," Rand said. "Did she tell you where he is?"

"No, I don't know if she knows exactly. I can't explain it, but I think she just has... knowings... like knowing someone is all right, or someone's going to get hurt. Like last year when she told me Joe was going to break Sheryl's heart. She didn't say when or how. I thought she was just being stubborn, but I don't think she knew, exactly— just that it would happen."

"Now, you're getting the picture."

"She said he was OK for now. Did she say for how long?"

Allie shook her head. "And I was afraid to ask."

■ ■ ■

SIDNEY HUNG FROM the fifth-floor girder. Dressed all in black, he was invisible against the black night. He was still taking a chance, and he had almost blacked out in pain climbing the goddamn ladders, but he didn't dare use the construction elevator. It squealed like a banshee, and someone might hear it.

He'd spent more than an hour feeding his idiot captive and had left him sleeping like a baby. He'd been afraid he'd be too late to rig up his latest surprise, but the gods were on his side. Once he determined Allie was gone, he had plenty of time. He even left another present for her inside, thanks to the spare key he'd stolen the last time he was there, one that would just seal the deal. He couldn't wait. The stupid dog had tried to bite him this time. If Sidney paid another visit, he'd have to drug some meat. It was just a little dog. Maybe a quarter of a pill. Maybe less. He didn't want to hurt it.

He shifted on his metal perch. What the hell were they doing down there? Making out? Hell, they had a whole house in front of them where they could make out and screw and whatever else they wanted in a whole lot more comfort. And it was cold up here. The cold always made his injuries hurt more.

He had to park his new ride down the block under the carport of a shuttered house. Battened down for the winter. Who the hell would close their Florida house for the winter? Maybe they were just away for a few weeks. As long as they were away, that was fine with him.

He was driving a motorcycle now. He'd made the switch yesterday. It was getting too risky to use Port Canaveral—the guy there had given him

a suspicious look the last time he came through—
and Melbourne Airport was inconvenient. Then,
he'd remembered some friends of his parents who
lived in Melbourne Beach. Richer than dirt. Spent
every winter in the south of France or Italy or
somewhere. Their garage wasn't alarmed, even
though the house was covered with the latest elec-
tronic equipment. Dangerous oversight.

He broke a garage window and climbed in,
cursing his lameness all the while. He'd intended
to steal a car, but the motorcycle was just too
inviting, and it used less gas. Even though he had
his mother's gas credit card now, he didn't want
to overdo the charges.

He had plenty of cash too. He knew her debit
card PIN was his birthday. She used his birthday
for all her PINs, which was stupid. If someone
got hold of it, he'd have access to all her accounts.

What the hell were they doing down there?
Then, the driver's side door opened.

Twenty

SPOOK DIDN'T COME OUT TO GREET them when they walked in, but that didn't surprise Allie. Spook never showed himself when she had company.

As she dropped her purse on the sofa, she heard a scratching sound at her bedroom door. Rand heard it too. He motioned Allie to stay put and disappeared down the hall. A moment later, Spook raced out of the back of the house and went directly to the back door, barking and jumping. Did the dog have to go out that badly?

Then, it hit her. Spook was shut up in her bedroom. He'd been behind the couch when she left. She was sure of it.

"It's all right," Rand said as he stepped back into the room. "The pup—"

"Someone's been in here."

Rand stopped. "Are you sure? Maybe you shut him in the bedroom by mistake."

Allie shook her head. "He was behind the sofa. I remember checking before we left."

"Maybe the wind—"

"All the windows are shut and locked. There was no wind."

"The air conditioner..." His voice trailed off at

the look Allie gave him.

"Sidney's been in here. I can feel it. It's like a miasma in the air. Slimy. Murky." She shuddered.

"Do you want to call 911?"

"Not until I'm sure." She took Rand's hand as she checked each room. Nothing seemed out of place until she reached the kitchen. The hook where she kept her extra key was empty.

"He has a key."

"What?"

She motioned at the hook. "Aunt Lou always kept an extra key hanging here in case she lost hers. It's gone."

"Maybe it—"

He broke off when Allie spun on him. "Why don't you believe me? He's been here, damn it!"

Rand pulled her into his arms. "I believe you, honey. I'm just playing devil's advocate here, trying to think of alternative possibilities."

Allie went limp against him. Why was she attacking Rand? He was on her side. "I'm sorry."

"Don't apologize. It's freaking me out too."

Spook was whining now, his nose pressed against the crack at the bottom of the back door. Allie reluctantly withdrew from Rand's arms. Maybe Spook really did need to go outside. She picked up his leash from the counter, but Rand took it from her. "Let me walk him. You don't need to make yourself a target."

"Aren't you making yourself a target instead?"

"Yeah, but I'm not the one Sidney's after. He doesn't have anything against me."

They stared at each other. Sidney hated Rand for being Cord's son.

"Go out the front door," Allie said. "I'll turn on the porch light." Rand nodded.

Allie watched them circle the yard. Realizing she was a perfect target highlighted in the doorway, she stepped back inside. It usually took Spook a few minutes to go, especially when he was upset.

Allie crossed to the back door, pulling the curtain aside. And she screamed.

■ ■ ■

SIDNEY ALMOST FELL OFF THE GIRDER when she screamed. In seconds, the little dog was somewhere on the ground below him, barking his head off. *Jesus.* What was he going to do? He couldn't go down. The dog's barking was sure to bring people. He gritted his teeth as he stood on the steel beam, and he began to climb.

■ ■ ■

RAND WAS BESIDE HER in an instant. "What is it? What happened?"

Allie was doubled over, her hands covering her face. Rand pulled her away from the back door. "What is it, Allie? Are you hurt?"

She shook her head violently.

Rand wrenched her hands away so he could see her face. Then, he pulled her into his arms. "What's wrong? What did you see?"

Allie shivered uncontrollably. She burrowed into Rand's arms, trying to dispel the vision etched on the back of her eyelids.

After a minute, her breathing slowed. The

shivering eased. She realized she was gripping the back of his shirt in a death grip. She released one hand and waved her arm in the direction of the back door.

When he moved, she moved with him, unwilling to leave the protection of his arms. She heard him pull aside the door's window curtain and draw in a sharp breath. She felt him reach into his pocket, for his cell phone, Allie assumed. She couldn't bring herself to open her eyes.

Before he had a chance to dial, Sheryl burst through the open front door. "What the hell's going on?" she demanded. "You were screaming like a crazy woman. Probably woke up half of Cape Canaveral."

"Back door," Rand said, his voice hard.

Allie opened her eyes. Sheryl was in her pajamas, her gun in her hand. She crossed to the back door and ripped aside the curtain. "Jesus fucking Christ," she spit out, switching on the back porch light and yanking open the door.

It was worse in bright light. Allie, or a dummy made up to look like her. It hung by a noose from the upstairs deck railing, it's long, blond hair trailing over its garishly made-up face. It looked like the throat had been cut. Blood, fake blood, she hoped, trailed down the front of what Allie recognized as her clothes, and it had pooled on the patio below. Some kind of landscape uplight had been rigged to shine up at its face. It was hideous. And believable.

Sheryl snatched the cell phone from Rand and dialed a number. "It's Levine. I need two units and a CSI at…"

She rattled off Allie's address and a bunch of other stuff, but Allie wasn't listening. This was vintage Sidney. No, that wasn't true. Sidney had never gone to these lengths to terrorize, not when they were kids, but this was a new Sidney, a grown-up, insane Sidney, and he was escalating. First, poop...

She spun on Rand. "Where's Spook?"

"He pulled away when you screamed. I—"

Allie was already halfway out the front door. If that bastard did anything to hurt her dog, she'd tear him apart with her bare hands.

She heard Spook before she saw him. He was barking, jumping around at the construction site next door. Allie picked her way gingerly across the debris-strewn ground until she reached him. Then, she scooped him up and held him close.

"My poor baby," she murmured as she headed back toward the house. "I thought I'd lost you. What were you doing over here? Were you trying to chase that bad man away? It's OK, baby. He's gone. The bad man is gone."

■ ■ ■

SIDNEY WAITED UNTIL ALLIE went back in the house and closed the door behind her before he began his torturous climb down. That was too fucking close. She couldn't have seen him if she looked up, but if she told the others, and they brought flashlights...

He climbed faster. He had to get the hell away from here before someone figured out what that little dog was doing. He had to give it to the mutt, though. The little guy had tried to climb the girders. What a tiger. He wouldn't mind having a little guy like that some time in the future. But his future—a future spent in a mental institution or jail—wouldn't allow a dog. If he went back.

He paused as his good foot reached the ground. Jesus, what was he thinking? He couldn't go back. What kind of life would that be? His thoughts raced as he dodged through the puny shrubs and palms toward his ride. He would vanish instead. He had his mother's credit cards. He knew she wouldn't report them missing, and his dad didn't know about half of them. They would carry him a long way from here. She'd had more than a thousand bucks in her purse. Plus, he could make a series of withdrawals over a matter of days. Later, he could contact her for more. He knew she'd give it to him without question.

Mexico might work. Or he could catch a boat over to the Bahamas. Enough of them sailed out of Port Canaveral every day. That would be a sweet life. They'd never catch him. He was too smart. Hell, he'd already been within two feet of the sheriff, not to mention Allie and Levine, and none of them had made him.

If he left for good, he didn't need that asshole he was holding in his trailer. He could kill Allie and Levine because they deserved it and turn the guy loose in the Everglades. Sidney didn't kill without a reason. The schmuck probably wouldn't last two days in the Glades, not with the snakes and gators there. Hell, Sidney and the sheriff almost hadn't survived the week they spent down there, even though the sheriff was a seasoned outdoorsman, but at least, the Grainger guy's death wouldn't be on Sidney's head.

He hurried his steps as he heard sirens in the distance.

■ ■ ■

THE CRIME SCENE TECHS had been going over the dummy and the area surrounding it for more than an hour. They had floodlights set up at intervals on the dunes to provide adequate light. Once they had photographed everything, sifted, picked, and whatever else they did, they would take the dummy down and transport it to wherever they took things for further investigation. At least, that's what Sheryl told Allie. Allie didn't ask any questions. She didn't care what they did. She just wanted it to be over.

After Sheryl raced home to tell Libby Allie wasn't dead and put on some clothes, she'd been here the whole time giving Allie periodic updates. They already determined that the blood was fake, thank God. They also said they'd have Allie's clothes cleaned and returned to her as soon as they could, but she said no. She never wanted to see that particular outfit again.

She sat in a corner of the sofa, making herself as small as possible, Spook clutched in her arms in a death grip, as various officers and sheriff's office personnel wove in and out of her house like fish swimming in a slow-moving stream.

It all was surreal. She kept expecting to wake in her bed knowing Len was safely in Atlanta being his usual obnoxious self and that Sidney was securely locked up wherever they'd been keeping him. But she knew she was awake—Len was missing, Sidney was on the loose, and she was in big trouble, no matter how you looked at it, with her parents and maybe with the police. Especially, because they found Len's cell phone on her kitchen counter.

Cord had come out of the kitchen holding the phone by one end with a paper towel. "Is this yours?" he asked Allie.

"No, mine's in my purse. Maybe it's Rand's."

"He says no. I checked the ICE number. It's your mother's name and number."

"ICE?"

"In case of emergency. First place we look."

Allie felt her heart stutter. "Then… it has to be Len's."

"Any idea how it got here?" Cord's voice was neutral, but he was in uniform, and her brother was missing, a presumed victim of foul play—at least, presumed by Allie.

"Maybe the dummy brought it with her," she said sharply.

Cord raised his eyebrows and looked at her for a moment before walking away.

Her temper was frayed beyond repair. She was sick of this. She felt as if she'd been the target of Sidney's vicious pranks for years instead of a matter of days, and it pissed her off that it's exactly how he wanted her to feel. If she could find him, she wouldn't need a gun; she'd rip out his throat with her bare fingers.

She jumped a foot when the phone rang, but she made no move to answer it. A moment later, the answering machine clicked on, and she heard her mother's voice.

"Allison, when you have time, will you call me back? I need to talk to you." That was it. No ranting or raving. No demanding, badgering, or belittling. The timidity in her mother's voice was infinitely worse. Allie almost climbed out of her corner cocoon to return the call, but it felt too safe, a feeling too rare these days to give up without a fight. Tomorrow morning would be soon enough to call back.

Sheryl walked over and sat down beside Allie, reaching over to pet Spook. "You holding up?"

Allie bit her lip and nodded, blinking back tears that sprang unbidden to her eyes.

"You must have been practicing your screaming. That was a doozy. And did you hear Spook here barking? He might turn into a watchdog yet."

Allie looked down at Spook. A tear slipped down her cheek as she looked up at Sheryl. "I hope he hurries."

Finally, they were all gone. All except Rand. He locked the door behind the last officer and came over to join her on the sofa. Without a word, he pulled her into his arms.

Allie lay against his chest, squashing Spook between them. Spook didn't seem to mind.

"I don't know why it scared me so badly," she said. "I knew it was a dummy the minute I saw it. Or almost the minute I saw it. But it was so horrible, so... so..."

"Sick," Rand finished for her. "It was cruel and sick. If the bastard was here right now, I'd tear him limb from limb, and I'd enjoy it."

Allie nestled closer, causing Spook to yelp. The dog scooted out from between them and settled on Allie's lap.

God, it felt good to have Rand next to her. The last few days had been a roller coaster of anger and tension and fury and terror. Allie felt like every nerve in her body was raw. "Your father thinks I kidnapped Len," Allie said.

Rand pulled away and looked down at her. "What gives you that idea?"

"He was asking me about the cell phone."

"He asked me too. Does that mean he suspects both of us?"

Allie thought about it. "I snapped his head off."

Rand settled back against the sofa. "He's a tough guy. He can take it. He knows you're a victim in all this, Allie. It's killing him that it's his protégé who's putting you through all this hell."

Allie looked up. "Did he tell you that?"

"No, but it's how I'd feel if I were him." He pushed her head back down on his shoulder. "He's got a real soft spot for you," he said, stroking her hair. "Like father, like son."

He made no move to kiss her, so Allie reached up and pulled him down to her. His lips were soft and warm. They felt safe.

After a minute, he pulled back. "As much as it hurts me to say this, we aren't going to do this tonight. You've been through way too much. I don't want our first time together to be—" He hesitated. "Anticlimactic," he finished.

"Nice choice of words," Allie murmured. She felt his chest move as he chuckled, and she realized he was playing with her. In a nice way.

"You won't leave, though?" she said after a minute.

Rand stretched out on the sofa and eased her down beside him, pulling her head down on his shoulder. "I'm not going anywhere."

Somewhere down the street, a motorcycle cranked to life. Spook gave one little woof before settling back down on Allie's chest, but no one was awake to hear him.

■ ■ ■

ALLIE AWOKE TO THE SMELL of freshly brewing coffee. She opened one eye, then the other, and looked around in confusion. She was on her living room sofa fully dressed. Then, it all came back to her— the dummy hanging from her balcony, the police.

Sometime during the night, Rand covered her with a blanket from her bed. She pushed the blanket down and struggled to a sitting position. She felt as if she'd been in an auto accident. Then, she remembered last summer when Sidney had tried to run her off the 520 bridge. Her car careened into the guardrails like a spinning top, and Allie had the bruises to prove it. No, it didn't feel like that. Nothing she'd experienced before or since had felt like that. Still, it was amazing that nothing more than emotional stress could make her ache like this. Or maybe it was the thirty-year-old sofa.

Rand stepped out of the kitchen carrying two steaming mugs. He didn't look a whole lot better than she did. His hair was rumpled, and his face was red and wrinkled on one side from sleeping on it. Adorable.

He handed Allie a mug. "How can you look so damn good in the morning?" he asked.

Allie laughed. "Is it morning?"

"I think so," Rand said, crossing to the window. He pulled the curtain aside and looked out. "Uh, oh. You have company."

Allie scrambled to her feet. "Who is it?"

"Some woman getting out of a taxi."

Oh, God, it had to be her mother. Allie hadn't called her back. She remembered Vivian's threat the last time she called—that if Allie didn't answer, she was going to jump on the first plane. What was she going to do? She looked around. The house was a mess. The furniture was covered with fingerprint dust or whatever it was, and her laundry was on the kitchen counter. Her bedroom was a mess, and—

She took a step back. *Whoa.* She hadn't invited anyone to her house. What did she care if it was a mess?

She heard someone poking at the doorbell, which hadn't worked at any time in Allie's memory. Then the knock at the door. Allie steeled herself and pulled it open.

Twenty-one

"*ELLA FAYE*," ALLIE SAID when she recovered her voice.

"Allie, *sweetie*, how wonderful to see you again." Ella Faye leaned forward and kissed the air on either side of Allie's cheeks. "Don't you look just *wonderful*? How I've missed you. You don't come home nearly enough."

Ella Faye. Len's wife. Allie could count the times they'd seen each other on one hand. She'd missed her? Ella Faye, with her dyed blond hair and oversized bust and Scarlett O'Hara wasp waist, a woman who would drive a hundred miles for a perfect French manicure, but wouldn't cross the street to fetch a cup of water for a man dying of thirst. At least that's the opinion Allie had formed from family hints over the years. She was dressed in form-fitting spandex and enough cleavage to put Dolly Parton to shame.

"What are you doing here?" Allie managed finally. "Did I know you were coming?" In the chaos of the night before, it wouldn't surprise Allie if something like that had slipped her mind.

"Well, sugar, I thought about calling, but Mom-Mom said you'd just tell me to stay in Atlanta, so I figured I'd show up on your doorstep and surprise you."

Mom-Mom? All the time she spoke, she was humping a huge suitcase across the doorframe and into the living room. Rand stepped over to give her a hand. Ever the gentleman. Allie could kick him.

Ella Faye beamed on him. "And you are?"

"Uh—Rand, this is Ella Faye Garrison, my sister-in-law. Len's wife," Allie added, as if there would be any doubt.

"I'm pleased to meet you," Rand said, extending his hand.

"And I'm pleased to meet *you*," Ella Faye gushed, clutching Rand's hand like a lifeline. She pronounced I'm like "aaahm." Ella Faye's Southern accent had always grated on Allie's nerves, and today, her nerves weren't at their party best.

Allie reached over and disengaged Rand's hand. "Rand is my boyfriend," she said. She caught sight of Rand's grin out of the corner of her eye, and violence again crossed her mind.

"Well, isn't that nice, sugar, after that nasty divorce and everything. I'm so glad you were able to find someone else." She looked around. "It's awfully small here, isn't it? Len said the place was tiny." She laughed. "Well, he actually said it was little more than a beach shack, but I can see he was exaggerating. And—" She squealed and lunged for the sofa. "Who is this little precious thing?" she asked, dragging Spook out from his hiding place. "I just love dogs, don't you? I told Len I wanted one, but he says they're dirty and have fleas. I'll bet you don't have fleas, do you, cutie?" She held Spook up to her face and made kissy noises.

Why didn't the damn dog bite her? Instead, the traitor licked her fingers. Maybe she'd been eating fried chicken in the taxi. Allie looked again at Ella Faye's tiny waist. Maybe not.

"What are you doing here, Ella Faye?"

"Why, I'm worried about my husband, Allie. Mom-Mom was all set to come, but I told her it was my place to do it. I mean, she's already going to have to do her work and Len's. She can't be traipsing all over creation because her son is missing. That's a wife's job. And here I am," she finished brightly, as if that explained anything.

"I know you're here, but what do you plan to do? I mean, specifically."

Ella Faye looked at her blankly. "Well... be here. You know, when they find him and all."

It sounded to Allie as if she was here to identify the body. The thought made her stomach heave. "There's nothing you can do here. I don't mean to be unkind, but it would have been better if you'd stayed in Atlanta. The police are investigating Len's disappearance. They don't need any help from us civilians."

"But I thought you were an investigator," she said, looking away from Spook for a second. "I thought maybe I could ride along with you. I mean, if it's not too dangerous."

The woman was an idiot. A beautiful idiot. Allie had to grant her that, with her piled-high blond hair and flawless face, but an idiot nonetheless. "I'm not a police investigator; I'm a reporter. We don't ride around investigating." Not true, but she did not intend to get into the details.

"That's OK, then. I'll just… be here. You know."

Allie was afraid she did. "You can't stay here with me," Allie said. "Len was right. The house is tiny. Too small, even for me. And I only have one bedroom. I use the other for an office. I'm so sorry, but you won't be able to stay here. If only you'd called…"

"Well, shucks, sugar, don't worry about me," Ella Faye said, twitching around the coffee table and perching on the sofa. She still held Spook, who seemed to be enjoying the attention. Allie would talk to him later.

"I'm used to roughing it," Ella Faye said. "I can sleep right here on this couch. Look, there's even a blanket here. Looks like someone's been sleepin' here already." She batted her impossibly long lashes at Rand. "Was somebody naughty last night?"

When Rand laughed aloud, Allie shot him a dirty look. "Look, Ella Faye, I'm really sorry, but you can't stay here. For lots of reasons. There's a man trying to kill me."

"Mom-Mom said you were always gettin' into trouble like that."

Allie gritted her teeth. "And I work. I keep odd hours."

"That won't bother me none, honey. I can sleep anytime."

Allie was seething now. Ella Faye was just like her mother, only Ella Faye did it with syrup and her mother—God, *Mom-Mom*?—did it with a sledge-hammer. "Well, I can't sleep anytime. It wouldn't work. We'd be bumping into each other all the time. I'm sure you'd be more comfortable at a hotel."

Ella Faye's forehead had puckered into a pretty frown at Allie's words. Now, it cleared magically. "A hotel? I just love hotels, sugar. You got a Four Seasons around here? That's my favorite, although the Ritz is pretty nice. Especially the one in Buckhead. I just love the spa there."

Allie was nearly speechless. It was that easy? Mention a hotel and poof—goodbye Ella Faye?

"We have a Hilton. It's very nice."

"I don't know," she said, stroking Spook's head. "I've never stayed at a Hilton."

"They have a pool deck overlooking the ocean. And a restaurant and bar."

Ella Faye bounced off the sofa as if she had a spring in her butt. "That sounds real nice, Allie." She turned to Rand. "Will you drive me there?"

Rand had watched the whole exchange with a bemused smile plastered on his face.

"*I'll* drive you to the hotel," Allie said, taking Rand by the hand. "I need to talk to you in the kitchen."

Ella Faye put Spook down on the sofa and checked her reflection in the television set. "You just go say a proper goodbye to your sugar. I'll wait here."

As they stepped around the corner into the kitchen, Rand pulled her to him and kissed her until she thought she would melt from the sheer pleasure. "What was that for?" she whispered when she got her breath back.

"You heard the woman," Rand whispered. "She told you to give me a proper goodbye. Was that proper enough?"

Allie grinned up at him. "Definitely proper enough."

"Is that woman for real?"

Allie made a face. "I'm afraid so."

"You have a very interesting family. I can't wait to meet the rest."

"I can wait. Let me get rid of her. Will you be around?"

"I'm going to be in town all weekend. I need to run over to the paper," he said in a normal voice. "I'll be back in a few hours." Then, he yanked her to him and gave her a kiss so noisy it was probably heard in Merritt Island.

The whistles and catcalls that started when Ella Faye stepped out of the house died an instant death when Allie stepped out behind her and shot Frank and his crew a look. Good to know she could influence someone's behavior.

"So your boyfriend doesn't live here?" Ella Faye asked when she was settled in her seat.

"No, Rand lives in Orlando."

"What does he do?"

"What? About what?"

Ella Faye trilled a laugh. "I mean for a living."

"Oh, he's an attorney."

"Just like *Len*. Isn't that wonderful?"

Not just like Len, but Allie didn't say it aloud. Ella Faye chattered on all the way to the Hilton. Allie tuned her out. She doubted Ella Faye was here out of wifely concern. It was more as if she wanted a beach vacation, and Len's disappearance provided her with a ready excuse. Why in the world had Len married her? He could have his choice of almost any woman in Atlanta. Despite his flaws, Len was handsome and successful. Ella Faye started out as Len's secretary. When she set her cap for a promotion, she went for the gold ring—literally—and somehow managed to win the prize. Allie remembered her mother's horror when Len announced his engagement. It was the first time her brother ever stood up to her mother. Maybe he really did love the ditz.

■ ■ ■

"WHAT DO YOU MEAN the credit card's no good?"

The desk clerk glanced around. "I'm sorry, ma'am," he said, his voice barely above a whisper. "When the police were here asking about him, we ran through his charges to date. They were denied."

"Do you know anything about this?" Allie asked Ella Faye.

Ella Faye shrugged. "I know Len is always short of money."

Allie was stunned. Len, short of money? He easily cleared in the high six figures a year. Maybe seven in a good year. What was he doing with all that money?

"So, I'm sorry, ma'am," the desk clerk said. "We'll have to release his room as soon as the police remove his personal effects."

Allie winced at the words. She winced again at the thought of taking Ella Faye back home with her. After only a brief hesitation, she pulled out her wallet and extracted her American Express card. "Put it on here. Put what Len owes too. Keep the room in his name. His wife is going to be using it."

The desk clerk looked from the card back at Allie. "I'll have to run the charges through now, you understand. Just in case…"

Allie almost laughed, but this was no laughing matter. "By all means. Run each charge through as it comes up. Carte blanche. Anything she wants."

Ella Faye beamed. "Room service and everything?"

"And everything," Allie said, nodding, handing the clerk her credit card.

Ella Faye was looking around with interest. "Is that a gift shop over there?"

Allie signed the charge slip the desk clerk handed her and took her receipt without looking at it. Whatever the cost, it was a bargain.

She went with the bellhop to retrieve Ella Faye's luggage from her Jeep. The monstrous suitcase was just the tip of the proverbial iceberg. Ella Faye had another suitcase, a carry-on bag, and a garment bag. How much room did it take to pack two bikinis and a cocktail dress? Maybe the rest was makeup.

Once Ella Faye was settled—but not without complaints about no ocean view—Allie returned downstairs. She almost headed back to her car, but at the last minute, veered into the bar.

It was early—not quite ten o'clock—and the bar was empty. The bartender, a young man who looked like a student earning his way through college, was polishing the bottles behind the bar. Ella Faye would be in heaven. Allie didn't know the woman was a slut; it was just an aura Ella Faye gave off like bad cologne. She pitied her brother, and not for the first time.

The bartender looked startled when he saw Allie. "I'm sorry, ma'am. We're not open. Not until eleven."

Allie smiled and sat down on a stool. "I'm not here for a drink. I wondered if I could ask you a few questions. About a customer."

An equal blend of wariness and confusion distorted the bartender's boyish face. "I don't know. I'll have to ask the manager. I mean, no one ever..." His voice trailed off as he looked at the bar entrance.

Allie didn't want to be blown off by a child. "Why don't I ask the questions, and if you need to call the manager, you can? What do you think?" She gave the boy what she hoped was a reassuring smile.

He took two steps toward her. Was he afraid she'd bite him? "OK. I think."

Allie maintained her smile. If she had to keep this up for too long, her face was going to hurt. "My brother was staying here. He's tall with dark hair. Very handsome." Now, what could she say? He was kidnapped? "He's not answering his cell phone, and Mom and I are worried about him. I wondered if you remembered someone like that."

The boy walked closer. "We get lots of people in here who look like that."

Allie searched her mind. "He would have been wearing a suit."

The child laughed. "Almost all our customers are in suits. They're businessmen. Usually at lunch or something. Do you have a picture of him?"

Allie cursed herself for not thinking of it. "I don't, but I have some at home. Could I bring one in? Maybe you'd recognize him."

"Sure," the kid said. "I work Saturday through Wednesday. Ten to five."

Allie spent a few more minutes cementing their

relationship—Jeff was majoring in Business and Environmental Studies at Florida Tech. He was twenty, and he had two brothers and a sister. Jeff desperately needed someone to talk to.

Allie had lied. She didn't have a picture of Len. Why would she? Then, a thought struck her. She took the elevator up to the third floor and knocked.

"That was really fast," Ella Faye said as she swung the door open. She was dressed in a robe that Allie was certain covered a bikini. "Oh, you aren't room service."

Room service already? "No, I need a picture of Len. Do you have one?"

"Of Len?"

Why had she bothered? "Never mind. I'll call Mother."

Twenty-two

ALLIE DREADED IT, but she had to do it.
When she arrived home, the locksmith's van was in her driveway. She'd forgotten she asked them to be there by ten. She parked on the street and hurried across the yard. The man—fiftyish and forty pounds overweight—lumbered out of his van in no particular rush. Was she paying him by the hour?

"I'm so sorry I'm late. I had an unexpected —situation."

"No sweat, lady. I was late myself. Damn cruise traffic."

Allie couldn't agree more. "I want you to change all the locks. Front and back."

"Only the two?"

He made it sound so paltry. "And install another deadbolt in each."

"You expecting trouble, lady? If you are, I have a brother in the security system business."

Allie smiled. She just bet he did. "No, I think the new locks will be adequate."

She led the way inside and left him to it. After several deep breaths, she dialed her mother's number.

Vivian answered on the first ring. "I assume

Ella Faye arrived."

"With her twenty suitcases."

Vivian barked what might have been a laugh. "I called last night to warn you, but you never called back."

"I had... company last night." There was no way she was going to tell her mother about being hung in effigy. "I was going to call this morning."

"I'm sorry she came, but she insisted. I'm handling both my client load and Len's. If things... change... I'll be down there. But for now... I'm sorry."

"Don't be sorry," Allie said. "I put her at the Hilton in Len's room." She paused, but she had to ask. "Did you know his credit card was no good?"

There was a long silence on the line. "I know Len was having some financial difficulties, which is why—"

Allie cut her off before she could get started. "But why? He makes good money. He and Ella Faye don't have the expense of children. What's he spending his money on?"

A longer silence. Then, a sigh. "I asked him the same thing. I know he's been stretched lately, so I had to ask. It appears that Ella Faye is very high maintenance. Her spa treatments and breast enhancements—"

"She enhanced *that*?"

Vivian ignored the interruption. "Apparently, she's had some minor plastic surgery done lately. Len said it cost thirty-five thousand—"

Allie choked. "That's not minor. That's a whole body makeover."

Her mother made a strangled sound. Was that a

laugh? "I'm sorry," Vivian said, "but those were my words exactly. I couldn't understand how someone who looks like Ella Faye could require such extensive... enhancements. You brother had no answer."

"But what does she expect to do here? I mean, why did she come?"

A long sigh. "She was furious when Len wouldn't take her with him. I think she saw it as some kind of impromptu vacation. When Len vanished..." A long pause. "...I imagine she thought she might help."

"No, she didn't."

Another sigh. "No, she didn't. She seized an opportunity."

"Do you know she calls you Mom-Mom?"

This time it was definitely a laugh. "I know. I gag every time I hear it. I've asked her to call me Vivian or Mother or something normal, but she won't."

"She's a flake," Allie blurted out without thinking.

"An expensive flake who is going to drive your brother to ruin. I warned him before he married her."

"Why does he put up with it?"

"What can he do? If he cuts off the funds, Ella Faye will leave him. She's threatened enough times."

"Would that be so bad?"

"According to you or me? No. It would be a gift from the gods. But it would kill Len."

"You don't mean that."

"He loves her, Allie. God knows why. She doesn't deserve it. She's a cheap moneygrubber and a social climber, not to mention a bit loose with her... favors. Or at least, I suspect she is, but Len can't see beyond the surface. I don't know why not. Otherwise, he's a very intelligent and perceptive man. He's—" Her mother broke off, and Allie thought she heard a muffled sob.

"I'll find him, Mom. I swear I'll find him. He'll be OK. But I need pictures of him. All the pictures you can find. You can fax them to me." She rattled off her fax number. "Send them as soon as you can."

"Allie, I can't thank..." Again, her voice faltered.

"You don't have to thank me. Just send the pictures."

When they'd disconnected, Allie stared at the phone. Had she just called her mother Mom, and had her mother called her Allie? Maybe adversity actually did bring families together. But the bigger question—had she just made a promise she couldn't keep? Then, she squared her shoulders. No, somehow, she'd keep it.

■ ■ ■

"How long are you going to keep me here?"

Sidney looked up from his calculations. He was in the living room of the trailer sitting at the makeshift dining table, a two by four slab of stained Formica. When that scumbag loser had promised him accommodations, he'd hoped for something a little nicer, but beggars couldn't be choosers, and at least, he knew Arnie wouldn't turn him in. He couldn't afford to—not with what Sidney had on him. A few times, Sidney had busted him for dealing. Sidney had kept quiet about it in exchange for information, but he knew all about Arnie's supplier—who it was and where the dealer kept the dope. Arnie was a small cog in a big operation. If Sidney told the cops about him, his bosses would get rid of him on the spot.

With a sigh, he reached over and picked up the cannibal mask. He pulled it over his head and looked around for the microphone, although why he was bothering, he didn't know. If he took out Allie and Levine, they'd know he did it. What did it matter if this asshole saw his face? His visitor was going to perish in the Everglades, anyway. Still, it was how he'd started, and it was how he was going to finish.

"Did you say something?" Sidney asked, stepping into the bedroom. God, the place stank of unwashed linen and sweaty body. If he were going to keep this up much longer, he'd have to shove him in the shower, restrained, and in his clothes.

"I asked how long you were going to keep me here," Len repeated, his voice slurring from the drugs.

His prisoner looked bad, trussed up there in bed with his hands cuffed and pulled over his head. Sidney had installed a utility hook on the wall, and the cuffs were tied to it. The hair that had been perfect when Sidney snatched him was matted now. Not with blood. Sidney had cleaned the wound. He didn't want the guy to die of an infection. But the shirt was streaked with dried blood, and the oh-so-perfect suit was now a mass of wrinkles.

"Not much longer," Sidney said into the mike. "Pretty soon, you and me are going on a little trip." Which meant he'd have to ditch the bike and get a car. He couldn't drive all the way to the Everglades with a prisoner on the back.

"Where?"

"Don't ask so many questions," Sidney said. "It's bad for your health."

As he started out the door, Len said, "Why are you doing this? Did you contact my mother? Is she going to pay the ransom?" When Sidney ignored him, he said, "I have to use the bathroom."

Christ. He knew he had to let him go. If he didn't, the guy would pee the bed—or worse. But that meant he had to go through all the unhooking his pants and pulling them down. It made Sidney feel like a pervert every time.

"I have to go bad."

Sidney reached and untied first his feet. Then, he released his hands from the hook. Len groaned as he pulled his arms down. Sidney knew it had to hurt, but it wouldn't do any permanent damage if he didn't struggle.

Sidney reached into the top of the closet and pulled down the gun. He motioned Len toward the postage-stamp-sized bathroom. "Do your business, and be quick about it, or you'll be sorry."

Once in the bathroom, Len turned so Sidney could undo his pants. This was the tricky part. Keeping the gun pointed on his prisoner, his eyes never leaving Len's, Sidney reached out with his free hand to undo the trousers. That was when the jerk spun his body into Sidney, knocking his gun hand away. Sidney lost his balance, but managed not to fire the pistol. He didn't want to bring the neighbors.

By the time he regained his feet, Len was half-way to the trailer door. Sidney tackled him from behind, grabbing his hair and smashing his forehead against the trailer floor. Then, he pulled himself upright and kicked the cowering man in the kidneys, hard enough to do some damage, but not too much. He didn't want to be lugging around dead weight when the time came.

"Get up," he snarled.

"I can't."

"Get up, or I'll blow you away right now." He jammed the gun into Len's temple.

With a lot of groaning and moaning, Len got to his knees. Then, his feet. Sidney backed to a safe distance. He wasn't giving the guy another chance. He looked at the front of Len's trousers where a wet stain had spread across the front. "I guess you don't have to go anymore."

"I know your voice."

Shit. He'd dropped the mike.

"You're that police officer from the hotel," Len said, his voice incredulous. "Why are you doing this to me?"

Sidney hesitated. Then, he pulled off the mask. The damn thing was hotter than hell, anyway. "I said you asked too many questions. *Why* is none of your business. And if you want to stay alive, you'll shut the hell up. Back in the bedroom." He motioned with the gun.

At first, he thought the guy was going to challenge him. Sidney wasn't prepared to shoot. He'd have to bring him down another way. Hell, even if Sidney was a crip, this guy was no match for him. He'd logged hundreds of hours in hand to hand.

He knew every pressure point in the human body. Sidney almost welcomed the attack.

Then, the guy started moving toward the bedroom, holding his side. Sidney never took his eyes off him. *Catch me once, shame on you*, he thought.

Once he had him tucked back in bed—which meant tied and shackled—he moved back to the living room. He took a pill from his dwindling stash and returned to the bedroom. "Take this," he said, thrusting it toward Len's mouth.

"I need some water."

Sidney looked down at his pants front and laughed. "You're wearing it. Screw the water. Chew it."

Len opened his mouth, and Sidney shoved the pill inside. He watched as Len chewed it, making a face, and then swallowed.

"Open your mouth," Sidney said.

Len's eyes widened.

"Open it, goddamn it."

Sidney knew all about cheeking meds. He was a master at it. The pill was stuck to the inside of Len's cheek. Sidney whacked him on the knee with his pistol, earning him a satisfying groan.

"I said swallow it."

This time, Sidney was sure he took it. Len almost gagged as it went down. Sidney leaned against the wall and waited until Len's eyelids began to droop before shoving the sock gag back in his mouth. He tied a handkerchief around Len's head to hold the gag in place.

He had some thinking to do, and junior here needed to be quiet.

■ ■ ■

HER MOTHER CALLED BACK. Vivian needed to go home to get the pictures. She said she'd fax them as soon as she could.

Allie had a little time to kill. She walked Spook on the beach. When she let herself out the door, she could see the dummy hanging from her deck rail, even though it was long gone. She still didn't know why it had freaked her out so badly. It was cloth and stuffing and fake blood, not a real person. She knew that, but it didn't help. She read in history class about people being hung in effigy, and she had always wondered what the big deal was. Now, she knew.

Spook enjoyed the walk more than Allie did. She expected Sidney to jump out from behind every bush, to shoot at her from every rooftop, but she'd be damned if she'd cower inside until he was caught. She wouldn't give him that power.

She checked the fax machine when they got back. Nothing. She knew it would take her mother more than an hour to drive home, retrieve the pictures, and then drive back to her office. She still had at least forty-five minutes to wait.

She folded the blanket on the couch and put it away. She shoved her laundry into the mini-washer in the hall closet and started it. Then, there was nothing to do except clean, and she wasn't dressed for it.

Knowing it might be unwise, which seemed reason enough to do things these days, she grabbed a Diet Coke from the refrigerator and let herself out the back door. She gave the fake bloodstain on her patio a wide berth and climbed the wrought-iron staircase to her rooftop deck.

She knew Sidney had been here. There was no sign, but there was also no other way to hang the dummy from the rail unless he brought a tall ladder, which she doubted. His mere presence here sullied her childhood play area in some way. Had he sat on her lounge chair?

"Allie."

She almost fainted until she realized it was Frank's voice from the construction site. She turned. Frank was leaning out an opening that would someday be someone's balcony door. He wasn't more than ten feet from her.

Allie and Frank had gotten off to a rocky start when Frank flattened her Jeep tires in retaliation for Allie calling the police on him when he threatened to run her over with a backhoe. Somehow, they'd gotten past that and become friends of a sort, despite the fact that Frank and his crew were methodically destroying her private paradise. She couldn't hold it against them. They were doing a job, not attacking her personally. Someone else was doing that.

"Hi, Frank. How's it going?"

"So-so," Frank said. "Gotten any more presents lately?"

Allie shuddered. "Yes, last night."

"Yeah? What'd the asshole leave last night?"

She wanted to tell him, but she didn't want to yell it across ten feet of open space. "You got time for a cup of coffee?"

Frank grinned. "I always have time for coffee," he said. "Give me five minutes."

Frank tapped on her back door as the coffeepot gurgled its last. Allie poured them each a cup, and they took them up on the deck. So he could watch the boys, Frank said, but Allie thought maybe he just enjoyed the view. Like she used to.

She told Frank about the dummy.

"Jeez, this guy really has it in for you. You know who's doing it?"

Allie nodded. "You remember last August when that cop tried to run me off the bridge?"

"That was a cop? I thought the whole Sheriff's Department was your friends."

"A lot of them are. Not this guy. He was arrested for trying to kill a bunch of other people and me, but he escaped. Now, he's trying to make me pay."

"For what? You didn't do anything."

"He thinks I did. He's convinced I caused everything, from losing his job to his injuries——."

Frank broke in. "What injuries?"

"He was injured when he was captured. A lot of bones were broken. I've heard there's permanent damage to one leg and foot."

Frank rubbed his jaw. "I saw someone... but that was a chick. Woman," he corrected. "She came by. She was limping. I remember because she was dead-dog ugly."

Allie felt a stirring of excitement. "What did she look like?"

He shrugged. "Average height. About your height. Maybe a little taller. Skinny. She had this bright red hair. Had to be dyed. The good Lord never gave nobody that color hair for real. Anyway, she was kind of shifty, looking around. I didn't think much of it at the time."

"Have you seen anyone else around?"

"Just all those couriers. One was a skinny little

dude, and one was a fat guy."

"Did you notice what they were driving?"

Frank thought for a minute. "Nah, but they were all new. I remember thinking that this courier stuff must pay pretty well." He rubbed his jaw. "And there was that other man."

"What other man?"

"Tall. Good-looking guy wearing a suit and carrying a briefcase. I saw him prop something against your front door. Was that him?"

Allie felt like someone had pricked her balloon. "No, that had to be my brother."

"I didn't know you had family around."

"I don't. He lives in Atlanta, and I think Sidney might have kidnapped him."

"Sidney?"

"The cop who tried to kill me."

"Jeez, girl, that's bad. Do the police have any leads?"

Allie rubbed her forehead. "Not that they're sharing with me. My mother is frantic. His wife flew down last night."

"She that lady I saw you with this morning?"

"Yes, I put her up at the Hilton. I'm going back over there in a little while to ask some questions as soon as my mother faxes me some pictures of Len."

"Boy, I wish you luck. That's really tough."

Allie heard a whistle. Bobby was leaning out the opening motioning to Frank. "I need you over here, Dad."

Frank put his cup on the little glass table between the lounge chairs and stood. "Gotta run, but I'll tell you what. Me and the guys will keep an eye out for anything going on. I mean, we're around here all day. Maybe we'll see something."

"God, I hope so. I can use all the help I can get."

Frank hesitated, and then he reached over and gave her shoulders an awkward hug. "You hang in there, little lady. You don't deserve all this bad stuff that's happening to you. You let us know if we can do anything to help."

The faxes were waiting for her when she returned downstairs. Ten pictures, all in color. Her mother had come through. Now, she was going to get some answers.

Twenty-three

FIRST, SHE CALLED CORD to tell him about the redheaded courier with the limp. It wasn't much, but it was something. Cord promised to circulate the information. Then, he cautioned Allie to stay out of the police investigation. As she promised, she was stuffing the faxes into an envelope.

Minutes later, she was out of the house.

"Is he still all right?" she asked her aunt.

"He is. For now."

"Is he scared?"

"He's terrified."

"Can you tell him I'm coming?"

"I wish I could."

Goddamn Sidney Finch. Allie hated him like she'd never hated another human being, even the serial killer who tried to add her to his list of victims. Going after her was one thing—she was getting used to that—but involving an innocent man was too much. Len wasn't equipped to handle this kind of life. His world had always been protected. The closest he ever came to violence was probably handling a divorce client's irate husband. *Terrified.* The word twisted her insides. She'd had her differences with Len, plenty of them, but he didn't deserve this. And certainly not because someone was doing it to punish his sister.

Allie's spirits fell when she saw a different bartender was behind the bar, but he told her Jeff was on his lunch break. Allie ordered a Coke and sat at the bar, prepared to wait as long as necessary. She was halfway through the Coke when Jeff appeared.

His face lit up when he saw her. "Hi again."

"Hi, yourself," Allie said, returning his smile. "How was your lunch?"

Jeff's grin widened. "It's the best part of this job. I get all my meals free, and the food here is really good."

Allie opened the envelope and pulled out the pictures. She saw Jeff's face go wary. "You can check with your manager if you want," she said, hoping he wouldn't take her up on it. Hotels were notoriously protective of their guests' privacy.

"I think it'll be OK." He picked up the first picture and frowned. "I remember this man," he said. "He stopped by here a few times. He wasn't much of a drinker."

That didn't surprise Allie. She knew Len only drank socially.

"He had to be carried out of here the last time."

That stopped her. "What do you mean?"

Jeff looked uncomfortable.

"It's OK. I'm his sister. I won't tell anyone."

"Well, he and this cop were talking about some woman, and the drinks really got to him. He was about to fall off his stool. His friend said he'd get him upstairs to sleep it off."

Allie's heart was stuttering in her chest. "The

cop was his friend?" When Jeff nodded, she asked, "Do you remember what he looked like?"

"Well, he was no athlete," Jeff said. "He was kind of puny. He had dark hair and kind of sharp features, if you know what I mean. And he looked like a wimp. I couldn't figure how he'd get the guy up to his room without help, but he managed. I guess he was stronger than he looked."

"Yes, he is," Allie said, her voice shaking. It had to be Sidney, but where would he have gotten a uniform? Hadn't they confiscated those when he was arrested? Did he still have friends at the sheriff's office? If he did, she was in more danger than she'd realized.

She thanked Jeff and over-tipped him outrageously before slipping off her stool and heading for her car. Her fingers trembled as she dialed the sheriff's office. Cord was out, so Allie called Sheryl.

"Sidney's got him," she said without preamble when Sheryl answered. "I talked to the bartender at the Hilton. I showed him a picture of Len. He recognized him."

She filled Sheryl in on the rest. "I don't know where Sidney got a uniform, but I know it was him. Sidney had to drug him. I know Len. He doesn't drink. He's too much of a control freak. Well, a beer or two, but he doesn't get drunk. I tried to call Cord, but he's out. I'll leave some pictures of Len in your mailbox. Maybe someone else will recognize him."

"*Jesus*," was all Sheryl said. Then, "I'll get the word out. What are you going to do next?"

Good question. What was she going to do next?

■ ■ ■

TERESA STARED AT THE COMPUTER screen. He'd made another withdrawal. If he kept this up, he'd empty her checking account, and Wally would notice and call Cord Arbutten. She had no doubt of that. She had to do something, and fast.

She checked their savings balance. More than twenty-thousand dollars. Most of that was in a money market, but she could transfer some in to checking. Wally would never notice. She paid the bills. She always had.

Two clicks and her checking account was ten thousand dollars richer. She breathed a sigh of relief.

"What are you doing?"

Teresa spun around in her chair. Wally loomed in the doorway, his face thunderous.

"I'm checking my e-mail," she said, trying to block the computer screen.

"On the bank website?"

Teresa looked back at the screen. The bank logo was obvious with its red, white, and blue. "I paid some bills. Then, I was going to check my e-mail."

Wally came over and edged her out of the way. He studied the screen for a minute. With a series of two clicks, the money was back in savings. When he turned around, the look on his face frightened Teresa.

"You're coming with me," he said, pulling her out of the chair.

"Where?"

"And I'm not letting you out of my sight until we've stopped this."

"Where are you taking me? Wally, you're hurting my arm. Where are we going?"

He didn't speak again until they were parked outside the bank. He turned in his seat and looked at her. She recoiled at his expression.

"We're going to change our password, and if you say one word in there, I'm going to turn you over to the sheriff for aiding and abetting a criminal. Do you hear me?"

Their next stop was the sheriff's office. Wally hadn't spoken once all the way to Titusville, and Teresa was afraid to anger him. She'd never seen him like this. Maybe the injury to his head had done something to his brain.

They only had a short wait before they were ushered into Cord's office.

"She's been furnishing Sidney money," Wally said.

"I thought you weren't going to tell..." Her voice trailed off at the look on his face.

"He came by the house night before last. He did this to me." He showed Cord his head. "He stole her purse. He has all her credit cards and our bankcard. I changed the password on the bankcard," Wally said as Cord began to speak, "but that leaves the credit cards. Teresa is going to give you all the information on them." He glared at her. "If she doesn't, I'm leaving her here with you. You can lock her up for aiding a felon or impeding an investigation or whatever."

"You don't mean that!"

His gaze never left her face. "She's enabled Sidney long enough. She's turned him into what he is today, a common criminal. We've both turned him into what he is, but it has to stop. It's going to stop. Right now."

Teresa felt Cord's eyes boring into her. "We know Sidney is currently involved in a kidnapping. He's been positively identified. His victim is a prominent attorney from Atlanta. Allie Grainger's brother. If he harms the man, he'll get the death penalty."

Teresa heard Wally draw in a sharp breath. She couldn't look at either of them. God, what had they driven him to now? "I don't have the information here," she said. "It's all at home."

"I'll follow you there," Cord said, standing.

■ ■ ■

ALLIE FOUND ELLA FAYE on the pool deck wearing the flimsiest bikini Allie had ever seen, her already tanned body slathered in suntan oil.

"Working on your tan?" Allie asked.

Ella Faye jumped. She shaded her eyes, and her mouth formed a little pout. "Well, you said I couldn't ride with you. What else am I supposed to do?"

Allie sat down on the next lounge chair. The air was cool, but the sun warmed the skin. Winter in Florida. "Ella Faye, what do you know about Len's money problems?"

Ella Faye swung her feet to the deck and sat up, startling several men at the outdoor bar who had been watching her. Allie looked, too, but she couldn't see any surgical scars. No surprise. For the kind of money her surgeons made, they'd better not leave scars.

Ella Faye pulled her beach coverup around her. "I don't know what you mean."

"I mean," Allie said with exaggerated patience, "how long has he been broke?"

"I don't know. A while."

"How long a while?"

"A few months. I don't know. Maybe a year."

"And all this time, this *year*, you've done what to help him?"

"I don't know what you mean."

"Did you get a job? Did you cut down on your spending?"

The pout deepened. "That's none of your business. And why are you being so mean? It's not like he was trying to get money from you or anything. He just wanted you to sell that ugly little house."

Allie stared at her for a long time before she spoke. "You don't have a clue what's going on around you, do you, Ella Faye? The world could come crashing down, and as long as you could still get your tan and your manicures and your breast enhancements, you wouldn't give a damn, would you?" She stood. "You know, I used to think you and Len deserved one another, but I was wrong. No matter what Len's been in the past, he deserves someone a lot better than you."

Ella Faye jumped to her feet, her suntan oil falling unnoticed at her feet. "Why are you saying these mean things to me? You're just—just *awful*. No wonder Len doesn't like you." Allie turned her back on her.

She had only returned to the hotel because she was at loose ends. She had no idea what to do with the information she'd uncovered. She knew Ella Faye had no more information to offer. The woman had nothing of any kind to offer anyone.

She drove aimlessly for a while. If she was making herself a target for Sidney, so be it. It wouldn't be the first time. She stopped by Cord's house. He was at work, but Rand's grandmother Frenchie was there entertaining some of her retirement home cronies. Cord had rescued Frenchie from that terrible place his wife stuck her in after her stroke and had finally convinced her to move in with him. He was that kind of man.

It took her a while to extricate herself from the "girls," who were getting sloshed on Cord's liquor, but she finally managed. What did it matter if they got drunk? They weren't going anywhere. They were all about ninety and hadn't had driver's licenses in years.

Her wandering took her to the newspaper office. Rand's car wasn't in the parking lot. Then, she remembered. He was probably at her house waiting for her. She'd call him in a few minutes.

The newsroom was humming, which meant there wasn't much happening on the streets. She got a tiny sheepish smile from Holly Miller when she walked in, and several people called a hello. That surprised her. Maybe Holly had done what Allie asked her to do.

She stopped at Holly's desk. "Is everyone speaking to me again?"

Holly blushed the color of her lipstick. "It was Alf. He talked to us."

"Alf Reed?" Alf had been Allie's nemesis here at the newspaper since the day she started. He was a veteran reporter who had scoffed at Allie's inexperience and belittled her for her naivety. Now, he was suddenly her champion?

She felt a presence at her elbow and turned. Alf stood there, short and unkempt as always, in a wrinkled shirt, with thin gray hair he swept across his head in a futile attempt to cover his male-pattern baldness. He looked good to Allie right then.

"Hey, girl," he said. "Good to see you back. I set these children straight about your brother. I was there that day and saw what he did. I can see through bullshit like that. The guy was playing us for all we had. Kids fell for it. I didn't."

Modesty had never been Alf's long suit. "Thanks, Alf. I appreciate it."

"Don't mention it. I don't suppose he'll be around here giving you any more trouble."

Allie felt tears spring to her eyes, and she was humiliated. Alf took her arm and steered her out of the newsroom and into the old owner's office. "What's up, kid?"

Allie sniffed and wiped her eyes. "He's been kidnapped. Sidney Finch kidnapped him." Then, she caught herself. "Don't you dare put that in the paper without running it by Cord Arbutten."

Alf held up his hands. "Hey, wait. I wouldn't do that to you." Then, he leaned forward. "Are you sure?"

"Yes, I'm sure. And I mean it. If you print a word without authorization, I'll— I'll—"

"Hey, Allie. Give me some credit here. I might do that to someone else, but not to you." He scratched his head and then caught himself, smoothing his hair back down. "Do you have any more details?"

"Not yet, but I'll keep you posted." The pigs with fluffy pink wings again came to mind.

She hoped Alf kept his promise. If he so much as printed an "unsubstantiated rumor," she'd get Myrna to throw him off the newspaper.

Speaking of Myrna. "Where's Myrna?"

"She had a doctor appointment. I'm holding down the fort while she's gone. And your boyfriend was here earlier. You just missed him."

How did Alf know about Rand? The answer was obvious. He was a seasoned reporter. He'd notice the slightest innuendo, plus Allie and Rand hadn't been particularly subtle about their relationship. Such as it was.

"I'd better give him a call." She pulled out her cell. When Alf made no move to leave, Allie looked at him and smiled. "Out," she said, pointing at the door.

"You sounded just like Myrna when you said that."

Allie's smile widened. "I've heard Myrna say that to you, and I didn't sound a bit like her." Her smile died when Alf left.

Rand was her number one speed-dial number. She punched the number and waited. He answered on the second ring. "Where are you?"

"I'm at the paper. Where are you?"

"At your house waiting for you. Maybe it's me, but we seem to be at cross purposes here."

"Sidney has my brother."

"Are you sure? I know you thought—"

"I got pictures of Len from mother. The bartender at the Hilton recognized Len. He said Len got drunk and left in the company of a sheriff's deputy. Len doesn't drink to excess. Sidney must have drugged him. The bartender described Sidney, right down to his ugly ferret face."

Rand whistled. "You've been a busy girl. What are you going to do next? And how can I help? Do you want me to come back there?"

Allie thought about it. What good would it do to be here? Maybe Sidney was following her. Maybe she could lure him out of hiding. She'd make a perfect target crossing the 520 bridge, one he'd remember well, but this time, it would be different. This time, she'd ram his car with everything her Jeep could deliver, and he'd be the one to go off the bridge.

"I'm heading home. Can you wait for me?"

"For as long as it takes, honey. I'll be here."

Twenty-four

I t WAS GOING TO TAKE HER LONGER than she'd planned at the rate she was going, but if Sidney was behind her, she didn't want to lose him. She laughed. With everything that had happened to her in the last year, this was the first time she'd intentionally set out to make herself a target. Wouldn't you know it wouldn't work?

She kept her eyes alternately on her rearview and side mirrors. No one was darting in and out of traffic. No dark sedans with tinted windows. No suspicious glints of light on jewelry or guns. The only vehicle that was consistent was a motorcycle whose driver was much more intent on the view than on her. Where the hell was Sidney?

When she turned into her neighborhood, the motorcycle kept going. Darn. He was her last chance.

Rand was sitting in his car with the door open when she drove up. When he stepped out, she felt a little thrill go through her. He was in his weekend clothes, which in winter consisted of jeans that fit perfectly and a turtleneck, this one navy. The man was a vision.

Frank intercepted them before they were half-way across the yard. Allie had never given Frank a second look, but now, she realized how he must seem to Rand, tall and stocky, with the weathered face and hardened muscles of a long-time construction worker. He was an impressive sight striding across her yard.

"This guy OK?" Frank asked, motioning toward Rand.

Allie put her arm around Rand's waist. "This guy is very OK. Rand Arbutten, this is Frank Gray. He's supervising the building next door. Frank, this is Rand Arbutten, the sheriff's son."

"And her boyfriend," Rand added, sticking out his hand and ignoring the look Allie gave him.

Frank took it automatically. "Nice to meet 'cha. Me and the boys kinda keep an eye on Allie."

"And I'm eternally grateful," Allie said, looking from man to man.

Frank's scowl remained in place. "Only other guy who's been by more than once was a skinny little guy on a motorcycle."

Allie blinked. "A motorcycle? When was that?"

"Early this morning. Then again about ten. Why? You know him?"

It had to be a coincidence, didn't it? "I don't think so. Will you let me know if you see him again?"

"Sure thing, Allie. You just keep safe."

"I'm trying to, Frank. Believe me."

With one final nod at Rand, Frank strode back to the construction site.

Spook held his ground when they walked inside. Was he really this much gutsier, or was he getting used to Rand? Whatever. It pleased her that he didn't bark at Rand because she hoped they'd be spending a whole lot more time together.

"Want to go up on the deck?" Rand asked.

"And have Frank and the boys watch every move we make? I don't think so. I feel like I'm living in a fishbowl now, and it's only going to get worse."

Rand nodded, but said nothing. Allie knew he wasn't the type to try to influence her one way or the other. It was one quality she loved about him. One among many.

She sat on the sofa and patted the cushion beside her, and then laughed when Spook jumped up.

"Want to go for a walk on the beach?" Rand asked.

"Are you asking me or Spook?"

"I thought the two of you were a package deal."

"You got that right, bud."

■ ■ ■

THEY WALKED SLOWLY, taking in all the day had to offer, the sun warm on their skin, the soft breeze off the water blowing their hair. Allie watched the pelicans circling overhead in precise formation. The sand was hot under their feet, the water icy when they strayed too close. Allie felt the tension melt off her like a wax coating. It was so much like their first walk on the beach. What? Not quite a week ago? Had all this happened in less than a week? It boggled the mind, but she refused to give it the attention it deserved. Not now, not when everything was so perfect.

A sharp crack pulled her attention to the dunes. When she turned to say something to Rand, he was lying on the beach at her feet. Allie saw the spatter of blood on the pristine white sand and almost blacked out. It was Joe all over again. The gunshot. Joe stretched out on the asphalt with blood pooling around his head. All this passed through her head in the time it took her to kneel beside Rand.

He was staring up at her looking as shocked as she felt. "I think someone just shot me."

"Oh, my *God!*" Allie started tearing frantically at his clothes.

"Allie. *Allie!*" He reached up and pulled her down beside him. "It just grazed my arm. I'm OK. Hurts like a bitch, but I'm fine. But whoever shot me is still out there. *Stay down.*"

He had pulled Spook into his belly. Now, he handed him to Allie while he fumbled in his pocket for his cell phone. Allie heard him tell the 9-1-1 operator where they were. "Gunshots are being fired, and we're on the beach without cover."

Two more shots were fired. One grazed Allie's toe, and she screamed. Almost simultaneously, she heard sirens in the distance. A motorcycle roared to life and squealed away.

Allie jumped to her feet and went down on one knee. "Hurts," she told Rand, who was still sprawled out on the sand.

"Tell me about it." He sat up, and Allie saw blood dripping down his arm.

"I thought you said it only grazed you."

"Grazed. Gouged. It's pretty much the same," he said with a loopy grin.

Then, the police were there, and the paramedics. They determined that both Allie and Rand would live and, when they both declined a trip to the hospital, bandaged them on the scene, Allie with a lot of gauze and Rand with a couple of butterfly sutures and more gauze. Sheryl was about the third officer to arrive. While Rand told the police the sequence of events, Allie pulled Sheryl aside. "It was Sidney. I heard the motorcycle."

"What motorcycle?"

Allie filled her in on what Frank had told her. "I saw him following me across the causeway. I didn't give it another thought because he kept going when I turned off into the neighborhood. Why not? He knew where I was headed."

"You're sure?"

How to convince her? "Do you remember when we were kids, how we always knew when Sidney was sneaking around us? We got that creepy feeling. Well, had it earlier when Frank told me about the motorcycle, and I've got it now."

Sheryl gave a brief nod and headed toward the cluster of officers. She was back in a minute. "Did Frank know what kind of motorcycle?"

Allie thought. "I don't know if Frank does, but I'll bet his son Bobby does. He notices everything."

■ ■ ■

BOBBY SQUINTED. "It looked like a 2010 Softail. Harley." He squinted harder. "Black or dark blue. Black, I think, with red flames. He was wearing a full-face helmet, so I couldn't make out his face or hair. He wasn't big, though. He looked like a kid sitting on that hog."

"Isn't he amazing?" Allie asked.

Sheryl ignored her, her attention on Bobby. "Did you get any of the plate?"

Bobby closed his eyes. "I remember the first letter was L. There was a Z, and either a 3 or an 8. I was up on the fifth level, so it was hard to tell."

Sheryl grinned. "Yeah." She cuffed Bobby on the shoulder. "He's pretty amazing. Thanks, Bobby. You've been a great help." She crossed to the curb and climbed in her cruiser. A minute later, she had the radio at her mouth.

"You're going to be an amazing—officer." Allie knew Sheryl didn't mind being called a cop, and Joe had considered it a title of honor, but a pre-rookie might take offense.

Frank's grin was almost wider than his face. "Didn't I tell you, Son? You're a natural."

Rand's good arm had been around Allie and hers around him since they left the beach, even in the squad car that brought them home, and they remained locked in that stance as they walked back into her house. They could pretend they were supporting each other, but Allie knew the truth. Both knew how close they'd come to losing the other.

He left her on the couch and vanished into the kitchen. She heard the refrigerator open and close, the squeak of a cork being pulled from a bottle, the tinkle of glasses, and she smiled. Her last bottle of wine.

"Now, we won't have any wine when we finally have our big date," she said as he rounded the kitchen door.

"When we have our big date," he said, filling each glass halfway, "we won't need any wine."

Allie felt her nerve endings tingle. It was a promise she intended to hold him to. If—no, *when* they
had their big date.

They settled back against the sofa like an old
married couple sipping their wine. Four bare feet
on the coffee table, one with a huge gauze bandage.

"You're pretty cool under fire," she said, taking
a sip from her glass.

"I went to a military school. We shot at each
other at recess."

"Not with real bullets."

"No, not with real bullets." After a minute, he
added, "But war games were a real part of our
curriculum. Strategy, tactics, offensive and defen-
sive moves. They were training most of us for
careers in the military. We were taught to be cool
under that kind of pressure."

"How do you teach something like that?"

"I don't know exactly how they did it. We spent
a lot of time at war games. If you went to pieces,
you hurt the team, and the team lost the game.
I guess a lot of it was peer pressure, although
I didn't think about it at the time." He grinned.
"I just wanted my team to win."

"Did you like it?"

He considered. "It was a real boy thing, you
know? Very macho. It was pretty cool. I wouldn't
want to do it for a living. From what I understand,
the real thing's a whole lot uglier than skirmishes
on a make-believe battlefield."

They sat in silence for a few minutes.

"I like you, Rand."

He looked at her. "What brought that on?"

"I don't know exactly, but I like that you're cool

under fire. I like that you're not a steamroller or a pushover. I like that you don't try to protect me—"

"Like you'd let me."

Allie smiled. "I like pretty much everything about you."

"You sound surprised."

"I am, a little. I usually find something to dislike about every man I've met."

Rand chuckled. "Give it time. We're in the honeymoon period."

Allie raised her eyebrows.

"So to speak."

She smiled. "So to speak."

"Once you get to know me, I'm sure you'll find plenty of things to dislike."

Allie swallowed. "I hope I don't."

Rand reached over and put a finger under her chin, turning her face to him. "I hope you don't, either."

The kiss started out gentle, but it intensified. Allie reached out to put her arm around his neck and hit his bandage, spilling her wine. Rand flinched.

"Oh, God, I'm sorry. Your bandage is all wet."

"It's OK," Rand said through gritted teeth. "The alcohol is probably good for it. Kills germs and everything."

Seconds later, they were both doubled over in helpless laughter.

■ ■ ■

SIDNEY KICKED THE MOTORCYCLE. Damn, he almost had them, both that bitch Allie and Cord's pansy son. Both of them. Fuck, when you didn't practice, your skills deteriorated in a hurry. He used to be able to shoot the cork out of a bottle at fifty feet.

He'd winged them both, though. That should count for something. But it didn't. Now, they knew he was gunning for them. It removed that element of surprise he'd counted on. No way could they know where he was shooting from, though, or what he was driving, so he still had that advantage.

When he reached the door to the trailer, he knew something was wrong. It was in the air, like the scent from a cat box, in undertones—not in your face, but perceivable.

He pulled his weapon out of his pocket and stepped into the trailer, his eyes darting from right to left. Nothing was out of order, which made it worse—because he *knew*.

He toed off his shoes just inside the door and crept toward the back of the trailer, toward the bathroom and bedroom. As he neared the bathroom, he paused. No movement. Still the same smell of old urine. No, there was a difference. He couldn't put his finger on it, but—

He jumped back as the bathroom door crashed open. He swung out with both fists and connected with flesh. He kicked blindly with his good foot and felt bone give. Then, it was over. Len Grainger lay on the floor of the hall, weeping.

Sidney fell back against the wall, winded. "You stupid bastard," he said, looking down at the sobbing man. "Are you trying to get yourself killed? Here I am busting my ass to keep you alive, and you're trying to get me to kill you. Do you have a death wish? Well, do you?" Sidney nudged him with his good foot.

Len made some kind of sound, but Sidney couldn't understand him. He reached down to pull out the gag, and the guy kicked him in the balls.

Sidney reached out blindly, grabbing the first thing his hand connected with, and he smashed the asshole in the head. Coffee and grounds went everywhere.

"You stupid *fucker*," Sidney screamed. "I'm going to kill you for that." He felt his body snap into full attack mode. He saw nothing, heard nothing, felt nothing. Red mist clouded his vision. He'd kill him. He'd fucking kill him. His left foot connected with the guy's face while his right hand came down on the back of his neck.

When he realized his target wasn't moving, he pulled back. Then, he scrubbed his face with his hands. What the hell had he done? Had he killed him? Jesus, he never intended to hurt the guy.

He heard a click and looked down into his own gun barrel. That's when he realized his quarry was totally unrestrained. He took a step back.

Len reached up and pulled out the gag. "Get back. More," he said, waving the gun.

Sidney watched every move. Len's hand shook with weakness. Hell, he'd only eaten maybe two meals in three days. And he'd been drugged most of that time, so he couldn't be as alert as he seemed. All Sidney needed was an opportunity, and he knew that would come.

He held up his hands in surrender. "OK. Don't get excited. I'm going."

Len advanced on him, his step unsteady. "Give me your phone."

Sidney reached into his shirt pocket with two

fingers, pulling it out for Len to see. "Here," he said, tossing it in front of Len.

As Len stretched to catch it, Sidney swung and clipped him on the side of the head. While Len was off balance, he pivoted on his good leg and kicked with the other. The pain almost brought him to his knees. Len's body shot across the room, and his head hit the sharp wooden windowsill with a satisfying *thunk*.

Then, he was still. Sidney half-hoped he was dead. The fucking bastard.

When he thought his leg could support his weight, he lurched across the room and leaned down to check the carotid pulse, his gun trained on the bastard's head. One twitch and he was a dead man.

The twitch didn't come, and the pulse was there, so Sidney set about restraining him again. Hand-cuffs on his ankles. Last time, he'd left them loose so they wouldn't cut off circulation. This time, he snapped them tight. Wrists in nylon restraints, tight this time.

Almost passing out from the pain, he dragged the unconscious man to the bed. Once he got him up on the mattress, he tied one foot to the bottom of the welded-in-place bed and raised the hook higher so there was no way the stupid bastard could get his arms down, short of pulling them out of their sockets. Too bad.

No good deed goes unpunished. The words trailed through his mind like the banner behind a prop plane. He'd tried to be the nice guy, tried to go easy on the son-of-a-bitch, and what had it earned him? A pair of sore balls, and he almost got his head blown off.

No way was he cleaning up the mess the bastard made. He'd make him do it tomorrow. Right now, Sidney was so tired; he was falling on his face.

He went into the kitchen and took another pill out of his stash. *One more for the Gipper,* he thought a little hysterically. He pried Len's mouth open and shoved the pill under his tongue. It could do its work while he was out, and if he died, what the hell.

Back in the living room, Sidney collapsed on the sofa. He was way beyond tired. He couldn't keep this up much longer. He hurt like he'd been beaten to a bloody pulp. His head was about to split wide open. His leg throbbed and his foot pulsed with pain. He almost wished the dumb bastard in the bedroom had finished him. At least then he could get some rest. He didn't believe in hell, which was a good thing. He also didn't believe in reincarnation. No, he knew this life was a one-shot deal. All the more reason to keep going. He only had this one life, and he didn't want to croak until he'd enjoyed at least some of it.

Tomorrow. He had to finish this tomorrow. Allie Grainger, the sheriff's bastard son, and Levine. They were the walking dead. He would have laughed if he'd had the energy. But now, he had to sleep. He had to sleep, or he'd die.

Twenty-five

ALLIE AWOKE TO THE SOUND of hammers and heavy equipment. It took her a minute to realize she was in her bed; another to realize there was a really big man stretched out beside her. Then, she moved her foot, and the rest of yesterday clicked into place. Blood, sand, confusion. How could something as small as a toe hurt so badly?

She looked over at Rand. His eyes were open, and he was smiling at her. "Good morning, beautiful."

Allie could get used to hearing that. "Hi."

Rand started to reach over for her and winced. "Oh, yeah. We got shot yesterday, didn't we?"

"We did. Do you forgive me for getting you shot?"

His smile warmed. "It'll take some convincing by you, but I'm sure I will. Eventually."

He rolled over and sat up, and Allie realized he was only wearing his shorts. He must have seen the look on her face.

"I hope you'll forgive me for taking the liberty, but I couldn't sleep in my clothes another night. I'd bring over a pair of pajamas, but I'm hoping I won't need them here."

"You won't." Allie feasted her eyes on the whole

man. God, what a sight. She'd seen Rand without a shirt before, but not in her bedroom. All her boy-girl nerve endings sprang to life, nerve endings they couldn't take advantage of in their current condition. Damn Sidney.

Rand watched her watch him and seemed to enjoy it. "Why don't you get a shower while I make some coffee?"

"I don't know if I should get my toe wet."

Rand crossed to the bed and pulled her foot into his lap, removing the bandage. "Look, it's almost healed."

"It hurts."

"Baby." Somehow, when he said it, it was a term of endearment. He leaned down and kissed her wound. "Get your shower, and I'll rebandage it for you. How's that?"

Rand was right. The skin had almost scabbed over, although a bruise spread over half her foot. She'd had worse.

She heard a knock at her front door as she was coming out of the bedroom drying her hair with a towel. "I'll get it," she called to Rand.

When she saw who was standing on her stoop, her face flamed. "Good morning, Allie," Cord said. "Do you have just a minute?"

"I— I—" She felt as guilty as a schoolgirl caught smoking her first cigarette.

"Morning, Dad," Rand said at her elbow. If he felt any embarrassment, it certainly didn't show. "Come on in. Coffee?"

Cord grinned. "Coffee would be fine."

Allie could see him take in her bathrobe, Rand standing there in his underwear. "Go get some pants on," she hissed.

He grinned as he leaned down and kissed her. "Yes, ma'am. Dad, help yourself to coffee while Allie and I throw on some clothes."

"You could have told him we didn't do anything," Allie said as they walked into the bedroom.

"Why? It's only a matter of time." The look he gave her seared her to her core.

He pulled on his jeans and left her to change. Allie's face was still flaming, but this time she didn't think it was embarrassment.

The men were sipping coffee in companionable silence when she came out. She'd taken time only to pull on shorts and a shirt and run a brush through her hair. She took the cup Rand handed her. When his hand brushed hers, she almost dropped it. Everything about Rand Arbutten screamed out to the woman in her. She wanted this man. Bad.

"I just came by to give you an update on Sidney," Cord said to them both. "We don't know where he's staying yet, but we know where he's been getting his funds. This isn't for public knowledge," he said with a glance at Allie.

She was a little insulted that he thought she'd put what he told her in the newspaper, but he *was* a cop, and she *was* a reporter. She held up three fingers. "Scouts honor."

Cord appeared satisfied. "He went by his folks' house. Stole his mother's purse. He had access to all her credit and debit cards."

"The little weasel."

"We've frozen those funds. He won't get another dime. He made a few purchases that we can trace before we could stop him. Some clothes and camping equipment."

"Where were the purchases made?" Rand asked.

"Merritt Island. We have officers checking for descriptions. He made another purchase. A cruise line ticket to the Bahamas."

"Did he think he could just jump on a cruise ship and not get caught?" Rand asked, incredulous. "How stupid is this guy?"

"Not stupid at all," Cord said, shaking his head. "He doesn't know we know about the cards. He probably thinks he's home free."

"When did he think he was leaving?" Allie asked.

"The cruise departs Monday at four p.m."

Allie felt her heart hitch. "Monday? But that's tomorrow? But what about Len? What's he going to do with Len?"

The two men looked at each other, but neither spoke.

■ ■ ■

THE CLOCK WAS TICKING. He only had thirty-six hours to steal another car, dump the jerk he had stashed in his trailer, and get the hell out of Dodge.

He was the perky redhead today. The fake boobs were driving him crazy. He felt silly driving the Harley dressed like a girl, but he knew women were less threatening. The hog was parked in a pay lot down the street. What the hell did he care? It wasn't his money.

Money. He needed more if he was going to vanish off the face of the Earth. He intended to hit the ATM and then start making withdrawals from every credit card he could. He knew he could get a bundle out of the money market account. Then, he'd hit the checking. Her Chase card should be good for a grand or two.

The bank hadn't been open that long, and it wasn't crowded. Still, there was a short line at the ATM. Sidney shifted from foot to foot as he waited. The pain was still bad, but soon he'd be stretched out on a towel sunning on some crowded beach, anonymous among the thousand or so tourists.

The gook at the front of the line was having trouble figuring out the screen instructions that any dummy could follow. Sidney almost left, but he was next in line. Finally, he reached around the guy and hit "Take Card."

The man looked at him in confusion, but something in Sidney's face must have alerted him that he was about to be in big trouble. He took his card and moved off.

Sidney slipped his mother's card in the slot and punched in her PIN. "Incorrect PIN," the screen read. Sidney tried again with the same result. Shit. The machine must be broken. That must be why the gook was having trouble. He tried one more time. No dice. Hell, now he'd have to hit another bank. He didn't have time for this shit, but he had no choice.

He punched the "Take Card" button, but nothing happened. The screen went back to the "Welcome to Bank..." He punched it repeatedly. Nothing.

The people behind him were getting restless. "Hey, lady," the guy directly behind him said. "You need some help?"

Sidney barely restrained himself from spinning

around and taking the asshole down. *Shit*. It had his card. Did it eat the card after three incorrect tries? But he'd put in the right code. He knew he had. It wasn't like he could waltz over to the counter and ask for the card back. His disguise was good, but he couldn't talk like a broad. Goddamn fucking machine. He needed that card.

"Come on, lady," the guy behind him said. "I have to get to work."

Sidney turned. Keeping his head low, he muttered, "Fuck you," as he headed out of the bank. He knew the guy was staring after him. He didn't give a shit. He *needed* that card. It was his golden goose. His folks kept a shitload of money in that account. What the hell was he going to do now?

He took several deep breaths as he climbed on the Harley. OK, so the machine was broken and it ate the card. No big deal. He could only have withdrawn so much in a twenty-four-hour period. He had other cards. He could get money from the other cards.

Chase was his next stop. When the machine ate that card, he knew he was fucked. Someone had changed the passwords. He knew his mother wouldn't have done it. It had to be his dad. The bastard. Sidney wished he'd killed him when he hit him. The man had always hated Sidney. Jealousy, that's what it was, because his mother liked him better. Well, maybe when he got settled, he'd send for his mother. He knew she'd drop everything and come. He could swear her to secrecy. She could be his cover. That would serve his dad right.

Man, he was in a world of hurt. Without additional funds, it was going to be tight, but he'd find a way to make it. At least for a while. Then, he'd contact his mom and get her to send him a new card and the current password. That would work. That's what he'd do. OK, he had a plan.

Feeling a little better, he cranked the Harley to life. He wanted to buzz by little Allie Grainger's house. Just a brief visit. Who knew what opportunity might present itself? He might not have time to finish her and the bitch Levine off before his cruise, but he could always come back. Grand Bahama Island wasn't that far away. Just a short hop across the water. He patted the Glock in his pocket. But if the opportunity presented itself, he was ready.

■ ■ ■

A CHORUS OF CATCALLS went up from the construction site next door when Allie stepped out of her house, but they went silent when Rand stepped out behind her. Allie waved to the guys just as Rand pulled her into his arms. His mouth came down on hers in a kiss that ended up as long as it was passionate.

When it ended, Allie blinked up at him. Rand grinned. "I thought I'd give them something to cheer about. I'll be back in an hour or so. Call me if anything happens."

He waved at the construction workers as he headed across the yard and received a resounding round of applause. He was almost to his car when Allie heard Bobby yell, "Hey, Allie, I think I see that motorcycle. Looks like it's headed for the Bee Line."

Allie and Rand exchanged looks before Allie launched herself in his direction. Rand had the engine started before she reached the car. She clicked her seat belt as he spun around the first corner. "Put on your seat belt," she yelled.

"In a minute," Rand yelled back.

He squealed out on A1A and headed north toward Port Canaveral and the 528 Causeway, weaving in and out of traffic like a lunatic. They'd be lucky if they didn't get stopped—or killed.

Allie didn't see the motorcycle, and she cursed herself for not having Bobby's cell phone number. From his perch, he could probably still see it. Here at ground level, they were blind.

Cruise traffic. Bumper-to-bumper cruise traffic clogged the entrance to the causeway. Still, Allie wasn't willing to give up. That man had her brother, and she was going to get him, whatever the cost.

"Go around them," she urged. "Drive on the grass."

Rand's head spun around. "That's not grass. It's sand. We'll get stuck."

"Try it, anyway. *Do it*! What do we have to lose?"

Rand veered off the highway and onto the sandy shoulder. His car fishtailed for a minute before it sank in the soft sand. He and Allie rocked back and forth trying to get it unstuck.

Finally, she yanked off her seat belt and jumped out of the car. "I'll push," she said. "You keep trying."

"Allie—"

"Just *do* it!"

She ran around the car to the back and threw all her weight into the trunk. A minute later, arms closed around her waist and pulled her away. She whirled around, furious.

"We lost him. It's no use. He's long gone by now." Rand pulled her close. "We tried. Look." He pointed to the first bridge. It was wall-to-wall cars. "Even if we made it to the bridge, it wouldn't help. The bridge doesn't have a shoulder. And a motorcycle can weave in and out between cars. We can't."

Allie rested her head on his shoulder. She knew he was right, but they'd been so close.

"It might not even be him."

"Oh, it was him," Allie said. "I can tell because my skin feels dirty."

Allie suddenly realized they were the speculation of a lot of curiosity. Countless pairs of eyes were trained on them from the cars lining the road. Humiliating, but there was no help for it.

They turned back and looked at the car, mired inches deep in soft, white sand. "Next time, we'll take my Jeep. I have four-wheel drive."

"And I," Rand said, pulling his cell phone out of his pocket, "have Triple A."

■ ■ ■

WHEN THEY ARRIVED BACK at the house, Bobby was on the ground before they were out of the car. "Hey, bad luck about the sand."

"How did you—" Then, she noticed the binoculars hanging around his neck. "When did you start wearing those? Are they standard construction equipment?"

Bobby scuffed the grass. "No, and a lot of the guys are razzing me, but I have a job to do. I'm going to do it right."

Allie smiled. "I'm grateful, but are you getting any building done at all?"

"Some, I guess," Bobby said, his voice sheepish, "but Dad's cutting me some slack. He's really pis— mad at that guy too. I know about when he tried to run you off the bridge. I wish I'd been there."

Rand stepped forward. "Why don't we all exchange cell numbers? Then, next time, we'll have an ally in the air."

Bobby grinned. "Cool."

They spent a minute programming numbers into their respective phones before Bobby waved goodbye and climbed back up the scaffolding.

"Bet you're glad now that you have a high-rise going up next door."

"I had the same thought when we were chasing Sidney."

"I didn't have any thought except trying to keep us alive and trying to keep you from jumping out of the car and pursuing on foot."

He turned as Sheryl approached. "What's with all the tire squealing? I heard you two take off out of here like a couple of bats outta hell. How's an expectant mother supposed to get any sleep?"

"Bobby spotted Sidney," Rand said. "And we got stuck in sand up to our hubcaps."

Sheryl snorted. "I know. I saw Bobby hanging off the girder like a monkey and asked him. Figured if you were landlocked, you didn't need my help. I tried to go back to sleep, but no dice. You guys had lunch?"

Allie and Rand looked at each other. "We haven't even had breakfast."

"How about Lester's in half an hour?"

■ ■ ■

SHERYL TOOK A BITE OF HER hamburger, and Del reached over and wiped the mustard off her chin.

"I'm not a baby," Sheryl said, slapping his hand away.

"Just practicing for—you know." The grins they gave each other were almost embarrassing in their intimacy.

Del was the only bartender working, but the bar was almost empty. Sunday morning wasn't a heavy drinking time unless there was a hurricane approaching, and hurricanes were a nonissue in February.

"I think I saw him in here a time or two," Del said, taking the stool next to Sheryl. "Now that I know about the disguises, I'll keep a close eye. If he comes here again, he won't get out."

"Alive," Allie finished. She looked at Del and Sheryl. What a couple of wonderful, overprotective parents they would be. Del could teach the baby martial arts, and Sheryl could show it how to handle a firearm. No one would mess with their kid.

"I wish I'd had my gun," Allie said.

Rand looked at her in surprise. "I didn't know you had a gun."

"It's a weapon—or a firearm," Sheryl said with derision. "You sound like a jerk when you call it a gun."

"Well, it is a gun." She turned to Rand. "It's a Glock 26. Gen 4, whatever that means."

"It means it's the fourth generation of Glock 26," he said.

"I didn't know guns had generations."

"Weapon," Sheryl said in exasperation. "Firearm or weapon, for Pete's sake."

Allie rolled her eyes.

"What would you have done with it?" Rand asked. "Shot out my tires?"

"I was mad enough."

Sheryl glared at her. "You don't need to be shooting anything until your permit comes through, or it's my ass for giving it to you. Except for Sidney, but only if you have to. We know what he's driving now, but we haven't spotted him yet. Hard to spot anything with all the snowbirds on the road."

"Most snowbirds don't drive Harleys," Allie said.

"You'd be surprised what's under some of those helmets. Anyway, it wouldn't hurt to have a few like Bobby in the department. That boy takes the work seriously. Not that the vets don't, but rookies always have that shiny enthusiasm. You know?" She took another huge bite of her hamburger. "Good news is Sidney tried to make a withdrawal from the bank this morning. Machine kept his card." She swallowed. "Same thing with his mom's Chase VISA. He won't get any more funds."

Allie frowned. "I don't know if that's good or not."

"What do you mean?" Rand asked.

Allie looked at him. "I don't want him to feel too desperate. Desperate men tend to do desperate things."

Twenty-six

SIDNEY PARKED THE BIKE in the Cape Canaveral Hospital parking lot. He knew he should take the time to find a better source of transportation, but time was one thing he didn't have now. Twenty-four hours to get the Grainger guy down to the Glades, return to Cape Canaveral, and board his ship.

He'd decided to travel as the redhead. She was his favorite. He sure as hell couldn't wear his uniform, and the fat guy outfit was too damn hot. The red wig was hot, too, and it itched after a while, but it was better than a sweatsuit.

He didn't need much time, just long enough to get to Cocoa, load his human cargo, and head south. He'd ditch the car in Clewiston, where he and Cord had embarked on their Everglades adventure back when he was a kid. It was about fifty miles from Palm Beach. He could ditch his new ride at the airport there and pick up another for the last leg of his trip. It would work.

He looked around the lot. He wanted the most innocuous vehicle he could find—something that blended in with every other car on the road. Not too new. Then, he spotted it—a '94 Honda Civic. White like almost every other car in Florida.

Four-door. And was that a SunPass he saw on the windshield? Sweet. He wouldn't even have to stop at tollbooths and take a chance of being spotted.

He strolled over to the vehicle as casually as he could manage with a bum leg and peeked inside. Nice and clean. CD player. Couldn't be better.

His hand was in his backpack reaching for his slim jim when a woman walked up. She smiled at him. "I'm sorry. This is my car."

Sidney felt panic grip him. Be cool. Be cool. "I'm sorry," he said in a high, breathy voice. "These silly things all look alike, don't they?"

"They sure do," the woman said, inserting her key in the door. "I can't tell you how many times I've tried to get into someone else's."

For an insane instant, he considered taking her out and grabbing the car. He gave himself a mental shake and backed away.

"I sure hope you find your car," the woman said with a smile and a wave as she drove away.

Crap. That was close. If she'd been ten seconds later, he'd have been busted. God was she lucky. Women made such targets of themselves. Hadn't she noticed he didn't have any keys in his hand? They were too damn trusting.

Okay, it wasn't worth the risk. He'd have to go over to Merritt Island. Merritt Square had one of those mega-theaters that showed a dozen movies at the same time. He'd check the show times. He could watch to see who entered and snatch one of their cars. That would give him at least a couple of hours of lead time.

The trip only took ten minutes, and he couldn't

believe his luck. The theaters were beginning to empty as he drove into the lot. How did so many people get off work to go to daytime matinees? But most were probably tourists. Good. The more the merrier.

He pulled the Harley into a space and waited. Soon, a man, gray-haired, pulled into an empty spot a few cars down. Malibu, another four-door. This one was a '96, but good enough. Not much power, but great gas mileage. Like he gave a shit.

An elderly man climbed out of the car and walked around to the passenger side. The woman who stepped out was younger than he was, probably sixty or sixty-five, plump and smiling, maybe looking forward to a matinee with her hubby. Probably the only kind of matinee they could manage these days. He kept his eyes on them as they went through the double doors and into the theater. Then, he made his move.

He dismounted the Harley and pulled off his helmet, careful not to disturb the wig. The disguise had worked on the woman at the hospital parking lot. Maybe it'd work here, too, if necessary.

He reached into his backpack and pulled out the slim jim, inserting it carefully between the window and doorframe. Keeping his head up so he wouldn't look suspicious, he worked the tool until he heard a satisfying click. He tested the door handle. Voila! He had new wheels.

He had just pulled open the door and started to duck inside, when he heard a voice yell, "Hey, you! What are you doing to my car?"

Christ. The old man was coming back. Then he saw the woman's handbag on the passenger floor.

Shit. He had to pick the forgetful broad.

The man was drawing a lot of attention. Sidney slipped out of the car and kept low as he dodged between cars to the Harley. He ripped off the red wig and tossed it under a truck. No way could he use that again.

Still low, he climbed on the Harley and walked it a few rows down without starting it. All attention was on the guy standing beside his target car, talking nonstop and waving his arms in the air. Old codger would have a heart attack if he didn't calm down.

At the edge of the parking lot, he slipped on the helmet. No one even looked his way when he finally started the hog and drove slowly away.

OK, that was it. It was clear that luck had turned on him. He wasn't going to push it. That meant he had to leave Grainger at the trailer. Someone would find him eventually. And who cared if Sidney was made? He *wanted* them all to know it'd been him all the time, moving around under their noses with them too stupid to catch him. It would also be good payback for the guy who'd loaned him the trailer, for loaning him a piece of shit. Payback was hell.

In a way, it was better. There was no more time pressure. He'd leave the Harley at the trailer and take a cab to Port Canaveral. He'd give his guest one more dose of sleepy juice in the morning, which was about what he had left in his stash—a little something to keep him out for twelve hours or so.

But before he returned to the trailer, he had one more thing to take care of. He'd have to be careful and law abiding. It wouldn't do to get pulled over now, but it was worth the risk. He had to pay one last call on another Grainger.

■ ■ ■

ALLIE'S HOUSE PHONE RANG as she and Rand stepped out of the car. Lunch had been a waste. Allie couldn't get a bite past the lump in her throat, and all they did was rehash what they all knew— Sidney had Len. No one could find Sidney, who was planning to skip town in less than twenty-four hours, leaving Len who knew where. If—her mind refused to go there.

"Hello."

"Did you check your caller ID before you answered?"

"Yes."

"So you knew it was me?"

"Yes, Mother."

"Well, thank you for answering normally. It's disconcerting when someone blurts out 'hello, Mother' when she answers the phone." There was a silence as she waited for Allie's comeback. Allie had none. "Do you have any news about your brother?"

"Yes and no."

"Well, pick one," her mother snapped. Then, Allie heard her draw in a deep breath. "I apologize."

"That's OK. I don't think any of us is at our best." She wiggled her little toe.

"What have you learned?"

Allie didn't want to give her mother false fear or hope, but Vivian deserved to know the truth. "We think we know who has him. His name is Sidney

Finch. He's a former police officer—"

"I know who Sidney Finch is. I read the papers. He's that man who tried to shoot you last summer. So he did this to Len because of you?"

Patience. Allie took the phone over to the sofa and sat. "He escaped from where they were holding him pending trial."

"I didn't read about that in the papers."

"The sheriff is keeping it quiet for the moment. All we know is that Sidney kidnapped Len from the Hilton—"

"Where you sent him."

"From the Hilton where I sent him, fully knowing that someone was going to kidnap him."

"There's no need to be sarcastic, Allison. What else?"

"We know what Sidney is driving, but we don't know where he's holding Len right now. He—"

Her cell phone rang. Rand had been standing watching her face as she talked to her mother. Now, he reached into her purse and pulled out her cell. "It's Bobby," he mouthed.

"Gotta go, Mom. This might be some information about Len."

She disconnected and took her cell phone. "Bobby?"

"I see him," Bobby said. "He drove by, but I must have had my head turned. I can see him now. He's just about to turn on A1A heading for..." Allie heard construction noise in the background. Someone yelled something unintelligible. "Looks like he's headed for the Bee Line again."

Allie was already reaching for her purse. "How's traffic?"

"Light. Well, moderate. No accidents I can see. I'm climbing to get a better view."

"Be *careful*. And don't hang up."

She raced toward her Jeep with Rand behind her. "I'm driving," she called as he headed for the driver's side. After only the briefest hesitation, he reversed direction and climbed in the passenger seat. "You'd better buckle up. We're not going to lose him this time."

She fishtailed as she spun out of her driveway. Rand grabbed the chicken bar. "You will be gentle with me, won't you?"

"Just hang on."

"Woman of few words."

"Where is he now?" Allie said into the phone, then she punched "speaker" and dropped it in her lap.

"He just entered the causeway. He's not driving fast."

"Doesn't want to get stopped," Rand muttered. Allie nodded.

"I can see your Jeep," Bobby said. "He's about six—no, seven—cars in front of you. If you want to catch him, you need to speed up."

"I don't want to catch him. I want to follow him. He has my brother, and I want to know where."

"I'll keep you in sight as long as possible. I'm climbing higher now."

"For God's sake, be careful, Bobby. Your father will kill me if anything happens to you."

"I'm always careful." She heard a sharp intake of breath. "Oops!"

"*What?*"

"Just kidding."

"Don't kid. Where is he?"

"Five cars ahead of you. Four. Three. You're driving like a bat outta hell. I'm going to lose visibility soon, so you'd better move up some… one more car. That puts two between you. He's riding toward the center lane, so keep toward the shoulder."

Allie and Rand exchanged glances. Allie said, "Bobby, when this is over, I'm going to give you a big kiss."

"Oh, yeah? What will your boyfriend say?"

Rand picked up the phone from her lap. "Her boyfriend will say 'Get to it.'"

"I've lost visibility of both of you."

"No sweat. We're on it. And thanks, bud."

Sidney took the US-1 exit and turned right toward Titusville. Allie kept two cars between them and hugged the shoulder as Bobby had told her. About three miles down the road, he signaled a turn into a trailer park. Allie kept going. As soon as she could, she pulled over and prepared to make a U-turn.

"Give him a few minutes to get inside."

Allie nodded.

"Do you have your Glock?"

"Glove compartment." She was having trouble getting her breath. They were so close. *So close.*

Rand pulled the Glock out of the glove compartment and checked the magazine. Then, he dropped it in her jacket pocket.

"OK, now. Take it slow. First, I'll call Dad. Remember, when we get in there, we're looking for the bike. When we find it, don't stop. Once we determine which trailer they're in, we can get the manager to knock on the door. We'll get him to say he heard some noises and wanted to make sure everything's all right or something like that. We'll stay out of sight."

"What will that accomplish?"

"We'll know for sure Sidney's there."

"Oh. What if the manager's not home?"

Rand stared at her. "We'll deal with that when it happens."

"Shouldn't we have a plan B?"

"Plan B is to barge into the trailer and shoot Sidney dead and hope Len doesn't get caught in the crossfire."

Allie shuddered. "Not much of a plan B."

"Not much of a plan A, either, but they're all we have to work with."

While Rand called Cord, Allie dialed Sheryl. "Where are you?"

"I'm still at Lester's. Where the hell are you?"

"I found him."

"Who?"

"Sidney. Len, I hope." She gave Sheryl her location. "Bobby spotted him. We followed him from Cape Canaveral to this trailer park. He's still on the Harley. We're waiting for him to go inside. Rand's calling Cord, but I wanted you to know."

"I'm on my way."

Allie heard the phone snatched out of Sheryl's hand. "We're on the way," Del boomed.

She pulled the phone away from her ear. God, the man had a set of lungs.

Twenty-seven

"CAVALRY IS ON THE WAY. Let's go," Rand said. Allie started the Jeep and eased back on the road. She'd have to be careful. Sidney knew her car. Intimately, she thought, remembering his shooting out her tires.

She turned into the trailer park at a crawl. Single-lane asphalt roads in various states of disrepair divided several rows of trailers. If two cars passed each other, one would have to pull off on the sparse grass. She slipped the Jeep into four-wheel drive just in case. They weren't getting stuck this time.

The place was tomb quiet. The first trailer they passed on the right had a cardboard sign propped in the window that read "Manager." No car on the gravel parking pad beside it, no lights in the windows. She and Rand exchanged glances. So much for Plan A.

They made their way down the first row without spotting the Harley. Then, the second. "Where is he?" Allie whispered. He was here; he had to be. She could feel her skin crawl.

It felt eerie. Not one person was in sight. No sound came from any trailer. It was as if everyone had vanished off the planet, only no one had thought to mention it to her.

There were six lanes between the eight rows of trailers, with ten to fifteen trailers in each row. The ones at the front of the park were nice, with tidy flowerbeds and window boxes, painted lattice around the bases to conceal the wheels and cinderblocks. The second row was not quite as nice; the third, even less so.

By the time they finished the fourth row, Allie felt panic clutching at her throat. If Len wasn't here… She shivered. But Sidney had pulled in here. If it really was Sidney on that motorcycle. If this were a wild goose chase, she'd lose her mind.

Many trailers had makeshift sheds and dilapidated outbuildings where he could have hidden the motorcycle. Had they given him too much time with their stupid delay tactics?

Row five, toward the back. The trailers here appeared seedier, more unkempt. Weeds, some of them nearly waist high, grew up in the sandy soil between the lots. Discarded propane tanks in various states of rust corrosion littered the ground. That had to be illegal. She felt a bubble of hysteria rise at the thought.

By the end of row five, she was feeling desperate. Where *was* he? If her brother was here, she intended to find him. She wasn't leaving this place until she did.

As she turned on to row six, her breath caught in her throat. There it was, parked in plain view beside the last trailer. Bobby's description was spot on.

Her gaze flew to Rand, who was making backing-up motions with his hand. Allie eased to a stop. Then, she put the Jeep in reverse and began to back slowly.

Where was Len? Was he inside?

She backed on to row five and braked. He motioned her to put the Jeep in park and turn off the engine. Allie did it. War games and strategy were second nature to this man. She'd defer to the expert.

He leaned close. "We have to take it on foot from here," he whispered. "We'll circle around the trailer from behind. That way we can make sure he doesn't sneak Len out the back way if he hears any sirens. I asked Dad to come in quiet, but one mistake..." He didn't have to finish the sentence. Allie knew what one mistake meant.

She started to open her door, but Rand's hand closed over her arm as he pointed at the keys still in the ignition. Allie shut her eyes and bowed her head in gratitude. The dinging would have sounded like the bells of St. Peter's in this quiet. She gave Rand's arm an appreciative squeeze before pulling out the keys and dropping them gently in her purse.

She eased her door open in unison with Rand. He came around the back of the Jeep and motioned that they should go down row five to reach the trailer with the motorcycle.

Allie swallowed hard. Where the hell was Sheryl?

■ ■ ■

SHERYL LAID ON THE HORN again, earning her several dirty looks from the other drivers. "Christ, I wish I had my cruiser."

They were on US 1 where traffic had come to

a standstill. Several motorists were out of their cars, milling about and chatting.

Del stroked her arm. "Honey, she said Rand called his father. The sheriff's on his way. Everything's going to be OK."

"Don't honey me," Sheryl said, blasting the horn again. "I want that bastard as much as Allie does."

"You're getting too upset."

Sheryl leveled a look at him. "Run up there, and see what the hold-up is," she said, pointing in front of them.

Del stared at her.

Sheryl snatched off her seat belt. "All right, then, I will."

She swung open her door, but Del pulled her back in the car. "I will."

Sheryl watched as he sprinted out of sight. People were watching her, and many eyes followed Del as he vanished from sight. What? Did they think it was a domestic dispute or what?

Sheryl drummed her fingers on the steering wheel. She squirmed in her seat. She smacked the steering wheel with her fist. "That's it. I'm going."

As she climbed out of the car, Del ran back. "It's a bad accident. An eighteen-wheeler and two cars. The whole road is closed."

"Any vehicles in the median?" she asked, jumping back in the car and throwing it in drive.

Del slid in the passenger seat. "No—" was all he got out before she floored it.

Del grabbed for his seat belt as Sheryl sped across the well-mown grass. As they neared the accident site, an officer stepped out and held up his hand. Sheryl pulled out her badge and held it up to the windshield, and the officer waved her on.

Once clear of the bottleneck, she pressed the gas pedal to the floor. She heard Del mutter, "This can't be good for the baby." Then, a few minutes later, "I need to get her a safer car." She would have smiled if she'd had time.

The miles vanished beneath their wheels. She passed everything she saw, zipping in between cars like a water bug on a pond. When she saw the sign for the trailer park, she slowed to a crawl.

Half a dozen cruisers were parked on the side of the road. She pulled in behind them.

Cord stood in the center of a group of officers. He nodded when Sheryl joined them. "I want the area fully contained. We have good reason to believe Finch is in there, and he has a potential hostage. We don't want this to turn any uglier than it has to."

"I'm going in with them," Sheryl said.

"You're not on duty, Levine."

"Allie's in there."

"So is my son," Cord said, his eyes hooded and his voice level. "We'll take this slowly. And carefully."

Sheryl stepped back. By God, they weren't going to stop her. That was Allie in there. If Sidney got his hands on her, she was a dead woman. Sheryl would obey a direct order, but Cord hadn't given her a direct order.

She took a few more steps back and turned, motioning to Del. They slipped between the cruisers and into the brush at the side of the road.

■ ■ ■

ALLIE FOLLOWED RAND'S LEAD. They walked slowly,

like a young couple out for an afternoon stroll. Allie felt the adrenaline surging through her like a tonic. Let her find him. Just let her find Sidney and she'd kill him for all the grief he'd brought to her and her brother and the rest of her family. He deserved to die. She remembered Del telling her to be a warrior. "Be ready to kill, Allie. If it comes down to kill or be killed, be ready to kill." Well, she was ready.

She couldn't imagine how Rand could look so calm. Maybe she looked calm, too, but she didn't feel calm.

As they neared the end of the row, Rand touched her arm. He motioned her to drop down low and gave her a hand signal that said, "Follow me." Allie nodded and slipped in behind him.

They plastered themselves against the last trailer in row five and eased around the corner until they had the trailer where the Harley was parked in sight. There were no lights showing from the windows, but it was still daylight. Still, the black at the windows looked too complete to be natural, especially because Allie couldn't see any curtains hanging there. Rand motioned her to stop. "I'm going to circle the back and see if I can see anything," he whispered. "You stay here in case someone comes out the door."

Allie nodded and watched as Rand made a complete circle of the trailer. Maybe if they couldn't see in, whoever was in there couldn't see out, either.

After what seemed like an eternity, he returned. "Not a sound in there. Let's go back to the car—"

"I don't think so," said a voice behind them.

Twenty-eight

ALLIE SPUN AROUND and cried out at what she saw. Len, gagged and bound, his eyes wide with terror. His face was swollen on one side, black and purple, his hair matted and his shirt stained with blood. He was unsteady on his feet. Sidney held him, one arm around Len's neck and a gun shoved under his chin. Allie could tell Sidney's arm was all that kept Len from falling to the ground.

Allie couldn't say a word. *Len.* God, what had Sidney done to him?

"Why don't you let him go, Finch?" Rand said, his voice soft and even. "He hasn't done anything to you. He's the good guy in all this. It's me and Allie you want."

Allie could have hugged him. Warrior mode, she told herself as she tried to recall what Del had taught her. Classes. Damn, she'd taken classes in self-defense. What had he told her? Her mind was a blank. This was the panic Del had told her about, the frozen moment when it's fight or flight, and flight simply wasn't an option.

It began to come back. Scream. He'd told her to scream, but if she did, Sidney might pull the trigger. Oh, God, what else had he taught her?

She could feel Rand edging over. What was he doing? She looked up, but he never took his eyes off Sidney. Was he trying to get her behind him? Very heroic, but what was the point?

He moved again. Was he trying to get *behind* her?

"Come on, Finch. You know the party's over."

This had to be his mellow courtroom voice. Soothing. Mellifluous. God, where did that come from?

"Let him go. You can get one of us, but not all of us. You can pick which one. You know how much you hate us. Allie because you think she got you into this. She ruined your life, didn't she?"

Allie could have kicked him. Why was he baiting Sidney?

"And me," Rand continued, "because I've got what you'll never have. I'm Cord Arbutten's son. His real son, not some relationship you made up."

"Shut up, you fuckhead pansy."

"And you know what? Since you were busted, dad and I are just getting closer. Hard to take, isn't it?" Rand said, edging closer to Allie. She felt his hand brush her side. "Here you've busted your ass all your life to please him, and I just had to... be."

Sidney shifted from foot to foot, swaying slightly. Len tried to make a sound. Sidney jammed the pistol harder against his chin. "You bastards," he choked out. "I fucking hate all of you."

"I'll bet you do," Rand said. "We have everything, and you have nothing. Doesn't that suck? So what is it, Finch?" He motioned at Len. "You want to take out this guy who's trussed up like a rabbit, or you want a fair fight with someone who's a little more of a challenge? What's it going to be? I never figured you for a pussy."

Allie heard a strangled sob as Sidney flung Len to the ground. And it all came back. Go for the weakest spot.

Allie lunged and stomped his crushed foot with her full weight. Sidney roared in agony. As he was going down, he turned the gun on Len, and Allie flung her body at him. The gun went off. Allie felt a sharp pain. Another gunshot exploded, and then nothing.

■ ■ ■

IT HAD TO BE ONLY SECONDS, but it seemed like hours. She heard Sidney cry out, and then his weight as he fell across her feet. Then, confusion. It was always confusion. Sirens. People everywhere. She needed to get up.

She felt arms pulling at her and someone saying, "Don't move her."

She blinked her eyes open, expecting to see Rand's chocolate brown ones staring at her, but it was Len. "Allie," he said, almost shaking her, "are you OK?"

She smiled up at him. "You aren't dead," she said.

Someone pulled Len away. Hands yanked at her jacket. She heard the sound of fabric giving way as she tried to remember the sequence of events. A sting on her arm. That jolted her to awareness. Where was Rand?

She must have cried out his name, because

a moment later, his face swam into her vision. That's when she realized she was crying. "Are you all right?"

He knelt beside her. "Better than you, I'd say. I'm fine. Sidney's dead."

Allie closed her eyes. She was glad... but...

"You're going to be OK."

Sheryl's voice. Allie opened her eyes in time to see Sheryl push Rand out of the way. "I am?"

"Yeah," Sheryl said, wiping her eyes on her sleeve. "He got you in the arm, but he missed the bone. It'll be fine."

"Who shot Sidney?" As Allie watched, Rand stepped close to Sheryl and slipped Allie's Glock into her pocket.

Sheryl glanced down, then back at Allie. "Me. I shot him. With that gun I bought you as a gift."

Gift? That's when Allie realized Cord had joined the party. She reached out with her good arm, and Rand helped her to a sitting position. It made her feel less vulnerable.

She saw Sidney lying on the ground three feet away and averted her eyes, but not before the tears started. What was the matter with her? Was she crying for the man who'd kidnapped her brother? Who had tried to kill her more than once?

Sheryl put her arm around Allie's shoulder. "It's all over, Allie. It's finally over."

Allie nodded. For her it was, and for Sheryl, but Sidney Finch had left a trail of pain behind him. She thought of Sidney's parents. Of Cord, who had struggled long and hard to turn Sidney into what he might have been. And she knew Sidney Finch would continue to inflict pain for a long time.

Twenty-nine

TERESA FINCH YANKED OPEN the front door. "Why are you here again? Haven't you hounded us enough? He's not here."

"I know."

Something in Cord's voice must have alerted her. She took a step back. Then, another. Wally appeared at her shoulder.

"Cord?"

"It's bad, Wally."

"How bad?"

Cord shook his head.

Teresa bit her hand and screamed. Wally grabbed her against him as tears started down his face.

Cord followed them into the house, into the living room. When Wally pulled his sobbing wife down on the couch, Cord perched on the edge of a chair and waited. There would be questions. There were always questions.

Finally, Teresa's sobs quieted some. Wally looked over.

"That man he kidnapped?"

"He's OK."

"Anyone else hurt?"

"He shot Allie Grainger, but she's going to be fine."

Teresa's head snapped up. "Her! She was the

cause of it all. I wish she'd *died.*" Her voice rose to a scream. "I wish he'd *killed her!*"

"Hush, Teresa," Wally said. "You don't mean that." He looked at Cord. "I'd better call her doctor and get her something. Can I call you later about... arrangements?"

"Sure." He noticed a suitcase by the front door. "Are you going somewhere? Where can I contact you?"

Wally looked from the suitcase and back to Cord. "Here," Wally said, stroking his wife's hair as she sobbed quietly against his chest. "Tessa will need me now. I'll be right here."

■ ■ ■

"ELLA FAYE'S HERE?" Len's voice was incredulous. He looked from Allie to Rand and back again. "Where? How long has she been here?"

Rand had driven them to Allie's house after a brief stop at the emergency room—or as brief as emergency room visits ever were. Allie had a bandage on her arm as big as Nebraska and a new prescription for pain meds. Shot twice in twenty-four hours. That was a new record for her.

Spook was curled in her lap. Maybe life would get back to normal after all.

"Allie?"

She remembered Len's question. How long had Ella Faye been in town? It seemed like forever. She thought back. "Since Saturday."

"Yesterday?"

Was yesterday Saturday? Was it possible that so much had happened in one day?

"Where is she?"

"At the Hilton," Allie said, dragging her mind back to the present. "I put her in your room."

Len glanced away. He appeared exhausted, but otherwise, he looked better. He'd showered and washed his hair, and Rand had loaned him a pair of jeans and a shirt. It surprised Allie that the men were so close to the same size. Rand had always seemed so much bigger.

Allie looked at Rand now. "Would you take Spook for a little walk? He probably needs to go out." Which was ridiculous because Sheryl had walked him when they got home before she left for work, but she didn't want to have this conversation in front of Rand.

Rand seemed to notice it immediately. Thank God for perceptive men.

How to begin? "The credit card you gave the Hilton when you checked in was no good."

Len hung his head. "It was good when I gave it to them. Barely, but it was good. Ella Faye must have put more charges on it."

"Why do you put up with it?" She knew the question was inflammatory. She expected Len to explode, but when he looked up, his eyes were moist, his face haggard.

"I love her, Allie. It's as simple as that." He scrubbed his hands down his face. "Mother asked me the same question—although in much stronger language. I gave her the same answer. She called me a patsy and a fool." He shrugged. "Maybe she's right, but you can't choose who you love."

Maybe not, but Allie believed you could choose what to do about it. She didn't say that to Len.

She doubted it would change the way he felt or the way he behaved.

"How broke are you?"

Len barked out a laugh. "Flat, as in teetering on bankruptcy. I have the house, but it's mortgaged to the hilt. The car is leased, and I'm a month late on the payment. I— uh—" He had been staring at the floor. Now, he looked up at Allie. "I kind of borrowed some money from the firm."

Allie tried to hide her shock. Len was pilfering money from the law practice? "Does mother know?"

"Are you kidding? She'd kill me."

Allie tried to make sense of it. Her successful, perfect brother, nearly bankrupt and dipping in company funds. "How did you let it get so bad?"

Len looked away. "I wasn't lucky enough to inherit a fortune," he said, his voice bitter.

That stopped Allie. Len was right. She had been lucky. When her inheritance came through, she had exactly fifty-six dollars in the bank. Her marriage was over. When she came back from Belgium, she might have been able to stay with her parents for a short while, but it would have been torture. Her only asset was her Jeep. She could have worked at the *AJC*—if they were hiring—but her starting salary would have been something like thirty-thousand a year if she was lucky. But instead of starting from scratch, she was handed a paid-for house on the beach and more than two million dollars, and she'd walked into a job that paid almost four times what she'd make at the *AJC*. Yes, she'd been lucky.

She reached down on the floor beside the couch and picked up her purse. "How much do you owe the firm?"

"Forty thousand."

"*Forty*—" She stopped. Water under the proverbial bridge.

When she'd written the check, she handed it to Len. When he looked at it, he gasped. "It's too much. I shouldn't take this."

She noticed he didn't say he *wouldn't* take it. "It's half what I inherited from Aunt Lou. It's been sitting in the bank collecting interest. I want you to have it. It comes with conditions, though."

Len looked wary.

"No more pressuring me to sell the house, and when I do, the proceeds are indisputably mine. So will the next house be mine."

Len grinned. "Deal. Jesus, Allie, you don't know what this means to me. This will save my life."

For a while, but if things didn't change… "Maybe you can convince Ella Faye to spend less. Maybe—"

She broke off as the front door swung open.

"Look who I found in your front yard," Rand said, as Vivian Grainger swept past him and into the room. Allie and Len just stared at her, their mouths open.

Vivian rushed to Len and embraced him. "You're all right. Thank God, you're all right. Why in God's name didn't anyone call me? I didn't know until this man told me." She looked at Rand as if it was his fault she hadn't been told and sat on the sofa beside Len.

"We just got home from the hospital, Mother," Len said.

"*Hospital*! Were you injured?" she demanded. Then, she reached up and touched his swollen face. "Oh, my Lord, you poor thing."

"Not me," Len said, pushing her hand away. "Allie. She was shot."

Vivian turned and looked at her daughter. "She seems all right."

Len's face flushed. "She got shot saving my life, Mother."

Vivian sat back as if she'd been slapped. "Well, none of this would have happened in the first place if it weren't for her, would it? That man was after her, not you. You wouldn't have been in Florida if she'd been fair-minded about that inheritance. You—"

"Mrs. Grainger," Rand said, his voice icy with rage, "Your *daughter* was shot when she threw herself in front of a bullet to save your son's life. I think she deserves a measure of gratitude for that, don't you?"

Vivian blinked rapidly. "Well, I— I— well, yes. But the facts remain—"

"The facts remain that your son is alive and sitting here beside you today because your daughter made it possible."

He advanced a step, and Allie jumped to her feet. Startled, Spook ran behind the sofa, and Vivian squealed. "Was that a *rat*?"

Allie smothered a laugh. "No, Mother. That was a dog."

"A *dog*?" She stood and took several steps away. "Filthy beasts, covered with fleas and—"

"He is," Allie said, seizing on it. "The whole house is crawling with fleas... and who knows what else? I have the exterminator coming tomorrow, but you know it does no good. They'll be crawling all over everything again in no time."

Vivian edged toward the door. "Come with me, Len." She looked at Rand. "I want you to drive us to the Hilton to pick up my daughter-in-law and then to the airport. We're flying back to Atlanta as soon as possible."

Allie waited for the explosion.

Rand regarded Vivian with raised eyebrows. "I'll be happy to call you a taxi. You can wait outside or in here. It's your choice."

Vivian's mouth opened and closed. Tossing her head, she stormed out the front door.

Len looked after her, shaking his head. He rose from the sofa, stuffing the check in his pocket. "Allie… I'm sorry." He made a helpless gesture.

Her big, strong, arrogant brother, or that's how he'd always seemed to Allie. Now, he just looked whipped. Defeated.

"It's OK," she told him. "Some things will never change. Just—just take care of yourself. OK?"

Len put his arms around her. "You, too, Sis. Don't stop anymore flying bullets."

Allie smiled. "I'll try not to."

The taxi must have been in the area because it was only a matter of minutes before they were gone. Allie sagged against Rand. "Thank you for trying," she said, looking up at him.

A muscle in his jaw twitched. "It was my pleasure. But promise me one thing, will you?"

"What?"

"Promise me you won't grow up to be like her."

Thirty

THE MONDAY MORNING sun shone on Allie as she lay on the rooftop deck, Spook on the chair beside her. Rand was in Orlando clearing his schedule for the next few days and picking up some clothes. He told Allie he'd be back in a couple of hours. They were overdue for that long-awaited weekend they'd promised each other for six months, and they'd both decided the waiting was over.

Allie arched her back, stretching her arms and legs and loving the warmth of the hot sun as it soaked into her aching muscles. Her arm didn't hurt much. Not *too* much. She smiled. Nothing was going to stop them this time.

The construction noise was muted today, as if Frank and his crew were using tools wrapped in felt. They must be working on the other side of the building. She wondered how long it would be before they finished it. She'd have to remember to ask Frank.

The quiet was—unusual—and Allie embraced it. The waves on the beach below whispered sweet nothings to the sand. Gulls circled overhead. Judging by the rolling cloudbank to the north, a front was moving in. It was hours away, and who cared if it came? She and Rand didn't plan to spend much time outside. Let it rain. Let it snow, for all she cared.

"I'm proud of you, Allie."

"For what?"

"For how you handled all of it."

"You mean Sidney?"

"That, and Vivian and Len."

"She was right. It was my fault what happened to Len."

"She was not *right. What happened was Sidney's fault. Or it was Len's fault. But it was not in any way your fault."*

"It wouldn't have happened if—"

"Allie, stop with the should-have-been and would-have-been. Focus on the what-is. This situation happened because Sidney targeted you and because Len was down here pressuring you. Neither of those things were your choice or your doing. You have to stop taking responsibility for other people's actions."

"I know, but it's hard."

"I never told you life was easy."

"You were wrong, you know?"

"About what?"

"You said she loved me."

"She does love you… in her own way. It's wrong to ask more of someone than she can give. It just leads to disappointment."

"I know. You were right about another thing, though."

"I'm right about a lot of things. Which one?"

"You can't protect people from life. They have to live it their way. I only hope Ella Faye doesn't break his heart."

"Hearts heal. You've seen that with your own eyes."

Allie thought of Sheryl and Del and smiled.

"You gave Len money."

"Are you angry about that? I know you said I shouldn't."

"I said you shouldn't let him bully you out of it, and you didn't."

"So I was right to give it to him?"

"It won't last long."

"Then, I was wrong?"

"Right and wrong aren't as simple as what people make them out to be. Life is full of gray areas. This was one of those."

"I just wonder what's going to happen to him when the money runs out."

Silence, but she'd expected it. Lou didn't predict the future. Allie didn't know if it was because she couldn't or wouldn't. It didn't matter. The future would come when it was ready.

She must have dozed, because the next sounds she heard were footsteps on the wrought-iron steps leading to the deck. Her heart stuttered, but then she relaxed. It was over. Sidney was dead.

First, she saw his head appear, then his shoulders. As the rest of his body appeared, she drank in the sight of him. Finally.

Things had changed. She no longer felt like a schoolgirl; she felt like a woman, and she intended to show Rand just how much of a woman she was.

She met him halfway, and they melted into a long, deep kiss. When she surfaced, she asked, "Got everything? Clothes? Toothbrush?"

He stroked her face. "They're in the car. I'll get

them later. Right now..."

As he pulled her back against him, Allie heard a whistle from next door. She took Rand's hand and led him toward the stairs. "I don't think we need an audience." He grinned and followed her.

In the living room, they picked up where they'd left off. Just as Rand started to pull Allie's top over her head, the front door burst open.

"Look!" Sheryl cried, waving a piece of paper at them. "I had a sonogram today. It's a picture of Rocco. Can you believe it?" She held it out for them to see. It looked like a picture of an alien, and the photo had the quality of a bad negative.

She collapsed on Allie's sofa. "Isn't he beautiful?" Then she noticed how Allie and Rand were standing, Allie's shirt half over her head. "Oh. Oops."

"That's *it*!" Allie pulled down her shirt and grabbed her purse off the floor by the sofa before running into the bedroom and returning a moment later with her Glock. "We're out of here, Sheryl. You lock up. Take care of Spook. Don't call my cell phone, and don't even *think* of trying to follow us." She waved the Glock in the air. "If you do, I'll shoot your tires out. I swear to God I will."

As she raced to the car dragging a grinning Rand behind her, she heard Sheryl say, "I never saw a broad who wanted to get laid so bad."

Epilogue

ALLIE STRETCHED HER ARMS over her head and yawned. She could hear Rand in the bathroom. Thinking back over the last few days, she smiled. When he asked her if it was worth the wait, she felt compelled to show him her answer. She wasn't even sorry they had to go back in a couple of hours. If they kept at it for much longer, they'd both die of exhaustion, albeit with silly smiles on their faces.

When she'd dashed out of the house dragging a willing Rand by the hand, she had no idea where she was headed—somewhere Sheryl couldn't find them easily. Out of instinct, she pointed the car south. About halfway down A1A between Melbourne Beach and Sebastian Inlet, she saw a motel that was perfect—Tiara by the Sea. It looked respectable, and the parking lot was U-shaped, meaning her Jeep couldn't be easily spotted from the road.

The nice woman who owned the place gave them a key and left them alone, which earned her Allie's everlasting gratitude. On top of that, there was a restaurant almost across the street, the New England Pub and Eatery. Exactly what a New England Pub was doing on the east coast of Florida, she had no clue, nor did she care. They could walk there for food when their energy flagged, further minimizing the risk of her Jeep being spotted.

Their only physical activity other than the obvious consisted of long walks on the deserted beach. There were few motels down this far and fewer high-rise condos. The area was populated instead with single family homes, many of them shuttered now. For the first two days, the only footprints they encountered in the sand were their own. Once, she saw a woman walking her dog about a quarter of a mile away. It was heaven.

"Just like Cape Canaveral used to be."

"Will it go the way of Cape Canaveral? Will these people sell out for big bucks to land developers?"

"Not a chance."

Allie blinked. *"So now, you can see into the future?"*

"I'm not looking into the future. Most of these homes have been here forty years or more, and many are passed down from generation to generation. Besides, what would draw land developers to this area?"

"What do you mean? It's perfect."

"For you, maybe. And for me. And for the people who live here, but think of it. There's only one grocery store within twenty miles. It's almost thirty miles to the nearest mall or theater. No swinging bars and nothing to entertain vacationing kids. Just the sea and sand and the pelicans."

"Which is all I want."

"Well?"

"Well what?"

"What do you intend to do about it?"

About the Author

Lynda Fitzgerald currently lives and writes in Snellville, Georgia, a small town just east of Atlanta, but she hails from Central Florida, where she spent most of her formative years. Florida still holds a special place in her heart, and you can see that influence reflected in her writing. Her most recent novels (*If Truth Be Told, LIVE Ringer, LIVE Ammo, and LIVE in Person*) have been set there.

She studied creative writing at both Georgia Perimeter College, where she was awarded a Creative Writing Scholarship, and through Emory University.

Lynda is an Active member of Mystery Writers of America, Sisters in Crime, the Atlanta Writers Club and the Florida Writers Association. More information can be found on her website. **www.fitzgeraldwrites.com**.

CPSIA information can be obtained
at www.ICGtesting.com
Printed in the USA
FFOW02n1759290414
5131FF